Ann Granger has lived in cities all over the world, since for many years she worked for the Foreign Office and received postings to British embassies as far apart as Munich and Lusaka. She is now permanently based in Oxfordshire.

Ann Granger is the author of three other hugely popular crime series: the Mitchell and Markby novels; the Fran Varady series and the Victorian mysteries featuring Scotland Yard's Inspector Ben Ross and his wife Lizzie.

Praise for Ann Granger:

'While Ann Granger's novels might be set in the familiar mode of traditional country crime stories, there is nothing old-fashioned about the characters, who are drawn with a telling eye for their human foibles and frailties. Granger is bang up to date' *Oxford Times*

'A clever and lively book' Margaret Yorke

'The plot is neat and ingenious, the characters rounded and touchingly credible' *Ham and High*

'Well-plotted, chilling and highly enjoyable' *Good Book Guide*

'This engrossing story looks like the start of a highly enjoyable series' *Scotsman*

'For once a murder novel which displays a gentle touch and a dash of wit' *Northern Echo*

'A good feel for understated humour, a nice ear for dialogue' *The Times*

ANN GRANGER

DEAD in the WATER

headline

First published in 2015
by HEADLINE PUBLISHING GROUP

First published in paperback in 2015
by HEADLINE PUBLISHING GROUP

1

Cataloguing in Publication Data is available from the British Library

ISBN 978 1 4722 0458 5

Typeset in Adobe Garamond by Palimpsest Book Production Ltd, Falkirk, Stirlingshire

Printed and bound in Great Britain by Clays Ltd, St Ives plc

HEADLINE PUBLISHING GROUP
An Hachette UK Company
Carmelite House
50 Victoria Embankment
London EC4Y 0DZ

www.headline.co.uk
www.hachette.co.uk

This book is dedicated to the memory of my dear husband, John, who so tragically passed away as I was putting the finishing touches to the manuscript. During all our time together, he offered constant support and encouragement to me in my writing, and in so many other ways.
I feel he stands at my shoulder still.

On one side lay the Ocean, and on one
Lay a great water, and the moon was full.

Alfred, Lord Tennyson
Idylls of the King

Prologue

The dead girl drifted silently onward on the rippling surface of the swollen river, rolling from side to side as the current buffeted her. It snatched at her long hair and played with it, fanning it out across the surface and then tangling it up in a cat's cradle before unknotting it again on a whim. It had stopped raining and the moon slid out from behind the clouds to touch the body briefly with silver fingers. The river made a turn here and the current pulled her towards the bank where the water had burst through its former corset and inundated an area of bushes and trees. Twiggy hands caught at her clothing but the current did not want to be deprived of its plaything. It began to worry at the body, trying to pull it loose. The moon disappeared again and left them to dispute in darkness.

Chapter 1

Mike Lacey, the vet, was on his way to Crockett's farm just after nine on Tuesday morning. He was keeping an eye on the river to his left, noting how debris borne on the force of the spate swirled past. He hoped he was not going to be called upon to rescue any trapped livestock. But it wasn't an animal he spotted. He braked, scrabbled for the binoculars he kept in the car, jumped out of his mud-splattered 4 x 4 and went to investigate. His eyes had not deceived him. Close-up scrutiny through the binoculars confirmed that the object, despite being largely submerged, was human in form and he thought he distinguished long hair. Drooping branches of the riverside willows, acting as a kind of filter for all the debris, had snared a body.

Mike stood transfixed at the sight and swore at length for a full minute, surprising himself because he was not normally given to profanity. Realising he was in shock, he made a conscious effort to pull himself together and review the situation. The wind blew sharply across the open water. High in the air, birds wheeled and swooped as they struggled to maintain a course. Below, the choppy water slapped against the mud, and the corpse rose and fell. All around him nature was moving, but he stood frozen. He forced himself to consider the situation as a problem to be solved, rather than a human tragedy.

To free it would require help. He briefly considered trying to drag her (the long hair suggested a woman) out of the river himself. But she was just too far out to reach from where he stood; and to wade into the water with no idea of the depth or the solidity of the ground beneath his feet would be to risk joining her where she floated face down. He estimated she had been at least several hours in the water, probably most of that time half under the surface. There was no hope of resuscitation. Behind him, in his 4 x 4, his mobile phone began to ring. They were waiting for him at Crockett's, and probably wondering where the heck he was. He returned to his vehicle, answered the call (it was indeed from the farm) and then phoned the police. He explained the situation, gave the location as precisely as he could, and promised to return to meet them there as soon as he'd dealt with the situation at the farm.

Sod's law meant that by the time he did return the police had duly arrived, both by land and by river. But of the body there was no sign at all.

Jess Campbell shielded her eyes and wished she'd had the fore-thought to bring sunglasses. The combined dazzle of the sun and sparks of light dancing on the surface of the water made it difficult to watch what was going on. As she squinted, a dark outline of head and shoulders surfaced briefly, only to disappear again below the glittering surface like some legendary river sprite. Around her, in the shade where the sun had not touched the ground with its fiery fingers, the overnight frost still spread a thin white blanket, for all the brightness of the day.

'No snow yet,' said a voice at her shoulder. 'We shan't have a white Christmas. Pity, the kids have been hoping for it.' A stamping of feet on the hard ground followed the words. DS Nugent was cold and restless and wanted to be back in a centrally heated office, sitting happily before his computer.

'I can't stand Christmas,' growled another voice. 'It costs a fortune, shopping is a nightmare, and it's all over in forty-eight hours. Why bother?'

'You want to shop online, if you don't like crowds,' retorted Nugent.

If only to put a stop to the squabbling, Jess said firmly, 'I like Christmas. I like the busy shops, the decorations in the high streets and on some houses. They brighten up a dark, cold time of year.'

There was a pause after she'd spoken. Then the other man, the modern Scrooge, muttered: 'Our neighbour, opposite us, he's got a Father Christmas climbing up his chimney. It flashes on and off all evening.'

His words conjured up a memory for Jess. Those sunspots on the water, glittering like tinsel, recreated the fairy lights draped around the Christmas tree of her childhood. Both she and her brother had loved the twinkling diamonds among the dark green fir needles. Then, one Christmas Eve while they were watching, there was an audible fizz and 'phut!' The tree lights went out, never to shine again. 'Mend it, Daddy!' they had pleaded with their father. But he had not been able to fix the problem. The whole necklace of lights was carefully unwound and removed, 'for safety'. Although the glass baubles remained hanging from the branches, and the crooked angel still presided wonkily atop, the tree had looked denuded and lifeless. Neither she nor her brother could bear to look at it. It was as though the tree's heart had stopped beating.

An elephant in the room, thought Jess. They were not in a room, of course, but out in the open. Yet the 'thing we do not mention' was there, all the same. The reason for the pointless discussion that had just taken place was that no one wanted to talk about what was actually going on, and the possible outcome. The three of them stood and waited. The water lapped at the sodden ground only a few feet away and the river's boundary ought to be out there, well away from the road. Only a slight rise in the land meant it had not covered that too. She wished she had been able to bring Phil Morton with her but he had just got married and was on honeymoon, skiing in the Tatra Mountains. She found Nugent's fidgeting distracting.

The man who resented Christmas went by the name of Corcoran and had arrived with the underwater search unit. She hadn't met him before. Now, as the divers surfaced signalling they had found nothing, Corcoran stumped down to the very edge of the water, his large gumboots making deep imprints in the sodden turf and brackish liquid seeping up to cover his feet. 'How's the current?' they heard him shout.

'Miserable blighter, isn't he, ma'am?' observed Nugent, now that Corcoran couldn't hear him.

Jess sighed agreement. None of them relished working in the run-up to the holiday season and certainly not on such a poten-tially grisly task. But Corcoran's grumbles made it worse.

Corcoran was returning now, scepticism writ large on his doughy features. 'There's nothing in the water; and nothing on the bottom but a couple of supermarket trolleys and some empty wine bottles. The current could have taken the body downstream as much as half a mile by now. That is, if we're not looking for a figment of *his* imagination.'

He nodded towards Mike Lacey's vehicle, parked behind them on higher ground on the edge of the road. The driver's dark silhouette could be seen seated at the wheel, drinking from a can. 'We ought to breathalyse that guy.'

'Hardly on the grounds that he's drinking Seven-Up,' Jess retorted. 'Anyway, it's still morning and he doesn't smell of booze. Also, he's a respected local vet, responding to a call when he noticed the body, face down, over there.' She pointed to where the tips of inundated growth thrust up despairing fingers.

'They all float face down at first,' Corcoran, the expert, said. 'Until they sink. Then they can lie on the bottom for up to two weeks before there's enough gas in the corpse to bring it to the surface. Depends on the depth of the water, of course, and the temperature. Some of them never come up.' He shook his head. 'Witnesses make mistakes, you know. It might have looked like a human body, but it could have been a large branch broken off a tree in that storm the other day; or a bag of rubbish chucked in by some fly-tipper, or a piece of clothing that ended up in the river somehow . . . or an animal cadaver. Whatever it was, the current's taken it and we'll have to go downstream.'

'The man's a vet!' Jess snapped. 'He must have seen enough dead animals in his time.'

'Sunlight is strong,' countered Corcoran. 'Plays tricks with the eyes.'

He was a burly man with weather-beaten skin and a straggling moustache. As he spoke, he raised his hand to stroke the straggling growth on his upper lip and Jess caught a glimpse of his teeth. They were startlingly white and very even. They had to be dentures.

Dave Nugent was also tall and solidly built. Standing between them, Jess was keenly aware that her slim build and cropped red hair must make her look like a child standing between two adults or – since this was something she saw fairly often – a young delinquent between two police or prison officers.

She opened her mouth to retort that Lacey had scanned the scene with binoculars and was certain. But Corcoran was set on being negative. 'Nip over there and have another word with the witness, Sergeant,' she said instead to Nugent; who squelched off towards the Range Rover with his fists jammed into his coat pockets.

Her mobile sounded its merry jingle. She put it to her ear and heard Ian Carter's voice.

'Found anything?'

'Nothing yet. I should tell you, Sergeant Corcoran thinks the witness may have made a mistake. Identifying objects in the water can be dodgy. Whatever it was, it's gone. We may have to follow the river down. Sergeant Corcoran's opinion is that the object – whether it's a body or a sack of rubbish – may have been carried as much as half a mile downstream by the current, since the witness reported seeing it caught up here. All the rain we've had means the flow is extra strong. All kind of debris has been racing by us. It makes sense that the body must have drifted.'

'How is access to the bank further down?'

'I think there is at least one house, a fairly big one, in grounds. We shall have to ask the owner to let us on to his stretch of bank.'

8

'He can hardly refuse in the circumstances. We've had no reports of missing persons. But you judge the witness reliable?'

'I'd say very reliable, a local vet. He says he saw long hair and had the impression of slight build. He thought it was probably a woman and her clothing had caught on some willows swamped by the flood. Dave Nugent is talking to the witness again, just to make sure. Unfortunately, he – the vet – carried on to make an urgent call at a nearby farm after he'd rung us. He returned here to meet us, but the body had gone and he wasn't here to see if that was down to the current, or somehow, someone fished it out. The strong current is still the most likely explanation.'

'If someone else saw it and hauled it ashore, we'd have heard about it. If you don't find anything in the next half an hour, call it off for the time being and come back,' Carter's voice said.

'We'll try further down, sir.' Jess returned the phone to her pocket.

Dave Nugent was back. The two divers had clambered out of the water and into their boat. Corcoran signalled to them to proceed downstream. The rest of them prepared to follow, with the exception of the witness who was driving off in the opposite direction.

'He's got work to do,' explained Nugent. 'I told him he could go. We can find him again if we need him. He's sticking to his story.'

They could be in for a long day.

Chapter 2

'Neil?' Beth put her head round the study door. Abandoned work littered the desk by the window; and on the computer screen a pattern of swirling multi-coloured lights signalled that he'd been gone some time. The waste bin, however, was full of crumpled pieces of paper. That had been emptied this morning, so her husband had managed some work, even if it had all been binned in despair or fury.

'Probably both,' Beth muttered.

She walked to the window and peered out. The day was bright and sunny and the puddles from the recent rain had almost soaked away on the lawn. The surface was still treacherously soft. A movement caught her eye. Her husband was sweeping up the autumn leaves still lying in a thick mulch. It was no easy task now they were so wet. They stuck to the brush bristles and Neil was shaking the broom furiously to dislodge them.

He was tall and thin. This wasn't because he didn't eat. Neil ate anything put in front of him, very often without bothering to establish first what it was. His untidy straight fair hair fell over his forehead and, as he made increasingly wild manoeuvres with the broom, the fringe almost reached the rim of his glasses. A smile tugged at Beth's mouth because he looked so comical out there, losing his battle with the garden debris. But Neil obviously didn't find it funny. As his frustration grew, his movements became more forceful as if, with his broom weapon, he parried some invisible opponent in single combat.

Several trees grew just inside the high wall of mellow local stone where the property met the road. Some of the trees were older than the house itself, like the oak presiding over its spindlier neighbours. That was listed and couldn't be felled. But she and Neil didn't want any of them felled, in any case. They provided a screen from the road and absorbed some of the noise from the heavy vehicles rattling up and down from the quarry. The lane wasn't suitable for heavy traffic, much too narrow, forcing any oncoming car to pull right over on to the verge or into the infrequent passing places. But because they were the only people crazy enough to want to live on it, despite the traffic, and because the house had been in desperate need of renovation, the property had been cheap, ridiculously cheap for the size.

'Double-glazing will take care of the noise,' Neil had said optimistically. 'It's the ideal place for me to work, nothing to disturb us.'

They'd sold up the London flat for such a good price it had almost frightened them, and come here. If you ignored the lorries: and to be fair they didn't use the road at weekends or after five in the afternoons on weekdays, yes, it was undisturbed. She'd quelled her misgivings. But within a month the isolation had begun to get to her.

Not so her husband, who told everyone (those who'd asked and those who hadn't), that coming here was the best decision they'd ever made. To be fair, until recently he'd put on a good show of being happy here, provided the writing was going well.

He'd bought himself a *Guide to British Birds* and watched wildlife programmes on the television. He would go out for long walks with a notebook and carefully list what he'd seen or found. He had to brave the crowds sometimes when researching a book. That might involve driving into Gloucester to catch the London train, or travelling by road all the way to Oxford for the Bodleian library or the University Museum of Natural History. Neil wrote novels about a fantasy world that had originally existed only in his head but now seemed to exist in the heads of numerous loyal readers. He was always hunting down what he called 'inspiration'; but Beth described as 'oddities'. Whenever he came home he would tell her how good it was to return. 'London is unbelievably awful, these days, Beth. I couldn't go back there to live. The pavements are packed; everyone is in a hurry. To get back here is bliss.' Neil had turned himself into an instant countryman.

'But it's no good,' Beth muttered. 'He doesn't – we don't – belong here.'

She yearned for the helter-skelter of big city life, the adrenalin rush from being part of the heart of things. Let's face it, they'd still be there if she hadn't lost her job. It wasn't healthy, she told herself, being stuck out here where nothing ever happened and the noise of the quarry traffic on a weekday was almost welcome. In Neil's books the hero or heroine, as the case might be, often found himself (herself) in a strange land ruled by unfamiliar laws and customs. That, thought Beth now, was exactly what had happened to her and to Neil. They were marooned in a foreign habitat.

She was still putting out feelers to people who might help her get another job, something which would let her work mainly from home but make the journey up to London, say, twice a week. In the present climate, it wasn't easy, as everyone seemed very keen to tell her. The labour market for her skills had become a desert. She had been nearly two years on the shelf and was beginning to gather dust, she often thought to herself with a wry smile.

The monthly statements from the bank had begun to be depressing reading. They had wildly underestimated how much it would cost to bring this house into the twenty-first century. The previous elderly owner had done nothing to it for years on the 'it'll see me out' principle.

'Mr Martin saw little benefit to himself in extensive renovation,' was the way the estate agent had phrased it. 'That is reflected in the price,' the man had added.

The house had indeed seen old Mr Martin out; and then languished on the market, the price reduced twice, before the Stewarts appeared on the horizon. Beth now realised the estate agent, and executors dealing with the former owner's affairs, must have seen them as the answer to their prayers. 'Fresh down from London with money in their pockets!' she imagined the estate agent chortling.

Well, the bonanza from the sale of the flat was disappearing like the frost on the lawn in the early-morning sun; ditto the lump sum Beth had received from her former employers. Neil left 'money matters' to her. She budgeted carefully regarding their day-to-day expenditure. But either he hadn't noticed, or it didn't bother Neil in his private world of bronze-helmeted, muscular heroes; mythical beasts; sword-wielding heroines; and sorcerers of both sexes. The books sold well, not in mega numbers but respectably, but with only one of them earning, the free-spending income they'd been accustomed to had suddenly been curtailed. This property, Glebe House, was like an ever-hungry monster that had escaped from one of Neil's plots and roamed outside demanding to be fed with large sums of cash. She had not yet told him just how fragile their financial situation had become.

She had also not wanted to worry him because lately even Neil had been, well, 'twitchy' was probably a good word. An ominous cloud had appeared on Neil's horizon with 'writer's block' emblazoned across it. The new book wasn't going well; and perhaps he had realised the writing was now their only source of income. He had not wanted to talk about the visit he'd paid his agent the previous day, returning monosyllabic and downcast in the evening.

The fact was that Neil had not been his usual self for the past couple of weeks. Not, in fact, since the end of the recent creative writing course he'd supervised at a local college. It was the second time he'd run such a course. The earlier one had been not long after their arrival here in the previous winter; it had proved very popular and the college had begged him to run another this year. Flattered, Neil had agreed. The second one had been oversubscribed.

Beth had been delighted he'd agreed to do it again, not only for the modest amount of money, but because the life of a writer was essentially a lonely one. She'd been pleased that he took to going for a drink with some of the students after the end of the evening session. He was a careful drinker, so she didn't worry about his driving home afterwards. One glass of wine and that was his lot. This frugality also meant the pub visits hadn't involved a sudden increase in expenditure. She'd believed he'd enjoyed the classes.

But writing also requires concentration; and possibly the considerable work involved in running the writing course had interfered in Neil's to the extent that the new book was suffering.

Beth sighed and turned to leave the study. She pulled on a lightweight quilted jacket hanging in the hallway and went outside. The crow perched high in the oak saw her coming and cawed a loud warning. Neil was still intent on sweeping the leaves into a pile. He paused in his labours to look up; and push his spectacles back up the bridge of his nose.

'Hello, darling. I'm not going to burn them. I'm going to leave them like that.'

'What for?' She'd almost asked, 'Burn what?' because the damp heap of leaves was very small.

'Hedgehogs.'

'I haven't seen a hedgehog in the garden for weeks. They're all hibernating.'

'At least one is still rooting about. I've heard him at night, grunting away, and he's left his calling card, look, just over there. They're almost endangered now, numbers falling fast, you know. I thought it would be a good idea to create somewhere it can over-winter.'

Anything but work! Beth thought in sudden exasperation. Displacement activity, or attempt to break the creative block? Or is it because we've got people coming for Christmas? He doesn't want the house full, the chatter and disruption to his routine. Susie's kids will be playing that running game, along the hall corridor, up the main staircase, along the upstairs passages and down the old servants' stair at the end, back to the hall and start all over again. But I'm looking forward to the noise, the company, the kids getting so excited over Christmas. I even don't mind them watching all those cartoons on telly.

She decided to tackle the situation head-on. Neil did not like confrontation and would do almost anything to avoid it, but sometimes he had to.

'I thought,' she said briskly, 'you might like to come and help me put up the decorations in the hall and dining room – since you're obviously taking a break from working.'

Neil's gaze slid away from hers and he poked the broom at the leaf pile. 'Just doing this . . . going back to the study now.'

'No, you're not. I need you for fifteen minutes. You can spare me fifteen minutes.'

He knew she was in earnest and he grew resentful. 'I don't know why we need decorations. None of the mob is coming until Christmas Eve and they're all leaving the morning after Boxing Day. It's not worth it.'

'The children will expect to see decorations, so will my parents and your parents and my sister.'

'Why have they all got to come to us, anyway?' He was getting mulish now, but they'd been through all this before.

'We decided, all of us. We are the only ones with enough bedrooms to put everyone up.' Beth flung a hand out to point at the house. 'Four spare bedrooms, five if you include the maid's room in the attic, Neil, and the only time anyone comes here to sleep in them is at Christmas!'

'Your parents were here at Easter,' he protested. 'And Susie and those blasted kids were roaring round the place for a whole week in the summer!'

17

'*Your* parents came to stay the last time they came over from Spain.'

'They don't run up and down the stairs,' grumbled her husband.

'Listen to me, Neil,' Beth said briskly. 'We are going to have a real old-fashioned family Christmas and that means decorations, Christmas tree, holly, the lot. I'm really looking forward to it and you will enjoy it, I know you will.'

'I refuse to have flashing lights.' Neil sought to have the last word. 'And that includes the sort you sling round the tree.'

'No need for those, I bought a fibre-optic tree last year, remember?'

'Tat,' muttered her husband. 'Tatty tree, tatty decorations – and holly is a pagan symbol. OK, but this is the last time. I refuse to do it next year.'

'That's all right,' she said sweetly, 'next year we can go on a Christmas cruise.' *If we can afford it, hah!*

He was so horrified he couldn't speak. However, just as they reached the house the silence was broken by a clang and rattle as a vehicle turned into the drive and began a noisy progress towards them. The crow flapped noisily away from its perch above, shouting news of an arrival.

'Wayne Garley,' said Neil with a groan.

'Oh, good,' Beth countered, 'he's brought the logs.'

'Why we have to have a log fire going when we've at long last got the central heating working beats me. You know, our native woodlands . . .'

'We won't have it going all winter, just for the holiday.' The truck stopped in a spray of gravel and a figure in faded blue overalls, a much-scuffed leather jacket and a woolly hat climbed down and stumped towards them.

18

'Got your wood!' announced the visitor. 'You're lucky, you know. Always a demand for logs this time of year. All the old pubs round here want to have a log fire. Brings in trade.'

'That means he's going to charge extra,' muttered Neil.

'Where do you want me to put 'em, then?' asked Garley. If he'd heard Neil's comment it hadn't bothered him. Wayne Garley was a law unto himself. 'If you don't like it, you can lump it!' was his motto.

When Neil and Beth had moved in to the house they had made inquiries locally to find someone who would do odd jobs without charging a fortune. At once they had been told by locals, 'You need Wayne Garley.'

Garley was the 'fixer' hereabouts. You name it, and he would arrange it, either doing the job himself or finding someone else who could (generally a member of his extensive clan). If you needed to hire a pony and trap for a wedding, or get your gutters unblocked, or have someone put up stalls at a garden fete, or rebuild a stretch of stone wall, you just asked Wayne Garley. All the Garleys looked the same. Male or female, they were small and wiry with nut-brown faces, bright eyes and snub noses.

Lettie Stone had informed Beth that Garleys were well known for always marrying 'in the family'. 'You know, cousins and that,' said Lettie, who came in once a week to lug the vacuum cleaner up and down the stairs and wash the stone flags of the kitchen floor. 'Mind you, there is a lot of them to choose from.'

'Weird,' said Neil, when this was relayed to him. He had sounded thoughtful. Perhaps a strange, tattooed tribe of blowpipe-armed Garleys was going to appear in a future book.

'Lettie says Wayne Garley won't let us down. He's not only reliable, he's kind-hearted,' Beth defended him.

19

'I'll show you where to put the logs, Wayne,' she said aloud now. 'There's a small shed just round the back of the house, by some bushes.'

'I knows it,' said Garley, 'no need for you to come. All right if I drive the truck round?'

'You'll churn up the ground,' objected Neil. 'It's very wet.'

'I can't carry 'em round meself, can I?' returned Garley. 'Take me forever to shift that lot and they're heavy, they are. Unless, of course, you wanted to give me a hand?'

'Oh, drive the truck round there, then!' snapped Neil and went indoors.

Beth thought she detected a faint grin on Wayne's face. 'Thank you,' she said. 'Did you bring the bill?'

'I got it.' Wayne searched his pockets of his leather bomber jacket and produced a crumpled scrap of paper.

'Cash, I suppose, as usual?' Beth asked.

'If it's all the same to you, I prefer cash. Saves me having to go special to the bank to pay in a cheque.'

'Well, just call by the house when you've got the logs stacked. The money's ready.'

Garley nodded and climbed back into the cab of his truck. As she went into the house she heard it rattle away round the side of the building.

Despite his earlier objections, Neil became quite keen on putting up the decorations and they made good progress. Beth was just about to suggest a cup of coffee when they heard Garley shouting from the direction of the kitchen.

'He's thinking about coffee, too,' said Neil.

But he was wrong. Coffee was far from Wayne's mind. When

they went into the kitchen, they found him standing in his work boots on the stone flags Lettie had washed the day before. A trail of muddy footprints led from the back door. It wasn't like him to be so thoughtless and it struck Beth that his snub features had taken on a look of shocked surprise.

'You been down to the bank this morning?' he asked hoarsely.

'I told you, Wayne, I've got your cash,' Beth reminded him.

He shook his head. 'Not that sort of bank! Where the river runs along the edge of your garden.'

No wonder Wayne had brought in so much mud on his boots. With the recent rain and the rise in the river level, that lower part of the garden had become virtually inaccessible. Well, thought Beth, to most people, but not apparently to Wayne Garley.

'Why did you go down there?' she asked. 'It's practically a quagmire, Wayne. We haven't gone there for a couple of days. If we weren't on a rise, the river would have crept halfway up the garden.'

'That's what I went to see, how much flooding you've got,' said Garley. 'The river's burst its banks all the way down, and that little mooring of yours is just underwater now. If it rains even more, the river could come up to, oh, about fifteen feet from your back door. You got any sandbags? I reckon you might need 'em. I can get you some.'

The mooring Wayne had referred to was a rickety wooden platform sticking out into the river. It wasn't safe at the best of times and was now waterlogged instead of standing two feet above the surface.

'Now you mention it, Wayne,' she said to him. 'I meant to ask if you could dismantle that mooring for us, later in the spring, when the water level has gone down.'

Wayne drew in a deep breath. 'There's something wedged up by it, most under the water. I reckon you . . .' At this point Wayne turned pointedly away from Beth and addressed Neil.

Neil looked startled. 'What?'

'Best you come and take a look yourself,' returned Wayne obscurely and started to walk back the way he'd come in.

'We'll both go,' whispered Beth. 'I don't know what it is, but Wayne is determined to show us.'

Garley had sharp ears. He paused and looked back. 'No, not *you*, Mrs Stewart, just your man there. Better you don't come.' He hesitated. 'It's something dead, I reckon.'

Neil decided to take charge of the conversation. 'Rubbish!' he said. Hastily, he added, 'I mean, it must be some rubbish, not a dead animal. All sorts of stuff has been coming down river this past week. Stay here, I'll fetch my boots and take a look.'

He followed Garley. Beth, left alone, hesitated, then muttered, 'Oh, for goodness' sake . . .' and pulled on the gumboots she kept by the kitchen door. As she stepped outside she heard Neil's voice, raised in something that sounded like horror.

That decided her. Whatever it was, she had to go down and find out. How bad could it be?

Neil and Garley were opposite what could be seen of the wooden mooring. They were pointing and arguing. Beth drew nearer, making a diagonal progress so that the two men were not between her and whatever it was. It was difficult going; the ground sucked at her boots and she wobbled alarmingly, throwing out her arms to balance herself. There was certainly something large, a hump shape, stuck by the platform. It floated, half-submerged and rocking on the swell of the current. She couldn't quite make it out.

She called, 'What is it?'

Neil turned and, seeing her, waved his arms as if he wanted to drive her away. 'Go back indoors!' he shouted.

'Don't be silly, Neil.' She ploughed on determinedly, even though it was like walking in glue, each step marked by a squelch and an effort to pull the foot out again. The trapped object bobbed up briefly and broke the surface, so she could see it better. It wasn't an animal. It seemed to be clothed; something else, too. Hair, long hair spread out across the water. The 'hump' was a woman's shoulders and upper torso.

Bile rose in her throat and made her want to gag. She swallowed hard. 'It's a − body,' she gasped.

Neil began to stumble towards her. 'We told you not to come out here—'

He broke off as they heard the sound of vehicles, certainly more than one, turning into the front gate. 'What now?' he growled. '*Go indoors, Beth!*' He set off to investigate the new arrivals.

Beth couldn't have done as he asked, even if she'd wanted to. Her legs didn't want to work. With difficulty, she twisted to watch him go and then realised Garley was at her shoulder.

Now she was here, he seemed to accept her presence. 'I reckoned it was a body,' he said to her. 'I knows rubbish when I see it.'

Neil was returning, not alone. Hurrying towards her with him were a trim young woman with red hair and two men. One of the men was fairly young, tall but of compact build; the other, older and bulkier, sported one of those untrimmed salt-and-pepper

23

moustaches that only the wearer could find flattering. Neil was trying to explain the situation to them, gesticulating towards the river. Behind her, on the water, she heard the put-put of a motor launch approaching.

Wayne Garley assessed the newcomers with a practised eye. 'Coppers,' he said.

Chapter 3

Minutes earlier, Dave Nugent, turning into the gates of Glebe House with a flourish, had almost knocked down a man who was running up the drive towards them.

The sight had not only been unexpected, it had been grotesque. The man was tall and thin, 'a regular stick insect' Nugent's granny would have called him. The pipe-cleaner figure was clearly in considerable distress, its long arms raised in the air and gesticulating wildly, conveying no clear message, only dismay and horror. Jess Campbell shouted a warning. There was a near-collision. Nugent braked in a shower of wet gravel and stuck his head out of the window.

The man panted up, his expression wild. 'Who the hell are you?' he'd demanded.

'Police, sir,' Jess called out from the passenger seat.

The man gaped at her, then exclaimed, 'Thank God! We've just found something horrible . . . It's in the river.'

He turned to lead the way, signalling wildly for them to follow him. Beside Jess, Corcoran – who had descended from his 4 x 4 to join them – muttered, 'Told you the current would have taken it downstream.'

The body had been trapped against one of the supports of a short wooden landing stage that stretched into the river; and must have cleared the surface before the rains had submerged it. It wasn't big enough to qualify as a jetty, but presumably someone had once kept a small boat tied up there. Not, thought Jess, the present owners. Or, if they did, there was no sign of the boat now and she suspected the platform was long disused and rotting. No one should try to stand on it when hauling the body out of the water.

But it had been sufficient to catch the corpse. No doubt about it being female. Here she was in shallower water than when Lacey had seen her. The swirling current had twisted her so that her bare white feet pointed towards them, breaking the surface as she bobbed up and down. Her shoes could have fallen off in the river.

Corcoran's men were in the water and lifting her out. They turned her over and her head fell back as they staggered ashore with their burden, their legs sinking into the mud. Her long hair trailed like riverweed, dripping a cascade of droplets. Earlier, the divers in the river had reminded Jess of water sprites. Now it was as if they had snared such a creature and carried her from her watery kingdom on to the land. She was very young. Jess remembered the owners of the house, who were standing just behind her. She turned and saw their appalled faces. The man looked as though he was going to throw up. The woman had opened her mouth as if to exclaim but no sound had come out and she remained frozen with her lips forming an 'O'.

The man in work clothing, who had apparently first found the drowned woman, was standing well back behind the husband and wife. Jess had the impression this wasn't because he was troubled by death but because he didn't care for the police. That didn't mean he was involved in anything criminal. He just didn't like people who asked personal questions. Jess understood he was a handyman of some sort and had been delivering a load of logs.

'Would you like to go indoors, Mr and Mrs Stewart?' she asked. 'I'll come and have a word with you shortly.'

They nodded and turned away obediently. The man put his arm round his wife's shoulders and she slipped her arm round his waist. If either of them removed that prop it looked as if the other one would fall down.

'Sergeant Nugent will take your details and statement now, Mr Garley,' Jess told the workman. 'Then you can go.'

Garley scowled but nodded. He followed Nugent back towards the parked vehicles. As they walked away, the rain began to patter down again on the already saturated scene.

Corcoran's men had deposited the girl, flat on her back, on the trampled mud and grass. They had handled her gently and now stepped back, faces impassive, like professional mourners, allowing the others to see her face. She was bleached white; the 'deathly pallor' romantic poets had liked so much. Her mouth was slightly open and her eyes stared unseeingly upward. In the pale winter sunlight her wet skin glistened as if polished. She appeared about to speak to them, as if to tell them how this had happened to her. She wore a single large, gold-coloured hoop earring. Its pair had presumably joined her shoes somewhere on the riverbed.

Jess balanced on her heels by the dead girl to study her more closely.

Nineteen, twenty years old? she wondered. The girl's bare feet could have belonged to a statue. Thin strands of dark green waterweed patterned her ankles and toes, increasing the appearance of marble. Her toenails were painted silver, as were her fingernails.

There was a Victorian painting – by Millais, wasn't it? – which depicted Shakespeare's drowned Ophelia lying in the water, surrounded by various bits of vegetation. Jess recalled being told by the school art teacher that Millais' model had been required to lie in a bath of water for hours and, as a result, caught a severe chill. But Death had laid his hand on this Ophelia.

The girl wore a flimsy top decorated with a swirled pattern of sequins. Not warm enough to be proof against winter chill and she must, at some time and somewhere, have had a jacket or coat. Her black trousers appeared to be made of some velvety cord. Fancy wear for an evening out, Jess thought.

Jess stood up, took out her mobile again and rang Carter again to tell him of the discovery. 'Any visible injuries to head or face?' he asked.

'Not that I can see, other than some scratches that might come from the bushes the vet saw her caught on earlier. She can't have been in the water long. Corcoran says she probably went in very late last night or in the early hours of this morning, anywhere between here and Weston St Ambrose. If so, any drugs she may have taken, if she did, could still be in the body. Tom Palmer will tell us more. But to my eye . . .' Jess paused.

'What?'

'I'd say she's dressed for an evening out, dark velvet-type trousers and a glittery top, big earrings, one missing. The water has soaked all her clothes but the sequin pattern is quite clear. Her shoes are missing, too. Her nails are beautifully manicured and lacquered, hands and toes. We need Tom to do a postmortem as soon as possible. I'm hoping the water won't have washed away evidence on the body.'

'Women's fashion's not my area of expertise,' Ian's voice said drily in her ear. 'But if she went out on a date, we'll have to find out who the guy was. That is, after we find out who she is! Fine, I'll get things moving.'

Jess returned the phone to her jacket pocket and surveyed the garden around her. It would soon be a hive of activity as others arrived, including the doctor to certify death. More vehicles would plough their way across what was left of the Stewarts' lawn. Her arrival with Nugent and Corcoran and the following activity had already wrought a good deal of damage. Jess felt sorry for the Stewarts.

She left Nugent in charge of the scene and began to walk towards the house, composing in her head, as she went, a suitably apologetic opening to a difficult interview. No one expects to find suddenly his or her home the centre of a police operation. Ahead of her, a door was open at the back of the house. It must be the kitchen. Jess made for it.

The Stewarts were indeed in their kitchen. They sat side by side looking towards the open door and the garden beyond, even though from there they couldn't see the river because of tall old laurel bushes and a woodshed. They appeared to have been sitting in silence, a pair of frozen figures. Warm air seeped from the kitchen, but they both clearly felt the chill of shock. Jess felt obliged to reach out and knock on the open door, even though they must see her clearly. She was relieved to note that the stone flags were already muddied because adding more mud was one thing she didn't have to apologise for. Nevertheless, she pulled off her gumboots and set them beside the door under the inadequate shelter of a small projecting ledge. If I lived here, she thought, I'd have a proper back porch built on.

She padded inside in damp socks and began, 'I'm very sorry about all this, Mr and Mrs Stewart.'

'Not your fault,' said the wife, almost inaudibly.

For all their immobility, someone had made coffee because it steamed untouched before them.

Mrs Stewart saw the direction of her gaze and got to her feet, stiffly, like an old woman, although Jess put her age at late thirties or early forties. 'You'd like a cup, too, I expect,' the woman offered, an automatic hospitality coming to the rescue.

'Thank you.' Jess nodded. Having something to do might relax her more. The husband would need a lot more than that to ease the tension. He remained in the same rigid attitude, his hands lying on the table surface. His complexion had a greenish tinge and was beaded with sweat. Though spare in build and bespectacled, he would be a good-looking man in normal circumstances. His face looked somehow familiar.

The wife was back, setting down a mug in front of Jess. 'My name is Beth,' she said. 'My husband is Neil.' She, too, was attractive, even this morning under strain. Her long tawny blond hair was tied back with a silk scarf, revealing regular features. She wore little make-up. Even though she had not removed her quilted jacket, she still managed somehow to look a professional woman. Her husband, still wearing his mud-smeared padded gilet, looked more the countryman. More so, but still not quite. They didn't match the surroundings. How did they come to be living out here?

30

Neil Stewart. She'd heard the name before. With a glow of satisfaction, Jess placed him. She had seen his photo in the local press and on the dust jacket of his books.

'You're the writer,' she said to him.

He raised his gaze from the untasted coffee before him and stared at her. 'Yes,' he said. He chewed at his lower lip and added with an effort, 'I'm sorry, I'm – it's thrown me, finding her, that girl.'

'Wayne found her,' Beth corrected him.

Irritation crossed his features. 'Yes, I know Wayne found her. But I meant, when I saw her . . . I didn't really think he had found anyone until then. After all, it's not the sort of thing that happens every day!' His annoyance had served to break the paralysis that had appeared to grip him.

'Tell me about it,' Jess invited them, hoping talking might help.

They exchanged glances. 'There's nothing to tell. Wayne Garley brought some logs. Beth told him he could put them in the shed.' Neil picked up his coffee mug and immediately put it down again, slopping coffee on to the table. 'We didn't know he'd find a body, for pity's sake!'

'What were you doing when Garley arrived?' Jess asked him.

'Nothing, well, nothing much. I was in the garden, sweeping up leaves.' He paused and then, as if he felt the answer inadequate, added, 'I'd been working on a book earlier this morning but I needed a break. I came outside and mucked about with the leaves to free up my mind.' He blinked. Perhaps the image of the drowned girl had appeared in his head, and he sought to drive it away. It would be a long time before he or his wife could do that.

'You didn't go down to the river? Could you see it from where you were working?'

He shook his head. 'I didn't go near the bank – or where the bank used to be before it chucked so much rain down. I couldn't see it, either, because there are shrubs – like those out there.' He pointed at the woodshed and dark bulk of the laurel bushes. 'Victorian planting, overgrown now. Whole garden needs clearing and re-landscaping. Even if I had, I wouldn't have seen anything in the water unless I stood right on the edge. It's like the Great Grimpen Mire down there. You found that out yourselves! Then Beth came out and asked me to help her string up some decorations.'

'We've guests, family, coming to stay over Christmas,' Beth explained. 'We were talking about it when Wayne arrived with the logs. I told him to put them in the shed and he drove off – Neil and I came indoors. We got started on the decorations and had just decided to stop for a coffee break when we heard Wayne calling from the kitchen here. He'd come to tell us there was something in the river, stuck by the old mooring. Really he only wanted Neil to go with him, sparing my sensibilities.' Beth grimaced. 'But I followed them. We would have called the police, of course! But there wasn't time before you came.'

Neil added, 'We didn't know you were nearby already and would turn up so quickly, even without our phoning. I heard your cars coming through the gate and wondered who the devil it could be.'

'A witness had reported seeing a body in the water earlier this morning, about half a mile upriver, so we were already searching for it.' Jess sipped her coffee but neither of the Stewarts made any move to drink theirs.

'She – she just fell in and drowned?' It was Beth who asked.

'We don't know. We have to await postmortem results. Did you ask Mr Garley to go and look at the mooring?'

'No. It was Wayne's idea to go down there,' Beth told her. 'There has been lots of localised flooding because of all the rain we've had. I suppose Wayne was checking.'

'Are you also a writer?' Jess asked her.

A small smile showed briefly on her unhappy face. 'No, not at all. I worked in the financial sector when we lived in London. The company I worked for got into difficulties and I was one of those "let go".'

She did not expand on this. Jess sensed it was a difficult thing for her to discuss with a stranger. From outside came the crunch of wheels on gravel.

Beth asked very quietly, but with a note of hope, 'Are they taking her away?'

'They will do, eventually,' Jess explained. 'The area has to be searched thoroughly first, photographs taken, that sort of thing. There's a routine to be followed. That may be the doctor arriving.'

'Doctor?' Neil moved so suddenly, it made Jess start. He bounced in his seat and banged his hands on the table. More coffee slopped from his mug. 'What the hell do you need a doctor for? He isn't going to save her, is he?'

Beth reached out to put a calming hand on her husband's shoulder and he sank back.

'It's a formality,' Jess explained. 'He has to certify death.'

Neil Stewart stood up wordlessly and walked out of the room.

'I apologise for him.' Beth looked Jess directly in the eye. 'You have to understand, Neil lives – he lives in his head. He can handle anything provided it's in a plotline.' She gestured towards the river. 'He's not so good in a real emergency.'

Jess smiled at her reassuringly. 'We'll do our best not to make too much noise. Sorry for all of this, the mess, having to ask you questions.'

Beth stared down at the stone flags. 'It doesn't seem to matter, does it? A little mud on a kitchen floor, some tyre marks in the garden . . . It's nothing compared to a woman being dead.' She raised her eyes to look at Jess. 'She's very young, isn't she? She looked very young from where I was standing.'

Jess nodded. 'Yes, she did.'

'I never wanted to come and live here, you know, not really. Neil was so keen and I had no job to go to in London any longer, so . . .' She waved a hand. 'But I shan't stay, not after this.' After the smallest pause, she added, '*We* won't stay.'

But she sounded less certain about that.

When the police had eventually gone and, to Beth's relief, the body had been removed, she went in search of her husband. He'd retreated to the study. The garden was no longer a haven. The deep ruts of the visitors' tyres across the lawn and along the drive were too immediate a reminder of the tragedy. Wayne Garley had slipped away immediately he'd given his statement.

Neil sat by the desk, staring at the flickering computer screen.

'You had better close it down,' Beth said. 'You won't work again today.'

He obeyed and the screen went blank. He still remained staring at it.

'I think,' Beth suggested, 'we ought to go out somewhere for the rest of the day. You know, get away from here.'

He turned his head towards her. 'Go out? Where? Doing what?'

It was a fair enough question. She sought desperately for inspiration. 'The garden centre.'

He blinked. 'What would we do there?'

'Look at the Christmas stuff, I don't know, have some lunch. We really should put some space between us and – here. Just for an hour or two, Neil. We can't just sit in the house, prisoners.'

Neil's face, already pale, turned deathly white. 'You're – you're not really suggesting . . .? After that, out there?' He raised a shaking hand and pointed in the direction of the river. 'It was nightmarish, horrible, that girl . . .'

'Yes, it was quite dreadful and I'm upset, too!' Beth snapped. 'That's why we need a break. We're shocked. We need other images in our heads. I'll drive.'

He shook his head and returned his gaze to the blank screen. 'You go, if you want to, I can't,' he said simply. 'I couldn't mix with crowds of people, all chattering, surrounded by tinsel and Christmas stuff everywhere. We'd be forced to listen to jolly music piped everywhere, even in the café – and I couldn't eat lunch, surrounded by people stuffing themselves with chips. All I can see is – her.'

He moved some scraps of paper on which he'd jotted notes. 'They'll come back, won't they?'

'You mean the police?'

'Of course, the bally police!' His voice rose. 'They'll keep asking questions.'

'They will probably come back but there isn't anything we can tell them. She floated down the river somehow, poor kid, and lodged up against our mooring. It's not our fault. We don't even know who she is or where she was from, much less how she came to be in the water.'

Beth kept her voice as brisk as possible. For Neil to be sunk in depression wouldn't help. She wasn't going to let herself go to pieces. She was tempted to shout, *Look, you write some pretty gruesome stuff yourself from time to time*. But that would be unjust and unkind because what exists in the imagination has nothing to with stark reality.

Neil muttered something. She didn't catch all the words but the few she did seemed to make no sense. 'What?' she asked. 'Sorry, what did you say?'

A little louder, and with some effort at sounding clearer, her husband said, 'I recognised her.'

Chapter 4

Millie knew, of course, that she ought not to phone her father while he was at work. But Millie was no respecter of adult rules when she had something urgent to impart, as now.

'Pantomime?' Ian Carter asked. 'That's a bit ambitious of your school, isn't it? I mean, it will be a lot of work for the teachers.'

'They're not going to be in it!' Millie's voice echoed briskly in his ear. 'We always do a Christmas play, anyway. So, this year, Miss Waterford suggested we do *Mother Goose*. Miss Waterford has written all the words.'

'And are you playing Mother Goose?' asked Carter, wondering if this was the cause of all the excitement.

There was a small, cross silence. 'No, I'm only one of the geese.'

'Oh, I see. Well, you won't have to learn any words, then.'

'I've got to learn three songs! We sing them together, all the geese, four of us, and we do a dance. We're all dressed as geese.'

Carter wasn't quite sure what this might involve, so said simply, 'Oh, that will be fun.'

'Mummy is making my costume.'

'Good for her!' said Carter before he could stop himself, adding quickly, 'I mean, that's very clever of her.'

'You will come and watch, won't you?'

Ah, this was the tricky bit. Carter's heart sank. 'You will have

37

to let me know exactly when and at what time this is taking place, sweetheart. I'll do my best.'

'Oh, all right . . .' said Millie, her voice suddenly glum.

'I want to come and see you, of course I do! But . . .'

'It's *all right*,' said Millie, and rang off.

'Damn!' said Carter aloud. 'Damn, damn, damn!'

Why had he never had a job that gave him family time? Was this why his marriage had failed? Worse, it meant he felt he had failed as a father. He had never been there when required and, true to form, he couldn't promise now. But he'd do his very best. Only it wasn't just a question of getting the time off and travelling fifty miles. There would be the embarrassment of sitting there with Sophie and a crowd of other parents. All of them would know who he was and why he rarely appeared. Even worse, suppose Rodney, Sophie's present husband, decided to come along? Carter had an image of the three of them sitting on hard wooden chairs, Sophie in the middle between two husbands. No, she wouldn't do that. Sophie had a keen sense of the ridiculous. What she would do, most likely, was phone later today and explain, very nicely, that it really would be better if he didn't come.

'Millie wants me there,' he muttered aloud, rehearsing his reply.

There was a polite clearing of a throat, over by the door. He looked up and saw DC Bennison. 'Sir?'

'Yes, yes, do come in, Constable. I was just – just talking to my daughter on the phone.'

Bennison smiled. 'That's nice, sir,' she said kindly.

That was the problem in any tightly knit work environment: everyone knew everyone else's business. They all knew he was divorced. They knew about Millie. Worse, they were sympathetic.

'Inspector Campbell is on her way back, sir. The body's been taken to the morgue.'

Carter thanked her and she disappeared.

It might turn out an accidental drowning. They were approaching Christmas. The season, extending it to include New Year, was one when people celebrated. They went out, to parties and pubs, and drank more than they usually did. They got stupid drunken ideas like going for midnight swims. The river was in flood. There were treacherous snares like submerged branches. The low temperature of the water caught the would-be skinny-dippers unawares. They panicked. It might be too dark for any companions to see where the troubled swimmer was and respond to desperate shrieks.

This girl still had her clothes on, though, although they did sometimes jump in fully clothed. That raised the possibility of a suicide.

Or, in another scenario all too familiar, she might have been making her way home alone, stumbled and fallen in. The body had first been spotted in open countryside with no sign of any house or anywhere the girl might have been walking from. But the swollen river could already have carried her some distance, just as it had carried her to Glebe House, the home of the Stewarts, after dislodging her from her temporary rest among the drowned willow branches. The girl had entered the water anywhere between Weston St Ambrose and the spot where she'd first been seen by the vet, Lacey, according to Corcoran, the expert. Carter was trying to calculate the amount of manpower required to search such a big area.

Carter got up from his desk and wandered over to the window, looking out at the wet, bleak car park below. Until Tom Palmer had done his postmortem examination, they would be no wiser. It might be difficult to establish the facts, even then. There was a lot of debris in the river at the moment and injuries to the body could be caused by collision. They would not necessarily mean she had been attacked.

To his shame, he found himself hoping for purely selfish reasons that the young woman's death would turn out to be accidental. If there were evidence to suggest it was not, there would be even less chance he'd be able to take a couple of days off. Just now he wanted to watch Millie, singing and dancing in her goose costume, more than anything in the world.

The last thing any of them wanted was a new case of murder.

Vehicles turned into the car park and he recognised Jess's car, mud-splashed to window level. Shortly afterwards she appeared in his office, pretty well mud-splashed herself, her features pinched with cold and her auburn hair, darkened by rain, plastered to her scalp like a swimming cap.

'For goodness' sake, get yourself a hot drink first!' he ordered.

'Bennison's bringing me a coffee.' Her teeth weren't chattering – quite.

Machine-dispensed coffee, Carter thought, just the thing after a morning out in the cold and mud, supervising the retrieval of a corpse from the water.

'Come back when you've drunk it,' he said.

Jess and Carter were both unaware of it, but Jess was not the only bearer of the grim news. Urban dwellers use email and Twitter for spreading gossip. In Weston St Ambrose they had the Garleys.

'Debbie Garley told me her Uncle Wayne found a body in the

river this morning,' announced Prue Blackwood to her husband, about the same time as Jess was detailing the morning's activities.

He looked up. She was standing by the door in her winter coat and boots, holding a supermarket plastic carrier bag in either hand. Her face was red either from the chill air or with excitement. Askew on her grey hair a gaily striped hand-knitted beret was balanced precariously.

'Debbie Garley isn't the most reliable informant,' he retorted. 'She probably made it up. Where did you have this illuminating conversation?'

'In the supermarket, at the checkout. She works there.' Diverted from her news for a moment, Prue added, 'I am so pleased that place has opened up on the edge of the village. It was awful before when we didn't even have a village shop. I know some people got up a petition against it, but I'm all for it – and you meet people there.'

'Prue,' said her spouse, 'can we stick to what Debbie said and why you believe her?'

'It's not the sort of thing she would make up, surely? She was very excited about it, telling everyone.' Prue dumped the carrier bags on the carpet and began to unwind her scarf and divest herself of her coat.

Henry Blackwood studied his wife. Her eyes were sparkling. Clearly, Debbie was not the only one thrilled by the gruesome find. He suspected there was more information to come and Prue was bursting to impart it. But, with an aspiring novelist's instinct, she was spinning it out.

'Go on,' he urged.

'You'll never guess *where* Wayne Garley found it.'

'Obviously not. Just tell me, can't you?'

'In the river.'

'What on earth was Garley doing on the river? I know he undertakes to do just about anything, but always, as far as I know, on dry land.'

'*He* wasn't on the river. He was delivering some logs to the Stewarts. You know, Neil Stewart and his wife.' Now, Prue saw with satisfaction, she really had got Henry's attention.

'You are sure about this?' he asked slowly. 'Debbie hasn't got it all wrong, has she? Why on earth would it have anything to do with the Stewarts?'

'They bought Glebe House, didn't they? Its gardens go down to the river *and it was there*, Debbie says. Wayne Garley found the body snagged up on some sort of landing stage. On the Stewarts' property – in their garden, or adjacent to it, in the river!'

Henry digested this added information. 'I never understood why they bought that place,' he said. 'It was in a wretched state. Right near the quarry, too.'

'They bought it so that Neil could write his wonderful books in peace, didn't they?' Prue paused to look wistful. 'I do hope he runs another creative writing course. This last one was marvellous. I found it very helpful, didn't you?'

'No,' said Henry. 'I found him very negative. He dissed all my ideas.'

'Dissed?' asked Prue cautiously. 'What is "dissed"?'

'It's a modern word,' said Henry, growing pink. 'One has to be up to date with modern jargon. I need it for my novel. It means to put someone down. He dissed my novel.'

'He didn't like your novel much, did he?' Prue recollected, adding hastily, 'He didn't, um, diss it. He wasn't criticising your writing skills. But he thought you ought not to be writing about gangsters when you, um, don't really know anything about gangland goings-on.'

'I know as much as the average reader,' retaliated Henry. 'I do my research, the same as he does. That's how I know words like "diss". Anyway, I don't take kindly to that sort of criticism by a man who writes books that are pure fantasy!'

'But that's the sort of book his are,' argued Prue. 'People know they are fantasy. They're marketed as fantasy. Readers know that when they buy them. He's very popular. Yours are supposed to be gritty realism.'

'To follow your argument through, the only people permitted to write crime fiction would be old lags, and most crime writers are utterly respectable. What about your romantic novel? He didn't enthuse about that!'

'He was very nice about my novel.' Prue reddened. 'He admitted he knew little about romantic fiction, so he couldn't give me much individual help.'

'I think he meant your novel is beyond help!' snapped Henry.

'That's mean, Henry,' said his wife loftily, 'and unworthy of you. If you can write about one-legged bank robbers, I can write about Regency bucks.'

'Oh, all right,' said Henry, 'sorry. But you did criticise my thriller.'

'Constructive criticism enables a writer to grow!' pronounced Prue. 'Neil said so.'

'He may have said it to you – and me – but I bet he doesn't like it when anyone criticises what he writes.'

He spoke to an empty room because Prue had scuttled back into the hall to hang up her coat and take off her boots. She usually did these things before walking on the carpet but, clearly, Debbie's information had sent routine out of the window. Henry, as vulnerable to curiosity as any other man (he told himself), left his chair and his crossword to gather up the abandoned shopping and carry it into the kitchen. Prue came pattering along behind him.

'I wonder,' he said, 'if the other club members will have heard.'

'I do hope not,' said Prue wistfully. 'I would really love to be the first to tell them. What luck we've got a meeting tonight.' She pulled a loosened hairgrip from her dishevelled mop, prised it open with her teeth and shoved it back into place.

'One ought not to revel in bad news, dear,' reproached Henry.

'I'm not revelling. It's dreadful news, of course. But the others will have to hear it from someone and I would just like to be that person.'

'As a writer,' observed Henry judiciously, 'it would be very useful to observe their reactions . . .'

'I just want to tell Jenny Porter something she doesn't already know,' said Prue frankly. 'She always knows everything first. It would be really satisfying to tell her the news. She'd hate it, not being the one to tell everyone else.'

There was a silence while they contemplated the likely reactions of the other members' of the writers' club to the startling turn of events.

Prue gave herself a shake. 'Scrambled eggs on toast all right for tea? It's never a good idea to have beans on toast before we go.'

'Recognised her?' Beth repeated incredulously. 'How? Are you sure?'

She was struggling to absorb the claim her husband had just made. It couldn't be right. She didn't think she'd misheard. Perhaps he was just in shock and gabbling nonsense.

But he spoke quite calmly. 'Yes, I think I am – sure. I didn't get much of a look at her but it was enough.'

Now Neil stood up and walked out of the study. Beth watched him agape. Just like that? Drop a bombshell like that and then stroll away, conversation over? She wasn't supposed to ask any questions? How could Neil know the dead girl? They'd hardly glimpsed her. They hadn't been near enough and the police had crowded round the body. Neil didn't know anyone locally. He didn't know any *girls*.

Oho! whispered an unkind voice in her head.

Shut up! she told it immediately. If Neil were having an affair with someone half his age, she'd know it. Anyway, why should he?

How many women have told themselves that? retorted the unwelcome voice.

Listen! she said firmly to it. I know more about it than you, whoever you are!

I, it sneered, am the Voice of Worldly Wisdom.

No, you're not. You're the voice of a daft idea.

The voice fell silent, probably sulking.

Beth followed her husband. In the hall the gilet he'd worn earlier in the garden lay discarded on a chair. She paused to hang it up next to her coat. The action wasn't due to tidiness; it gave her a little time to think. She had to get this right. It was always possible he'd had a breakdown, gone off his head temporarily. He hadn't been at all himself recently, she reminded herself. I was thinking that only a couple of hours ago.

He'd gone back into the dining room where he stood staring up at the festoons of tinsels, waving gently in the draught from the open door.

'Neil,' Beth said carefully, 'I don't think you're very well. I think you are suffering from some kind of strain. You ought to go and see a doctor.'

'No,' he said.

Despite her resolve to keep calm and logical, Beth began to give way to irritation. 'Neil, you have just made an extraordinary, unbelievable statement. Then you walked away without any explanation. You can't leave it like that.'

He didn't answer and so she added, 'Well, all right, then. You recognised her. Who is she? What's her name?'

'Courtney.'

That he put a name to the dead girl was more shocking than his original statement. Surely this wasn't really true? He *did* know her?

'Who *is* she, anyway? How do you know her? Neil, for pity's sake!'

He heaved a sigh and turned to face her. 'She's a barmaid.'

'You don't know any barmaids. You don't go out to the pub . . .'

But he had been going to a pub during the weeks of the creative writing course. He went with the students, after the working part of the evening ended. 'Which pub?' Beth asked tightly.

'The Fisherman's Rest. You know that creative writing thing I let myself be dragooned into running for the college? Well, several of the students belonged to that writers' club they've got in Weston St Ambrose. They wanted to mark the end of the course in some way. We went to a pub after every meeting, the Black Horse in

Weston. But it's a bit of a dump and doesn't do food. They decided this was special and wanted to go further afield; have a meal and a pint somewhere interesting. Someone suggested the Fisherman's Rest at a spot on the river called Lower Weston, well off the main road. So we went there. I saw no reason not to go along with the idea. You weren't here. You'd gone to spend a couple of days with Susie. I could either come back here and stick a ready-meal in the microwave – or go to the Fisherman's Rest with the others and have steak and chips. I chose steak and chips.'

'You didn't tell me,' Beth said, trying to sort all this out in her mind.

'You weren't at home, I told you. You were at Susie's.'

'Yes, but I mean, you never mentioned it when I got back.'

'It wasn't important. Not worth mentioning.' Neil shrugged.

Nor would it be in character for Neil to mention something he'd probably forgotten about by the time Beth had returned.

I spend four days away from here, travel time included, to help out Susie, she thought crossly. In that short time, Neil, left alone, gets involved in something like this. He goes off to eat at a pub we have never visited together, and to do it with a group of people he barely knew. Three weeks later, the corpse of someone working at the pub that night comes bobbing down the river to rest against the crumbling landing stage belonging to Glebe House.

'You are sure this is the same girl and her name is Courtney?' she spoke slowly. She had to get a grip on this. 'It sounds a bit wild, Neil.'

'I know it sounds impossible. But I'm sure that was the kid who was our waitress. I saw her close to. She brought drinks to the table on a tray when we first went in and sat down. Some of the others chatted briefly to her. They knew her. Perhaps they ate there often. They called her Courtney. She was a cheerful sort of kid. Later she came back to take our orders and brought us our food. I pretty sure she was – the girl in the water.'

'Even so, after one visit to the Fisherman's Rest, you remember her well enough to recognise her again, dripping wet and covered in weed, when they lifted the body on to the bank? We barely glimpsed her, Neil! The police ushered us indoors.'

Neil thought about this. 'Yes,' he said. 'I'm pretty certain. I took a good look at her in the pub because I'm trying to decide what Astara, the lost daughter of King Zar, looks like.'

Oh, fine. The inner voice was back again. Try that as an explanation on the cops!

'OK . . . what's her other name, her surname?' she managed to ask aloud calmly.

'Good Lord, I don't know! No one calls pub staff by their surnames. People always just call them by their first names, don't they?'

'You tell me about it!' Beth heard herself snap. 'You seem to know a lot about pubs all of a sudden!'

'Don't be silly, Beth,' he reproached her. 'Don't exaggerate.'

'Don't exaggerate! Is it possible to exaggerate this weird situation?'

This whole business was quite crazy. Beth felt she was going mad. Perhaps Neil really had gone mad? 'You don't seem to realise the importance of what you're saying, Neil. She was wedged, drowned, under our landing stage! Not just anywhere, *here*!'

The implication of all this suddenly seemed to strike Neil, too.

'Will I have to tell the police?' he asked her nervously.

48

'Yes, of course you'll have to bally tell them! They will want to identify her!'

'I mean, they might think . . .' Neil was beginning to panic.

It wouldn't do if they both panicked. 'Now, listen,' Beth said. 'I'm going to ring the cops and tell them you think it is possible – although you can't be sure.'

Neil had opened his mouth to say he was sure.

Beth didn't let him. 'No, Neil, you are not sure, no matter if you think you are. You only saw this girl one evening at a pub you'd never been to before. She was alive, talking to the people she knew, probably grinning away at them, right? You only glimpsed the girl in the river when they lifted her out. Then the police told us to come back here into the house. You cannot be *certain*. Even when you saw a girl at the pub, you began recasting her image into that of some lost princess in your book. But we ought to tell them, even so, because if we don't tell them and it turns out it's her – well, it's better if we get in first.'

A strand of tinsel fell down. Neil was staring at it as if he'd never seen such a thing before. Beth was beginning to feel nothing was as it had been before. Another thought struck her, probably inspired by watching TV crime series.

'Neil, they – the police – might ask where we were yesterday. I was here except for an hour and a half in the morning when I drove to Weston St Ambrose. They were holding a farmers' market. I bought some produce but I didn't know the stallholders and they wouldn't remember me. I didn't see anyone I knew. But you weren't here all day, were you? You went to London.'

'Yes.' He brightened. 'I was in London and so I couldn't have anything to do with this.'

'You can prove it?'

'Of course I can! I met with people who do know me.'

Beth drew breath. 'Only you did get home rather later than usual.'

'I caught a later train. I bumped into Jack Calloway at the entrance to Tottenham Court Road tube station, and we decided to go off and have a drink and catch up. We hadn't seen each other for a long time. We went to some dive Jack knew. He and Jodie have split up, by the way.'

'What was it called, this dive?'

'I don't know. I told you, it was a place Jack knew. I just followed him in there. It was packed out, full of City types downing booze as fast as they could and boasting about the deals they'd pulled off.'

Beth was about to say he hadn't told her about that, either, or that a couple with whom they had at one time been quite friendly (because Jack and Jodie had lived in the flat above theirs) had parted. But her mind had thrown up a roadblock. She didn't know whether she wanted to know everything he hadn't yet told her; or if she'd rather remain in ignorance. Whatever else could there be?

See? sniped the voice in her head. You don't know as much as you think you do about Neil! Serve you right for being so complacent.

Chapter 5

'Tom Palmer will carry out his autopsy as soon as possible,' Jess said a little later, at the close of her verbal report to Ian Carter. 'In the meantime, we'll keep trying to identify her. There was nothing on her to tell us anything. Local press and radio might be the best bet. Someone must miss her, a flatmate, employer, family members . . . It's party time. People will be asking where she is. It's always worse at this time of the year when everyone is looking forward to Christmas. If a tragedy like this can ever be made worse, I mean.'

She didn't look so much of a drowned rat as when she'd arrived earlier, Ian Carter thought. She'd presumably drunk the coffee and certainly dried her hair. Her pale face was now flushed pink. Someone, one of the men from the look of it, had lent her a pullover. She'd rolled up the sleeves but it bagged out round her slim form. He found himself repressing a smile despite the grim content of what she was telling him. Mentally he ordered himself to get a grip. He stood up and walked back to his previous station at the window. It was still raining. The tarmac of the car park glittered like black satin. Drenched figures scurried between vehicles and the building. He thought that Lowry could have chosen such a subject for a painting.

'Christmas!' he repeated. 'Yes, bad at any time but worse

51

somehow now . . .' He paused and, with his back still turned to her, said, 'My daughter – you remember Millie? Well, she's in the school panto. They're doing a version of *Mother Goose*. She's one of the geese.' He turned back to face Jess now and gave a rueful smile.

'How could I forget Millie?' Jess smiled back at him. 'She'll be great in the panto.'

She had met Millie when Carter's daughter had been staying with him while her mother and mother's new husband went on a business trip. Ian worried a great deal about his daughter, she knew. He didn't doubt that his wife took good care of the child, but he worried that Millie somehow felt he – her real father – had let her down. Jess suspected that it was Carter himself who felt he had let down his daughter. Jess had wondered whether Millie, as could happen, also felt a responsibility for her father, living alone as he did. The little girl had assessed Jess rather closely during the visit and clearly decided that Jess could be the answer. That was flattering – but alarming.

'She'll be doing a dance with three others, and singing songs, all tricked out in some sort of costume her mother is making, I don't know what she'll look like.' Carter sounded despondent.

Jess asked cautiously, knowing it would be wiser not to become involved, 'You won't be going to watch?' She was sorry for him, and it was rotten for the kid, too. But she couldn't help.

'I'd like to, of course I would. She wants me there, phoned me to tell me so. It's – complicated.'

Jess tried to think of something constructive to offer by way cheering him up, but couldn't. When Ian Carter had first arrived, about eighteen months earlier, they'd all been wary of him, as they would be of any new superintendent coming to take over. He was a tall, solidly built man, not yet to be described as 'burly' but one day he might be, if he didn't watch out and keep going to the gym. Always supposing he went to the gym now. Jess had no reason to suppose he did. He had a liking for tweed and the look of a country gent when he was in repose. When he was agitated, he looked more like a fraught headmaster. Not that he lost his cool much. He was a controlled sort and had an unnerving way of waiting for others to speak first . . . It meant you never knew quite what to say, as Jess didn't now. Sometimes, while waiting, he'd keep his hazel eyes fixed on you in a way she found particularly disconcerting because she always found herself trying to decide if the colour of the irises was more on the pale brown, or on the green, range.

She'd been disconcerted, too, a few minutes earlier, when he'd been grinning at the sight of her swathed in a pullover DC Stubbs had provided. But she supposed she must look a bit of a freak in the garment. Stubbs was a six-foot-tall rugby player.

With relief, Jess saw DC Bennison's cheerful face and bobbing black braids, peering in through the doorway. 'Sorry to interrupt,' she said cheerfully, 'but Mrs Stewart is on the line, from Glebe House where the body was found, I mean, found in the river at Glebe House . . .' Bennison made a circular movement with her right hand indicating that she knew she could have phrased the information differently. 'Anyhow, ma'am,' Bennison addressed Jess, 'she's asking if you could go back there. There is something she and her husband want to tell you. She asked for you.'

'I'll go!' Jess said hastily. 'I wonder what she wants.'

'You've only just thawed out. I'll go,' Carter offered.

'I'm fine. Don't worry about it.'

'Then I'll come with you,' Carter said. She suspected he was relieved to have something practical to do. He moved briskly towards the door, unhooking his waxed jacket from the peg as he passed it.

Jess followed him. What had happened, she wondered, that Beth Stewart wanted to speak to her again so quickly? She pushed Carter's domestic problem out of her head. It was, after all, his problem: not hers. She had an unexplained drowning to think about. So did he.

Twilight had shrouded the landscape by the time Jess and Carter arrived at Glebe House. This time of year, thought Jess, it always feels as if the day is over and it's only late afternoon. A spot of moisture struck her cheek. She thought it had dripped from the branches overhanging the drive at the approach to the front door. But when she looked up, she saw that it was not only the fading day that had darkened the sky, but an ominous gathering of smoky clouds. It was going to rain.

Carter was standing back a little and surveying the frontage of the building. He had asked her, before they'd left, to describe the house to him. Jess had had to admit she really hadn't taken too much notice of it on her previous visit. It had been the background to the grim discovery in the river, registering in her memory as large, foursquare, of weathered pinkish brick, not the yellow stone of so many old buildings hereabouts. A late-Victorian building, perhaps, built for another time, certainly when the owners could afford a staff of servants, indoors and out. This time, on their arrival, the gloom made it impossible to make out any detail of the exterior, so only the vague impression of a large, square struc-ture remained.

Their arrival had been heard. The front door, as solidly built as that of a church, was pulled open and a woman stood there, with the tiled entrance behind her. She looked past Carter to Jess, whom she obviously remembered from that morning.

'You'd better come in,' she said. Then, after the barest break, 'Thanks for coming back, sorry to be a nuisance.'

Inside, the rooms on the ground floor had the same nineteenth-century spaciousness. The architect had further increased the floor area of the room in which they sat by the use of large bay windows. The ceiling was high and moulded. It must cost a fortune to heat the place.

The room was sparsely furnished for the generous space avail-able, and the attempt to make a comfortable area had not really worked. There were two large leather sofas set at right angles and a long, glass-topped coffee table. A sheet of A4 paper lay on the table, either blank or printed surface down.

The television set had its own stand. There was a low cabinet, consisting of an open space filled with books above closed cupboard doors. On the mantelshelf above the tiled Victorian fireplace two red-glazed pottery cats perched, one crouching and its companion with its back arched.

The only other piece of furniture was a hoop-backed Victorian chair, in need of some restoration. That was presumably genuine and might have been picked up at an antiques market. It didn't match the rest of the aggressively modern furniture. Perhaps its acquisition was an attempt to match the style of the building. Instead it just struck an incongruous note. Jess guessed that the

Stewarts had moved into this large house from a much smaller home. The original wood floors had been stripped, sanded down and polished. One very modern painting hung on the wall. Jess couldn't make out what it was supposed to represent.

There was a faint tension between the Stewarts that suggested they had been arguing. But they presented a united front to their visitors as Jess introduced Carter.

'It has been a great shock,' Beth Stewart said, still taking the lead in the conversation. Her husband sat beside her on one of the two sofas, silent. He looked drawn and unhappy. He had risen to his feet to greet them, but almost immediately sat down again, as if standing required too much effort of him.

Jess and Carter, seated side by side on the other sofa, nodded sympathetically. Neither of them said anything. They had been invited here to listen to some presumably important detail, and they were waiting to hear it. Their professional detachment seemed to unnerve Neil Stewart even more. He began to pick at a fingernail.

'All that business this morning threw us completely.' Beth paused and glanced sideways at Neil. 'We haven't been able to think straight. It upset Neil very much. Tell them why, Neil.'

Forced into speech, Neil Stewart stopped fidgeting and looked directly at the visitors for the first time. Both of them recognised the signs. They'd seen them before in others. They were about to hear a confession, not to murder, but to some private embarrassment. Witnesses often found it hard to speak of something embarrassing to them, if trivial to others. They felt they were somehow stripping themselves naked. They had to wind themselves up like an old-fashioned clock to do it. Neil Stewart had wound himself up to that point.

When he spoke, the words were blurted out. 'The thing is, I only glimpsed that girl's face. To be honest, I didn't want to look at the poor kid. It was horrible, water dripping from her . . . But, well, after you left I began to think she had seemed somehow familiar.'

Perhaps he saw new alertness in the visitors' expressions. 'No!' he corrected himself quickly. 'Not *familiar*, not someone I would know well. Just someone I might have seen somewhere. Then it occurred to me she might be a girl who works – worked – at the Fisherman's Rest, a girl named, I think, Courtney.'

'You didn't mention this earlier, Mr Stewart, when we were here,' Jess observed calmly. She didn't want to sound as if she were accusing him of anything, but she was reproachful. They had, after all, had to make a return journey to hear this, a journey at the end of a long day, and which they could have done without. Would have been without, if Stewart had spoken out earlier.

'Look, I wasn't sure!' he burst out. 'And you arrived so suddenly, unexpectedly. I couldn't think who you might be. That's why I was running up the front drive, to find out. If you hadn't come, we'd have phoned you to tell what we'd found, of course we would – and by the time you came I'd have got my head together enough to think what I was going to say—'

He broke off. 'That didn't sound right,' he said miserably. 'I meant, I would have decided to mention it to you. But, as I said, I only got a quick look at her when your divers carried her out of the water and put her on the grass. Before that, when Garley and I went down to investigate, she was wedged face down, under the platform. I didn't want to mislead you.'

His wife joined in. 'Look, he's really very shocked. Anyone

would be, if they saw a body like that, at the bottom of the garden, in the river . . . After you left, he told me he thought he might know who she was, and we – I called you.'

Jess looked at Carter. 'Fisherman's Rest?' she asked.

He shook his head. 'Don't know it.'

'The Fisherman's Rest is a pub, more of a restaurant, really, at Lower Weston. There isn't much more there than the pub,' Neil explained. 'It's just a collection of buildings on a minor road that follows the course of the river across country, before joining the main road.'

Beth added her support. 'I have heard that it's quite well known for its food. Not that Neil and I have ever been there together.' A barbed note in her voice recalled the tension Jess had sensed between them on arrival.

'And I only ever went there *once*,' Neil added defensively. 'That was with a group of people who attended my creative writing course, at the Elsworth Arts and Media College. We – the people on the course and I – used to go and have a drink at a local pub after the end of each session. The pub was near the college and called the Black Horse. But after the last module of the course, someone suggested we splash out and make more of a celebration of it. Go for a meal, you know. Beth was away visiting her sister, so I thought I might as well go along – and I did. The Black Horse doesn't do food, other than packet snacks and sandwiches, so someone suggested the Fisherman's Rest. The others all seemed to know of it, so I agreed. One of the reasons I went along with the others was that it is near here and I hadn't far to go home.

'This girl, Courtney, was working there. Some of the people

with me called her by name, knew her.' Neil drew a deep breath. 'I can't tell you any more than that and I could be quite wrong.'

'You can see why Neil hesitated to tell you straight away,' supported Beth. 'He could still easily be wrong. Perhaps it's not this Courtney girl, after all.'

They both sat waiting for the visitors' reaction.

Carter stirred. 'Well, you did quite right. We will follow this up, of course. We may need to speak to all the other people who went along to the Fisherman's Rest that night – the students from the course you spoke of.'

Beth leaned forward and took the sheet of A4 paper from the coffee table. As she picked it up, Jess could see that it was printed on the side that had been face down.

'I've listed their names and telephone numbers. But we don't have their home addresses. You'd have to get those from the college. There were more people than this on the course, but these are the ones who went to the Fisherman's Rest last night, with Neil.'

'Thank you,' said Jess, taking the paper.

Neil had brightened. 'It was a popular course. I'd run one like it before and the college asked me to do it again. We had thirty people register but some dropped out after a week or two. With one exception, you'll find the names listed there are of people who belong to a writers' club in Weston St Ambrose. They never missed an evening. They came along as a body.' The word 'body' wiped the animation from his face. 'Um . . .' he mumbled.

'Who is the one who doesn't belong to this writers' club?'

'Graeme Murchison. He has something to do with antiquarian books and I'm not sure why he came on the course. I don't think he was actually trying to write anything. He just seemed to want to listen.'

Jess marked a cross against the name 'Murchison' and folded the sheet. 'What sort of people are they, who sign up for your courses?'

'Oh,' he frowned, 'all sorts, you know. There are a lot of people who try their hand at writing. Some have a go at short stories; others aspire to novels of various kinds. I must say we had a couple of talented people on this last course. The usual couple of deluded ones, too. Not all of them belonged to the writers' club I mentioned. That seems to be made up of people who live in and around Weston St Ambrose. For some of those I suspect the club provides a social life. Weston St Ambrose is pretty quiet.'

Jess, who knew Weston St Ambrose from previous investigations, could have told him that, despite being a small place with few amenities, quite a lot went on there behind closed doors.

'Can you remember which of them knew the waitress by name?'

'No, not really.'

'And you don't recall seeing her anywhere else? Or you, Mrs Stewart? Did you recognise the girl in the river?'

Addressed directly, Beth said, 'No. I'd never seen her. I didn't know her at all. She could have worked at the pub at Lower Weston, but I was never in there, as I explained. The fact is, in the eighteen months we've lived here, we've hardly ever gone out for a meal, or even a drink. The move down here from London has proved expensive. We don't waste money.'

'Just for the record,' Carter took up the conversation, 'where were you both yesterday evening? Don't be alarmed. It's a question we'll be asking all the people on this list.'

They did indeed both look alarmed, Neil particularly so.

'I was here,' Beth said. 'On my own, all day, except for a trip to the farmers' market in Weston St Ambrose. I didn't see anyone I knew, I'm afraid. The stallholders probably won't remember me. I had a cup of coffee in a hotel lounge, a place called the Royal Oak. It was pretty busy in there, too. I don't suppose the waiter would remember me either.'

'I was in London all day,' her husband took up the tale. 'I left early to drive to Gloucester to catch the train. I visited my agent and looked in at the British Museum. I particularly wanted to see some Fayoum mummy portraits they have there.' Perhaps he detected some puzzlement in his visitors because he added, 'They're panel paintings. During the time that Egypt was part of the Graeco-Roman world, the local custom was still to mummify the dead but it became the fashion to add a panel portrait to the wrappings of the body. A number were excavated at a place called Fayoum. I wanted some inspiration for the book I'm working on. The faces are extraordinary.'

'And you got back here?' Carter asked.

'Oh, quite late because I ran into someone I knew and we went for a drink. I didn't get home until after eleven. When I got to Paddington, I found that I'd just missed a train and had to wait an hour for the next. I got a coffee from a stand and just sat around, reading through the notes I'd made at the museum – and the book I'd brought with me to read on the train: *British Fungi*. It was cold and uncomfortable. There was a big crowd waiting for the train and a stampede down the platform to get on. I fought my way to a seat. I spent the whole journey wedged like a sardine in a tin. I couldn't even read comfortably. The guy next to me was working on his laptop. It was hellishly distracting. Then I had to drive home from Gloucester station to here.'

Beth said quietly, 'You had better give them Jack Calloway's details, in case they want to check.'

'Why should they want to check?' Neil snapped at his wife.

'It's what they do,' said Beth flatly.

'Then they can have Jack's latest business card! He gave me a couple before we parted. It's in the study – hang on.' Neil got up and strode out.

In his absence, Beth said, 'Neil isn't a pub person. He doesn't much like crowds these days. He lives for his writing. He begrudges time spent on anything else. I was pleased when he agreed to run the two writing courses for the college. Only, now this has happened, it will put him off ever running another one.'

Neil was back, holding out a business card. 'There you go, Superintendent Carter. I don't think I can help you any further. But that should do it.'

As they drove away, Carter observed, 'Impossible to prove he was at the museum. As for just sitting round Paddington waiting for a train! Yes, he had a drink, he says, with an old acquaintance. He could have contacted Calloway before his wife called us, and asked him to provide an alibi. It does seem very convenient for him that he "ran into" this old pal. Do you think he realises we might not be convinced by his giving us that business card – or by his whole story?'

'I don't know whether he realises it,' Jess replied. 'But I'm pretty sure his wife does. On the other hand, it was bad luck the body was found on his stretch of bank. Lacey, the vet who called us, had seen it earlier much higher up the river.'

Carter grunted. 'Did he? It wasn't there when you and Nugent arrived, together with Corcoran and his team of divers. Perhaps Corcoran was right and Lacey was mistaken. OK, so now we'd better drive over to this pub called the Fisherman's Rest. Do you know it?'

'I've driven past it. I've never been inside. It looks a tourist trap.'

As the Stewarts had described, Lower Weston clung mostly to the sides of a B road that was itself clinging to the category of 'B'. It hardly qualified to have a place name of its own, but perhaps it had once been a larger settlement. If so, little of it remained, but there was the suggestion of former importance in a medium sized Georgian house on its outskirts. The house was just visible through wrought-iron gates in a high wall, but the twilight made it impossible to distinguish details. Security lights over the front door and at the corners of the building bathed the exterior and immediate surrounding garden in white light. But all the windows in the house were dark, not even a thin beam slipping through chinks in a curtain: no one at home.

After that came a row of former labourers' cottages, most now expensive homes. Finally, and on the opposite side of the road, stood the Fisherman's Rest. It was a long, low stone building suggesting two or more original dwellings joined together. In deference to the approaching festive season, a string of lights designed like icicles decorated the eaves. Like the Stewarts' home, Glebe House, the pub stood on the riverbank. Also like the Stewarts' home, Jess guessed that the swollen river must threaten the grounds at the rear of the building. But the pub was still in business.

The building fronted the roadside directly, without even a strip of footpath, but there was a car park alongside it. They turned in. Three vehicles were parked there already. As they drew up, another turned in behind them, a large Range Rover.

'This might be a red herring,' warned Carter beside her. 'We'll walk in and find Courtney pulling pints. You lead the way and start the questions. I'll ferret around.'

There was an entrance into the pub directly from the car park. They found themselves in a warm bar, low-ceilinged, discreetly lit, and welcoming. Jess decided she had been wrong to judge the Fisherman's Rest a tourist trap. The people here had presumably come in the cars already parked; or owned the cottages across the road. Possibly there were more dwellings tucked, like Glebe House, down lanes and not visible from the main road. These regulars looked a prosperous lot. They leaned on the bar and chatted affably with one another and with the barman.

'No,' the barman was telling them, 'the water isn't threatening the building yet but it is halfway up the garden. We've got sand-bags all along the back.'

There was a chink of glassware from the right and, glancing in that direction, Jess saw that it came from the restaurant in the next room, where a trim young woman was setting up the tables. She was about twenty, professionally turned out in a black skirt and white shirt. Her long hair was tied back with a black bow at the nape of her neck. Could she be Courtney? Were they, after all, about to eliminate one possible identity for the corpse?

Behind them, the entrance door opened and shut. A brief chill breeze invaded the warm space. The driver of the 4 x 4 had followed them in. The man behind the bar was now coming towards them with a welcoming smile.

The smile vanished to be replaced by a look of concern when Jess produced her identification. Silence fell on the bar and the cheerful regulars became as alert as gundogs. All conversation ceased. The chill breeze briefly swept the area behind her as the entrance door was opened again. The driver of the Range Rover had changed his mind about a pint.

Carter was aware of it, too. He left Jess at the bar and slipped outside.

'We'd better talk in the office,' the man at the bar said. 'Amy, come and take over here, will you?'

Not Courtney, then, thought Jess, as the girl who had been busy in the restaurant left what she was doing and came to replace the barman. She followed the barman, whom she was beginning to think managed the place, through a mini maze of stone-flagged passageways until they reached the office. The roundabout route confirmed Jess's original impression that the Fisherman's Rest had once been more than one property. The barman/manager was holding open the door for her to enter.

'I'm Gordon Fleming,' he said. 'I run the Rest. What can we do for you, Inspector?'

Chapter 6

Ian Carter had stepped out into the car park. But he was just too late to intercept the driver of the Range Rover, who was apparently unwilling to consort with coppers. The vehicle was turning out on to the road where the driver made a left, rolled past the frontage of the pub, and in seconds was out of sight. Carter ran to the car park exit and stared in frustration down the road. It was now quite dark and there was no way he could attract the driver's attention. By the time he returned to his own car, and set out in pursuit, the quarry would be long gone. He could still see the rear lights of the Range Rover but they were growing smaller. He heaved a sigh and was about to turn back to the pub when the pinpoints of red seemed to waver and then vanish.

The road ran straight ahead until it joined the main road, as Ian knew from having driven along it on the way there. The Range Rover could not have reached that junction yet. So, where and how had the vehicle disappeared so suddenly? It had turned in somewhere. He tried to remember if they had passed any gaps in the stone walls and hedgerows and cursed the poor light. He did remember something – a possibility – the Georgian house. Could the driver have turned in there?

Carter set off at a jog-trot down the road. He was soon wishing he were fitter. It was a chill evening but he was sweating within a couple of minutes, sealed inside his waxed jacket. He couldn't shed the garment, so he had to persevere, lumbering on until he had almost reached the house when he was obliged to slow to a walk, gasping. The wrought-iron gates loomed out of the darkness and he halted to control his ragged breathing. Apart from the worst-case scenario in which he pitched forward and expired from a heart attack, he did not fancy even the less dramatic one, in which he presented himself, panting and wheezing, to the house owner.

There were lights on in the ground-floor rooms now. The owner had returned home. Carter could see the outline of the 4 x 4 parked at the front of the building, dark against the illuminated frontage. The gates had already closed. He put out a hand and rattled them experimentally, but they were obviously controlled from the house. With some difficulty (he should have retrieved a torch from the car before he set out), he managed to locate a button on the nearer gatepost and pressed it. Dragging a handkerchief from his pocket, he mopped his brow and tried to appear composed as he waited for a reply from the entry phone.

It seemed a long wait, and he was preparing to press it again when the still night air was broken by a crackling noise. A tinny voice inquired who he was.

'Police – Superintendent Carter,' he told the phone. 'We are making some inquiries at the Fisherman's Rest and I believe you were there a few minutes ago.'

Another silence while the man inside the house thought about this. Was he going to be stupid and deny he'd been at the pub?

There was no verbal answer, but Carter heard a buzz and the gates began to creak slowly open. He stepped through and started down the gravel drive, his footsteps crunching on the surface. Behind him the gate hissed and scraped closed. At the same moment, clamour broke out, piercing the quiet air. Dogs – definitely more than one. Their sensitive hearing had picked up the sound of his feet on the gravel. Their cries became shrill as they yelped and howled their frustration at not being able to intercept the intruder.

They were not in the house. They were certainly outdoors in the grounds somewhere. He couldn't retreat through the gates now, too late for that. Were the wretched beasts running loose? But although they continued to kick up an alarming racket, the animals didn't appear. They were confined somehow; Ian felt himself relax. The likelihood was that these were guard dogs, not spoiled indoor pets. This was a lonely area and a large house standing alone might well attract criminal attention. Perhaps he ought not to be surprised. But at the same time, this represented a high degree of security.

Ahead of him the door opened and a man was silhouetted in the yellow light of the hallway.

'Don't mind the damn dogs,' he greeted his visitor. 'You won't mind showing me your identification, will you?'

Carter obliged.

The man scrutinised it and raised his eyebrows. 'Bit of a senior man to be making house to house inquiries, aren't you?'

'I like to get out from behind a desk sometimes,' said Carter, retrieving his identification. 'You are the owner of the house, sir?'

'Yes. My name's Graeme Murchison. Come in.' He stood back to allow Carter to enter and closed the door behind his visitor. 'This way.'

Murchison . . . Carter was thinking. Graeme Murchison was the name of the only person who was not a member of the writers' club in Weston St Ambrose to accompany Neil Stewart to the Fisherman's Rest, on the last night of the writing course. Had this man, Murchison, been the one to suggest the party drove out to eat at his local pub, because it was convenient for him? The Stewarts had told them that Murchison was not trying to write anything, but had a connection with antiquarian books. Carter glanced around him. Did old books pay well? It seemed so.

This house had all the comfort that Glebe House lacked. It had been restored, decorated and furnished with taste and empathy with the period of the building. Such attention to detail cost money. Murchison had led him into a large, but not over-large, drawing room. A log fire crackled in the hearth. There was a long sofa set before it and at one end, on a small table, stood a glass of whisky. It hadn't been touched, by the look of it, suggesting Murchison had just poured it out on his return.

Perhaps Murchison had noticed Carter looking at it because he now offered, 'Care for a drink?'

'Thank you, I'll have just a small whisky, please,' Ian Carter said. He wondered if his host would make some crack about police officers not being supposed to drink on duty, but Murchison merely nodded, and fetched another tumbler. 'Make yourself comfortable. I'll just go and silence those animals. Once I tell them it's all right, they'll settle down again.'

When he had returned and both were seated before the fire, Carter said: 'You're well protected here, dogs and security gates. Do you let the dogs run loose when you're not here, or you've turned in for the night?'

'The days we live in, Superintendent, require good security. Lower Weston is a very small place. It doesn't run to street lighting. I live on the outskirts, it's a large house in grounds and, after dark particularly, lonely. Just the place to attract the wrong sort of interest. Someone might decide to scale the wall, break in and help himself to anything he fancied might fetch a price. He might not appreciate my extensive collection of books, but I have other things of value, like the silver in that display cabinet over there.

'I've not had anyone actually getting as far as breaking in, so my security, the outside lights and the gates, must be working, touch wood.' Murchison tapped the table top beside him.

'As regards the dogs, they are not guard dogs, they are pets. I'm aware of the law. They are in no way dangerous. They are kept outside because there are two of them, German Shepherds, and I don't want them running round indoors knocking things over. They have a purpose-built kennel they can go in and out of at will, and a pen they can move round freely, and that's where I put them at night or if I go away from the house. But during the day, if I'm here on the property, they run loose around the garden. I also take them out and exercise them in the woods behind the house . . . or down to the river. Riverside walking is off limits at the moment, too much mud. We quite often meet another dog walker without incident. My two, Max and Prince, are very obedient. They do set up a racket from time to time at night because they have sharp ears. I go out and investigate but, as you've just experienced for yourself, they are easily quietened if reassured. They would call attention to an intruder but I am confident they would not attack. They might keep him rooted to the spot until I got there. If so, that would be because of nerves on the part of the intruder.' Murchison smiled.

'Yes, you have looked up the law,' Carter returned drily. 'Well, I am sorry to have disturbed you and your pets. We are making just a few inquiries at the pub. We'd like to talk to anyone who is a regular there.'

Murchison nodded. 'Yes, I saw the woman officer brandishing her ID at Gordon. If she was preparing to talk to him it didn't seem a convenient moment to place an order, so I decided to come home here and have my evening snifter.' He smiled and raised his tumbler of amber liquid in salute to his guest. 'I didn't leave because I was avoiding you, Superintendent!'

My, my, you are a cool customer and a quick thinker! thought Carter, returning the salutation. He cast an eye over his host as Murchison raised the tumbler to his lips. Hard to put an age to the man, but probably just entering his fifties, so much of an age with Carter himself. To the way he'd made heavy weather of jogging here was added a consciousness that his build was heavier than his host's. Murchison was tall, lean, fair-haired and, when he went grey, would do so almost imperceptibly. His skin sat taut over his aquiline features with barely a wrinkle or frown mark. Murchison would probably always look younger than his years. *Must start going to the gym*, Carter told himself. The sweat that had built up on his body during his jog to the house was drying now and he feared he might start steaming like a racehorse.

Murchison was comfortably dressed, country style, in corduroy trousers and a pullover. The collar of his check shirt protruded through the neck of the pullover. The movement of raising the tumbler had revealed an expensive wristwatch. He wore no wedding ring.

'Anyway,' said Murchison unexpectedly, 'if you are asking questions at the Rest, I'd like to know. I own the place.'

Carter couldn't help but show his surprise and a faint smile on Murchison's face showed that he enjoyed the reaction he'd caused.

'Gordon Fleming runs it for me,' the man added.

That gave Carter an opening. 'Who hires the staff? You or Fleming?'

'Oh, I leave all that to Gordon. He knows what he's doing. He found a good chef and someone to assist him – and a couple of girls to help out in the restaurant and at the bar, if needed.'

'Where does he find staff?' Carter swirled the whisky in his tumbler and watched how the flickering flames in the hearth played on it. Golden lights flashed in the liquid. 'This is a very good whisky,' he added.

'Thank you. The chef was someone Gordon knew already. He managed to persuade him to come to us. The chap who helps in the kitchen, he calls himself a sous-chef, is the chef's partner. If you hire one, you hire the other, I understand. The girls, I don't know, he probably found them through a job centre.'

'No problems with them, the girls?'

Murchison shook his head. 'No, not as far as I know. They're good kids. Gordon wouldn't keep them on if they were shirkers or broke everything they touched.'

'Is owning pubs or restaurants something you do on a big scale?' Carter asked.

Murchison shook his head. 'No. I only bought the Rest because it came on the market and it was my local. I thought it had the potential to make money. That sort of place can do very well round here. In the summer there are tourists; but all year round there is trade of the upmarket sort.' He smiled faintly. 'No use running a business like ours if the customers don't have any money! Around here, it's not obvious, but there are some fairly affluent residents in the general area.'

Of whom you are one, thought Carter, with another surreptitious look around him.

'I understand you signed up for a recent course on creative writing at the Elsworth Arts and Media College? The course was tutored by Neil Stewart, the author of fantasy novels.' With this question Carter had the satisfaction of seeing his host look slightly disconcerted.

'Yes, I did. How do you know? Why is that of interest to the constabulary?'

'I also understand,' Carter went on, not replying to the question, 'that at the end of the last session of the course, a group of students, if that's what you call them, went for a celebratory dinner with Neil Stewart at the pub here.'

The pause before he answered and the look of appraisal Murchison openly gave his guest showed that he was assessing Carter anew, and wondering where all this was leading. 'Yes, we did.'

'Whose idea was it to choose the Fisherman's Rest? Yours?'

Murchison relaxed again. 'Because I own it? I don't know who suggested it, to be honest. I might have done. Or old Pete Posset might have done, he's a regular diner there, generally they see him for Sunday lunch. Or, come to that, the Blackwoods. They turn up fairly often. Someone on the course, anyway.'

'Do the others know you own the place?'

Murchison carefully set his empty tumbler on the end table beside him. 'Probably not. That's not because I'm trying to keep it secret. It's just irrelevant and I don't make a point of mentioning it. My business interests are my own affair. I told you, Gordon Fleming runs it. I do nothing but drop in for a pint from time to time, or for the occasional lunch.'

'But, apart from Neil Stewart, you were the only person at that celebratory meal who wasn't a member of a writers' club.'

Murchison looked as if he thought he detected the drift of the questioning. He seemed to relax. 'Ah, yes, the Weston St Ambrose Writers' Club. You're right. They all, Posset, the Blackwoods and others, meet regularly. I don't belong to it because I'm not any kind of writer.'

'What attracted you to sign up for the course?'

Murchison laced his fingers together. 'Well, there are other aspects to being interested in books than trying to write your own! I deal in antiquarian books and some modern first editions. There are a lot of collectors for both.'

'You have a shop somewhere?'

Murchison shook his head. 'No, all my business is done online. A lot of the inquiries about modern first editions come from the USA.'

'But you must have some stock? Where do you keep that?'

'Here, Superintendent Carter. I can show you the library, if you are interested.' Murchison stood up and walked towards the door.

Carter followed. At the other end of the central hallway, Murchison opened a door and switched on the lights. The library was just what such a room in a period house ought to be. Carter guessed it was lined with the original bookcases, all packed with volumes. Some looked very old indeed, their leather spines cracking, but there was a whole bookcase of new volumes, mostly shrink-wrapped.

'Where do you get them all from?' Carter asked, genuinely puzzled.

For the first time, Murchison grinned broadly. 'Originally, quite a lot of the really old ones came with the house. They've always been here. Occasionally I sell one, but I've already disposed of the ones that had any value. The remaining ones are what I'd class as curiosities but not particularly interesting. That's why I moved into modern collectable first editions.' He indicated the wrapped volumes. 'Collectors of those, particularly in America, like them pristine. That's why they're shrink-wrapped.'

Carter had moved to the books and began to study the titles. '*A Guide to London 1815. The Gentleman's Book of Etiquette 1849. An Essay on the Properties on Minerals. Collected Sermons of a Country Clergyman. The Diary of a Lady's Travels in the Orient . . .*' Carter read aloud.

He turned towards Murchison, who shrugged and said, 'Not a lot of call for those, but what the heck? I even dip into them myself from time to time. They have entertainment value. Plus, they've lived in this house longer than I have, so who am I to turf them out into the cold, cold world?'

Carter was genuinely interested. 'That's always been your line, old books, or any collectable books?'

Murchison shook his head. 'It's always been a sort of hobby interest, but I didn't take up the dealing side of it until I came back to England from America about ten years ago and bought this house.' He saw Carter's inquiring expression. 'I worked in New York, in the art world: paintings and ceramics rather than printed matter. I did quite well, made a lot of money. I was also in a – I thought – permanent relationship. But that ended.' He pulled a wry expression.

'I'm divorced myself,' Carter heard himself say.

'Really? Kids?' Murchison raised an eyebrow.

'I have a little daughter, well, growing up fast now,' Carter admitted. He reminded himself that he was breaking the cardinal rule. Never give the interviewee, however innocent the question might appear, any personal information about yourself. It can always reveal a chink in your armour, should anyone want to use that, one day. But Millie was on his mind and the words had slipped out.

'At least you have that from your marriage,' said Murchison. 'I have nothing. Barbara and I weren't married but we'd been together for six, seven, years. Then it petered out as a relationship. It wasn't my decision to finish it, but she saw it differently.' Murchison's former direct gaze became a stare into the middle distance.

'Anyhow,' he concluded. 'There was clearly no point in arguing. Maybe she was right? We divided the stuff we'd bought together, sold the flat, and went our separate ways. I can't deny I was hurt. I decided it was time to try my hand at something new, not a new relationship but a new lifestyle. After all, I'd got money in the bank; I could afford to swan around for a bit. I came back to England, bought this house, and decided to go for book-dealing, since books had always been an interest and here I had a ready-made stock of them to start me off!' Murchison waved a hand at the surrounding shelves. 'I discovered, once I'd got settled, that I like living on my own. I cook. I travel a fair bit, both hunting out old editions and on holiday. Odd things come along to take my interest, like that creative writing course. I was interested to hear a professional author's point of view. That's it.'

That speech almost qualifies as an official statement, thought Carter. Am I supposed to stop asking questions now? No, Mr Murchison, it doesn't work like that!

'Who takes care of all this –' he indicated their surroundings – 'and the dogs, when you go away?'

'Old Charlie Fallon. He lives out in the woods in a shack with a corrugated iron roof and without any amenities. He collects rainwater in a drum and uses oil-lamps for lighting; and a spirit stove for boiling water.'

'No heating? In this weather that must be a problem.'

Murchison shrugged. 'He's got some sort of a home-made wood-burning stove in there, with a pipe going up through the roof to serve as a chimney. He's what they called a bodger. He makes wooden items, pretty simple stuff, but useful. It's an ancient craft and he must be one of the last. I fancy he used to be a poacher, too. He has an affinity with animals. I trust him with the dogs and the dogs trust him, which is important. He comes and does a spot of tidying up outside for me, between the professional gardening company's visits.'

'How does he enter the property, when you're away? The gates, presumably, are locked fast.'

Murchison made a mild protest. 'If you must know – and I don't see how this is relevant to any inquiries, I must say! But there is a door in the back wall. There used to be a walled kitchen garden in former times. That's long gone. I suppose the old-time gardeners used the door. Now no one uses it but Charlie, who has a key. From outside the property you can hardly see it for the bushes growing by the wall. But Charlie can squeeze through; he's a little chap. It's a mutual arrangement. He helps me out. I let him go on living in his shack. I own that bit of woodland, too, you see.

'But that, Superintendent Carter, really can't be of interest to you.' Murchison had tired of his visitor and Carter's last question did appear to have annoyed him. His tone became brisk. 'Is there anything else I can help with?'

Carter told him, no, not for the time being. He thanked him for his hospitality and willingness to be interviewed, and walked slowly back to the car park at the pub.

Chapter 7

'We're making some general inquiries in the area, Mr Fleming,' Jess told the pub manager. 'Please don't be alarmed by our turning up on your doorstep.'

'Not at all, the police are welcome.' Having made this unlikely statement, Fleming pulled out a chair, removed a pile of what looked like advertising material, and indicated she should sit down.

Jess sat down. She didn't know where Ian Carter had taken himself off to, but something must have attracted his attention. Fleming took the seat before the computer, swivelling it to face her. He put his hands on his knees and waited. He was a pale-complexioned man who perhaps spent too much time indoors. His sandy hair was cropped short and sparse and he had almost no eyebrows or eyelashes. Jess was unfortunately reminded of one of those vegetables grown shielded from sunlight to ensure their whiteness. The colour had not leached out of Fleming. It had never been there. Yet he was not albino. Jess found him somehow disconcerting.

'This is a very old building,' she commented by way of an opener.

'Yes, and it stands on a very old road. You might not think it now, but this was once a main road to Cheltenham. I'm talking of three or four hundred years ago. The buildings date from

81

around the time of Elizabeth the First. I say "buildings" in the plural because the present pub is made up of the original hostelry, its stables and a blacksmith's forge. When horse traffic stopped, the stables and forge were no longer required.'

This is the little speech he makes to tourists, Jess thought.

'I thought the layout a bit eccentric,' she admitted. 'Can you tell me how many staff you employ here, Mr Fleming?'

'Four,' he replied promptly. 'Our chef and his assistant, they are very important to us. We value the reputation of our food. Then there are the two girls who help me in the bar and restaurant.'

'I saw one of them out there, Amy? She took over the bar?' Jess indicated the direction of the bar, somewhere at the end of the maze of passages.

'That's right, Amy Fallon. She lives with her parents in the last cottage across the road from here, looking to your right. She's worked here for two years. She's very reliable.' Fleming frowned. 'I'd have said the other girl, Courtney Higson, was also very reliable. But she failed to turn up for work today and I haven't been able to get in touch with her. I've left messages on her voicemail but she hasn't replied, not even with a text message.'

It was beginning to look as if Courtney was indeed the girl taken out of the river earlier.

'I would like to talk to both girls,' Jess said, 'since they deal with the public who use this pub.'

'You can talk to Amy now. You'll have to seek out Courtney. I can give you her address and her mobile number. If you get in touch with her, could I ask you to tell her we'd like to see her here, *at work*?' His tone was pettish.

It was too soon to tell the man he was unlikely to see Courtney again. If they failed to find a family member, they might have to ask Fleming to identify her. But surely a youngster like Courtney must have some family, unless of course she'd emerged from the care system.

'The girls get time off, I suppose?'

'Oh, yes, there's a rota, and the restaurant is closed on Mondays, so neither of them comes in then. Amy had asked if she could have today off; and it was agreed with Courtney, who should have come in this evening. I don't think Amy's too pleased at having to change her plans because Courtney has let us down.'

'Do you know anything about their social lives, friends, interests, that sort of thing?'

'Nothing at all,' said Fleming firmly. 'I'm a busy man and I don't have time to chat to a pair of youngsters about whatever it they get up to in their free time. Not that they would be likely to tell me,' he added. 'You'd better talk to Amy. I think they got on well together.'

He was rattling the keyboard of his computer as he spoke. The printer whirred and delivered a sheet of paper with Courtney's home address and mobile number. Fleming handed it to Jess, who looked at it and frowned. 'This estate is on the outskirts of Weston St Ambrose, isn't it? How does Courtney get to and from work?'

'She's got a car, a Mini Cooper.' Fleming shrugged. 'It's a new one. We pay a decent wage but even so, I'm surprised she can afford it. Help from family, perhaps.'

'Do you have an emergency contact address or phone number for a member of her family?' Jess asked hopefully.

But it wasn't going to be that easy.

'No!' said Fleming curtly. He stood up. 'I'll send in Amy. I have to get back to the bar.'

Amy arrived within minutes. Viewed close at hand she looked a little younger than Jess had earlier guessed, and the professional gloss had vanished, leaving her a teenager pink with curiosity, but also simmering with some resentment. Fleming had not been able to curtail his interview with Jess fast enough. But Amy clearly had a grievance and wanted to inform the world about it.

'I don't know why Courtney's not come in today,' she said. 'I had to ring my boyfriend and tell him I couldn't go to the cinema. He was going to drive out and pick me up here and then we were going to his mum's for some tea and to the cinema afterwards in Cheltenham. I was really disappointed. I've wanted to see that film for ages and ages. I've tried texting Courtney and emailing her. She doesn't reply. I've also tried to ring her, but all I get is voicemail.'

She stared at Jess belligerently with gooseberry-green eyes. She would be a lot more attractive, thought Jess, without that sulky look. She guessed the look was permanent and did not relate particularly to Amy's grumble of the moment.

'You both had the day off yesterday, Monday,' Jess said. 'Did Courtney tell you how she meant to spend it?'

Amy's expression became slightly shifty. The gooseberry eyes fixed their gaze somewhere over Jess's shoulder as if an old sepia photograph of the pub hanging on the wall were suddenly of deep interest. 'Well, not directly, you know.'

'What *did* she say?' Jess persevered gently but firmly.

Amy reluctantly turned her gaze back from the photograph to the questioner. 'Nothing much. I thought she might be going to meet a boyfriend and go to a party or something. But I'm not sure.' With a sudden burst of energy, she added, 'Look, I mind my own business and Courtney minds hers! We only work together. We're not, you know, *friends*.'

'But you think she has a boyfriend?'

Amy looked even unhappier. 'Well, yes, sort of, but she doesn't talk about him.'

'Why would that be? I accept you and she are not close friends, but you must talk to each other. Do you talk to her about *your* boyfriend?'

'Yes,' said Amy simply, 'but my dad's not Teddy Higson.' She looked at Jess as though she expected the name to be recognised. When Jess said nothing, Amy added impatiently, 'You're a copper. You gotta know Teddy Higson. He's in prison.'

Somewhere in the back of Jess's mind a bell rang. 'GBH', signalled the bell. Teddy Higson, professional enforcer, at present the guest of Her Majesty on account of a spot of grievous bodily harm. Oh, oh, cat among the pigeons.

'Why,' Jess asked carefully, 'would that stop Courtney telling *you* the name of her boyfriend?'

Suddenly in a position to take temporary charge of the conversation with this nosy plainclothes police officer, Amy decided to plump for confidentiality.

'Well,' she said, leaning forward, 'he's coming out soon, her dad. He's very funny about her boyfriends; so she keeps them secret, doesn't tell anyone. Her dad's overprotective, seems to think she's just a kid, but she's nineteen. I told my mum about it and she reckons it's because Courtney's dad has spent so much time inside. He only sees her between his coming out and getting put away again. He doesn't twig she's grown up now. He can't do much while he's inside, but once he gets out he can make trouble, chase them away, you know? If he doesn't like them, that is, and generally he doesn't like them, Courtney says.'

Amy's smooth brow puckered. 'If you ask me, I think the one she's been seeing lately is married. She's been really secretive about him . . . and she's been really worried about her dad coming home. Don't get me wrong!' Amy added earnestly. 'She's not frightened her dad might harm *her*. It's what he might do to the boyfriends that worries her.'

'I see. Did she say anything at all, Amy, even vaguely about this boyfriend?'

Amy shook her head. 'Only one time she was acting really fed-up and she said, "I might have to tell him I can't see him for a bit," that's all.'

A thought struck Jess. 'Did Courtney ever warn any of these boyfriends? Tell them who her father was?'

'Course not!' said Amy, and looked at Jess in genuine surprise. 'It's not exactly a come-on, is it? "My dad is Teddy Higson and he breaks legs for a living!"'

No, Jess had to agree; it wasn't exactly a 'come-on'.

Jess had expected to find Carter waiting for her in the car park; but there was no sign of him. She let herself into the car and, this being a lonely spot, locked the doors. But about ten minutes later there was a tap at the window and Ian peered in.

'Sorry to keep you waiting,' he said when she'd let him in beside her. 'I went after that guy in the Range Rover, who didn't want to talk to us in the pub. He drove off in a hurry.'

'You managed to catch him?' Jess asked.

'Only by luck. He turned off into the drive of that Georgian house we passed. So I jogged down there . . .' (Carter was not going to describe his laboured and painful progress.) 'I pressed the intercom at the gates and he let me in. He turned out to be Graeme Murchison.'

Jess frowned. 'Isn't that the name of one of the students on the creative writing course? He went to this pub with the writers' club and Neil Stewart?'

'That's him. By the way, he owns this place.' Carter indicated the Fisherman's Rest. 'But I think he keeps it quiet. I doubt Stewart and the others knew the night they all came here.'

'What's he like, other than rich?' Jess asked.

'Very smooth, quick-witted, hospitable and – this is my gut feeling – hiding something. Don't ask me quite what. He was very forthcoming with information about himself; but I had the feeling that he was answering the questions almost before I asked them, getting in first. Then, when he felt he'd told me enough, he politely, but firmly, turfed me out.'

Carter paused. 'He lives alone, protected by security gates and dogs he insists are pets. He said a gardening company takes care of the grounds. I suppose a cleaning company takes care of the house in the same way. When he goes away on business or on holiday, a key to a separate garden door in the rear wall is left with an old fellow called Charlie Fallon, who comes in to take care of the dogs. The little door in question is tucked away and half-hidden. Charlie is the only one to use it. The arrangement appears quite feudal. Murchison also owns the patch of woodland where the old man lives in a corrugated iron shack. The old boy drinks rainwater and doesn't pay rent, so Murchison tells me.'

'Fallon?' Jess asked. 'That's interesting. I think I may just have been talking to his granddaughter. She lives with her parents in one of those cottages across the road. She told me something really interesting about Courtney.'

She recounted her conversation with Amy. 'You might not know about Teddy Higson. I think he started his present term just before you arrived here.'

Carter heaved a sigh. 'Teddy Higson may be the nearest relative, then. We'll have to ask for him to be brought from gaol under guard to identify the body. If the dead girl isn't his daughter, it won't worry him. But if she is . . . we could have trouble with him.'

When he got home that evening, Carter decided to phone his ex-wife and tell her he was hoping to attend the performance of *Mother Goose*. Get in first, he told himself. Tell her you're going to be there and put her on the back foot. If she doesn't want me there, let her start making excuses. I don't have to apologise for wanting to see my daughter. Millie wants me there to see her do her stuff.

Millie would be in bed at this time of night. She wouldn't pick up the phone.

But Rodney did. Cheery, self-satisfied, successful-in-everything-he-undertook Rodney, bellowing his bonhomie down the line. 'Ian, old chap, good to hear your voice! How are you?'

'I'm very well,' said Carter. 'How are you?' This was ludicrous. As if he cared two hoots how Rodney was. Rodney would be fine, anyway. He always was.

'Couldn't be better!' Rodney's voice assured him.

'I was wondering if I could have a word with Sophie,' Carter said impatiently. Why be so apologetic about it? he asked himself. Why not just ask if Sophie could come to the phone.

But it transpired she couldn't.

'No can do, Ian, sorry. She's gone out to her keep-fit class. She'll be back later, around half past nine. Can I take a message? Should she call you?'

'No, I'll call again, at a better time,' Carter told him.

'Tomorrow night we're going out to dinner,' said Rodney, still relentlessly cheery. 'If it's urgent I can give her a message – or you could call her mobile or text her.'

Carter had an inner vision of Sophie in a leotard, determinedly working out in a crowd of yummy mummies, and of her mobile phone ringing unanswered in her kitbag in the changing room. He felt even more unfit than when jogging from the pub car park to Murchison's place.

'I'll try some other time,' he said. 'Thanks, Rodney.'

'Good to have a word with you,' said Rodney.

Carter put down the phone and, now that Rodney couldn't hear him, made a little speech in which he told Rodney just what he thought of him. He was probably being unfair. But life was unfair. Murchison had split with his long-term partner in New York and come home to dear old England to live in luxury in a Georgian mansion. Having split with Sophie, he, Ian, was now living in a nondescript flat with a jumble of hastily assembled flat-pack furniture from Ikea.

He went into the kitchen and put a chilled cottage pie in the microwave, then took a bottle of cheap wine from the fridge and poured himself a glass. He thought of Murchison relaxing in his comfortable drawing room before his log fire with his whisky. He wished he'd had the presence of mind and courage to ask Jess to go out for a meal. Rodney, in his shoes, wouldn't have hesitated for a minute.

Then he began to wonder if Jess was spending the evening with Palmer, the pathologist who investigated the corpses police investigations brought him. True, Jess always denied that she and Palmer were anything other than friends, but Palmer, for all his grisly occupation, was a good-looking enough chap, Carter supposed. He was younger than the superintendent. He went in for outdoor activities at weekends, tramping up hill and down dale, and had a healthy glow that Carter always felt must contrast strangely with the deathly pallor of his clients.

This line of thought reminded Carter of how he'd puffed and sweated while jogging down the road to find Murchison. He really ought to join a gym.

Later, when he'd rescued the cottage pie before it completely dried out, he regretted even more not going out for a meal, with or without Jess. (Although preferably with.) He couldn't call the cottage pie tasteless, but he wasn't sure what it tasted of. It didn't fill. It didn't appease the taste buds. It was like an illusionist's trick. You thought you had a square meal on a plate and you had a cottage pie that wasn't.

He went to find some bread and cheese to make up for the lack of bulk in his dinner and the absence of taste. As he ate he began to think about Millie again. Whatever happened, he would make it to the pantomime.

Chapter 8

The monthly meetings of the Weston St Ambrose Writers' Club generally took place at the home of one of their founder members (he liked to call himself *the* founder member), Peter Posset. Peter lived alone in a terraced cottage. He had lived there originally with a male partner, but it had been so long ago that no one could even remember the partner's name, let alone his appearance. There had been a falling-out, as they'd heard, and the partner had taken himself off one weekend, never to be seen again. Peter had lived on happily alone in the cottage and the ex-partner was never mentioned.

Peter himself had taken early retirement, at fifty-eight, from his job at the bank. This was in order to have time to devote himself to his many interests, he explained. His hair, he also informed anyone who'd listen, had begun to turn grey when he was in his twenties. He was now sixty-five and it was snow-white. Defiantly, he wore rather it long at the back and had grown luxuriant mutton-chop whiskers. Together with the rimless spectacles he wore, he fancied he bore a strong resemblance to Henrik Ibsen. Others – not in his hearing – were less kind.

Everyone had turned up to this meeting because everyone had heard that a drowned body, as yet unidentified but rumoured to be female, had been pulled from the river. What they had not known, and Prue had the hoped-for pleasure of telling them, was that it was certainly that of a young woman; and had been recovered from the river at Glebe House, home of Neil Stewart.

They had all attended Neil's creative writing course at the college, and had a drink with him after lectures. They'd all celebrated 'end of term' with him at the Fisherman's Rest. They looked upon Neil as quite an old acquaintance. They were proud of their association with him. Prue's news left them stunned.

Predictably, Peter Posset cleared his throat and made the first comment. 'That's most unfortunate.'

'Honestly, Pete,' Jason Twilling burst out. He was a slightly built, fair-haired young man, at only twenty their most junior member. 'You are the limit! Is that the best you can come up with? Unfortunate? Talk about understatement! It's sensational!'

'I don't go in for sensationalism,' retorted Peter, folding his hands over his Christmas pullover, oatmeal in shade and patterned with dark red reindeer. 'Anyone who knows my writing will know that. I don't aspire to be a tabloid journalist.'

Jason reddened. 'I don't aspire to be a journalist. I am a novelist!'

Jenny Porter asked aggressively, 'How do you know that, Prue? It wasn't on the local news.'

She thrust her head, and untidy long grey locks, forward and fixed Prue like an interrogator.

'Debbie Garley told me when I was at the till paying for my groceries.' Prue smiled. She had known Jenny would be upset at not being first with the news. Good, teach her to be a know-it-all. 'Her Uncle Wayne found it – the body.'

'Her uncle being Wayne Garley?' retorted Jenny, not giving up the fight. 'Wayne Garley found the body? Rubbish. It's one of Debbie's flights of fancy.'

'He was delivering a load of logs – for an open fire – to Glebe House. That's how he came to be in the gardens. He went down to the river to see if it had flooded the bottom of Neil's garden; and he saw the body. Then the police arrived.'

The additional detail caused them all to sit thinking for a moment.

'You mean either Neil or his wife called the police?' Peter demanded.

'No, they just arrived. They'd been searching for a body already, following the river down. Wayne told Debbie the body was that of a young girl – it had long hair, anyway.'

There was a silence. 'At the Stewarts'' hung in thought bubbles above their heads.

'Coincidence,' observed Jason and gave a little snort that might have meant anything.

'It's not amusing, Jason,' Lucy Claverton spoke up. She had been listening in shocked silence. 'It's – it's awful. What a terrible thing for the Stewarts.'

'I wasn't laughing,' Jason defended himself. 'Yes, of course it's really bad.'

Henry Blackwood said, 'It might only be on local news now, but when the national press hear a girl's body has been found in the grounds of the home of a well-known writer, it'll make the TV news and all the main newspapers.'

They drew in a collective breath.

'Oh, dear . . .' said Lucy tremulously. 'Will they think poor Neil had anything to do with it?'

'Why should they?' snapped Henry. 'The police were already looking for a body along the river. Someone must have reported it or seen someone fall in. The current carried it along and somehow, I don't know how, it got stuck at the Stewarts' place. Snagged on something, probably. We must not—' Henry leaned forward to make sure he had the attention of all. They waited. 'We must not start any rumours about the location of its discovery being in any way significant.'

'Of course not!' Isolde Evans spoke up. 'I help out at the library. I know how people gossip. They hide behind the stacks to pass on the latest. They think because no one can see them, no one can hear them. But they whisper so loudly, everyone can!'

Opera-buff parents had saddled Isolde with her name. Parents, she often thought, ought to think more about it before they did something like that. All you can do, carrying a name like Isolde, is live up to it. She wore long, floaty garments and scarves and wore her long, red-brown hair in a single plait hanging down her spine. She fancied her appearance conjured up the heroines of Arthurian romance, though she had to admit her glasses spoiled the image.

'Don't you tell them to keep quiet?' asked Jason unkindly. 'I thought that was your job?'

'Well . . .' Isolde flushed. 'Of course I remind them if they get too noisy. It's not my full-time job, is it? I only help out now the library's run by volunteers. I can't throw my weight about. If the pupils behaved like that when I'm working as a supply teacher, then I would tell them very firmly.'

'How can we start any rumours?' Jenny asked resentfully. 'We don't know anything. Besides rumours start when people like Prue go round telling others – like us – something which she learned from Debbie at the checkout and which might not be true. Debbie Garley invents things. I used to teach her. I know.'

'Prue was not starting a rumour!' snapped Henry.

'No, I wasn't!' Prue joined in. 'I believe Debbie. She said her uncle found the body. If she'd said *she'd* found it, I wouldn't have believed it. But I believe Wayne could find it because Wayne Garley goes everywhere around here, in and out of people's gardens and homes, doing odd jobs and so on. If you ask me, not a thing goes on round here that Wayne Garley doesn't find out about first!'

'That's very true,' remarked Peter thoughtfully.

'Thank you, Peter,' said Prue to him.

Dennis Claverton spoke. Dennis rarely made any suggestions and was generally assumed to come to the meetings because his wife did. He occasionally read out a poem he'd written. It was always about the garden birds he took delight in feeding. His last poem had been called 'The Blackbird'. *At dawn the blackbird gives a cry and wakes . . .*

Prue thought Dennis's poems were rather sweet. Lucy thought them wonderful. Jason always sank down in his chair and pressed his lips tightly together as Dennis read aloud. The others always said, 'Well done, Dennis!'

'Do you think,' asked Dennis – ('out of the blue', commented Jenny later) – we ought to write Neil a letter of support?'

This caused visible consternation.

'It might read,' Henry said, 'like a letter of condolence.'

'He might need our support.' Dennis proved unexpectedly attached to his suggestion. 'That's what friends are for. We are his friends, aren't we?'

Another confused murmur ran round the room.

'After all,' Dennis went on, 'suppose the police start bothering him – and his wife, what's her name?'

'Beth!' the others chanted.

'That's it, Beth. Suppose the police keep going to Glebe House asking Neil and Beth questions?'

'They've probably already interviewed them,' said Jason. 'Young female victim found at popular novelist's home, you know . . .'

'What do you mean, victim?' demanded Peter angrily. His face, in the frame of white whiskers, glowed as red as the reindeer on his pullover. 'There hasn't been any crime! Some poor soul got trapped in floodwater.'

'Don't get hot under the collar, Peter. Anyway, people talk about the victims of accidents, don't they? All right, this was an accident, if you insist.' Jason added in the next breath, 'But, hey, she was in the river. Why should she be in the river? It's not like she was trying to cross some area that wasn't usually flooded and miscalculated. Got stuck in a car down in a dip where water had built up, that sort of thing. The river is always there, however much higher it might be at the moment.'

'Perhaps,' suggested Lucy, 'she went in to rescue a dog. It seems to happen every winter. Someone tries to rescue a pet and is drowned. It's very sad.'

'The dog generally gets out all right by itself,' said Jenny Porter, 'nearly every time. People drive their cars into rivers sometimes, by mistake.'

'They'd have to be pretty well pissed,' said Jason.

Lucy winced. Isolde looked as if she wanted to say something, but decided against it and huddled into the shapeless knitted garment she was wearing over the mediaeval draperies, in deference to the winter cold.

'See here,' rumbled Peter, 'I do agree with one thing Henry has said. We must not start rumours. I appreciate that you want us to show support for Neil, Dennis old chap. But I think it might be early for that, as yet. If the coppers have been bothering him and Beth, then a letter from us might just – er – feed the flames. He might think we'd been listening to gossip.'

Prue flushed.

'We can keep it in mind, though. Let's see how it all goes – and what the coroner rules. As far as we know, this is an accidental death: tragic, but not unfamiliar in times of flood and high water. We must not, absolutely not, start talking about crimes. There has been no crime.' Peter pronounced the last as if it were a verdict.

'I thought we had to wait and see what the coroner rules?' Jason said sarcastically.

'Quite!' snapped Peter. 'Now then, that's enough about that, I think! Has anyone managed to do any work since our last meeting?'

Over the rustle of paper, Lucy Claverton's voice could only just be heard, whispering to Dennis, 'Oh dear, will the police want to interview *us*?'

It was dark and drizzling with rain when they all left Peter's house later. Jason pulled the hood of his jacket over his head and hunched his shoulders. He could have driven here, but the aged vehicle he owned ate into his limited finances and just keeping it on the road was a nightmare. A couple of months ago, it had coughed and broken down without warning in the middle of the countryside, leaving him to tramp home on foot.

'You need to get yourself a new car, mate,' the garage mechanic had advised. 'This one won't get through the next MOT.'

Buy a car with what? Jason asked himself resentfully. Not on warehouse work wages. His parents, on the rare occasions he saw them, urged him to return to education full time, get some qualifications. But if he did that, his studies would interfere with his writing. He just couldn't make them understand how important his book was to him. Important as a creative artist: important as a future source of income. If he could just finish the damn thing and get it published . . .

People told him that most writers made very little money. But Neil Stewart did all right with his books. He and his wife lived in a ruddy mansion with grounds. Mind you, he'd heard that Neil's wife had held some sort of power job in London before they came here. They'd probably bought Glebe House with her bonus money. Life was unfair.

He had hoped, when he'd signed up for Neil's creative writing course at the college, that Neil would have offered him more individual help with his book. After all, he was writing something very like the sort of stuff Neil wrote. But Neil had not been at all helpful. Perhaps he feared a rival. Funding the cost of the creative writing course had been difficult for Jason. He'd had to phone his mother. No use phoning his father. He would have said: if Jason wanted money to sign up for a course that would finish with some qualification he could show a future employer, then he would stump up, but for creative writing . . .

His mother was more soft-hearted. She'd sent the money but she would find it difficult to hide what she'd done from his father;

because she wasn't the sort of person who liked what she called 'secrets in the family'. The old man would find out.

After all that, Jason didn't feel he'd learned anything from the course. For two pins, he wouldn't have gone along with them all to that meal at the Fisherman's Rest but he hadn't wanted the others to realise just how broke he was. So he'd gone, only to find that Courtney Higson still worked there and she was the last person he'd wanted to see.

The pub had been packed out, everyone having a great time. Neil Stewart was declared guest of honour, so did not have to pay for his meal. The others insisted on treating him. What for? The guy had already been paid by the college to lecture to them. Let him pay for his own nosh. But Jason had to do as the others did and divvy up his share.

Peter Posset, looking like Father Christmas with all that white hair, and wearing one of his mad pullovers, held forth on all his favourite topics. That snooty git Murchison didn't say much (never had done during the whole six weeks), but behaved like lord of the manor. Whenever he wanted something, he simply held up his hand and a staff member scurried over. An impressed Isolde had cast him admiring glances (which Jason was pleased to see Murchison ignored).

On the other hand, when Jason wanted to order another drink, he appeared to be invisible, no matter how often or desperately he signalled. He had to get up and go to the bar and order it.

Then it came to the menu. You wouldn't believe the prices there. It was a pub, not the Ritz! But money was no object for the others. Prue Blackwood had ordered lamb tagine. Jason didn't know what that was, but when it came it smelled great. The rest of the group had ordered big juicy steaks, except for Lucy Claverton and Isolde. They weren't meat-eaters and had ordered the Tuscan bean casserole. That had come in individual earthenware pots with lids and had looked pretty good (though not as mouth-watering as the lamb tagine). Jason, after a panicked scrutiny of the menu, had ordered a pizza with basic topping and when it came, it looked as if he'd ordered something off the children's menu. Courtney had served it up to him with a knowing smirk. 'Not yet made a fortune out of that book, then, Jaz?' she'd whispered in his ear.

Right opposite him, as she said it, had sat Neil Stewart, setting about steak with all the trimmings, partly at Jason's expense. Courtney's gaze had drifted across the table. 'Not like your friend there . . .' she'd added breathily.

Neil must have heard her, because he looked up from his steak and smiled at Courtney, who gave him a dazzling smile in return and swayed off bearing her empty tray. Just about every man in the place, even Murchison, must have had his eyes fixed on Courtney's bum.

So, a body had turned up at the Stewarts' property and they had cops crawling all over the place. Serve them right.

Anyway, he didn't really need Neil's help. He thought he could even have given Neil Stewart a few tips.

The thought made him feel much better and he began to step out briskly. Just then, a small silver car overtook him, slowed and stopped. The driver beeped the horn. Jason's heart sank.

It was Isolde, in her little smart car. She was going to offer him a lift. It was another embarrassment to be offered a ride in Isolde's car because he couldn't afford to take his on the road. Plus he didn't fancy riding in a vehicle that did nothing for his image. But he got in because it was raining.

'Isn't it awful?' asked Isolde as they set off. 'Poor Neil and Beth.'

'They'll be OK,' Jason said.

'A writer like Neil must be so sensitive.' Isolde sighed.

Jason muttered. 'Sensitive, my – my foot!' He managed to amend the last word just in time.

'I wonder how that poor girl came to be in the river,' Isolde went on. 'I do hope she didn't drown herself, you know, like Ophelia.'

Jason didn't answer. Perhaps Isolde would get the message and talk about something else. She did, but just as potty.

'Prue Blackwood's novel is coming along really well,' Isolde said next. 'I wish I could say the same of mine. I'm really quite stuck. I want my hero to be decisive and a little bit arrogant but I don't want him to appear sexist. I want to show somehow that he has a softer, more feminine side but he's hiding it. Until the heroine eventually releases it, of course, and he returns her devotion with his love.'

'Drop me off at the pub!' Jason burst out, unable to stick any more of this. 'Look, just over there, the Black Horse.'

Isolde slowed and drew up. 'Oh, the dear old Black Horse,' she said sentimentally, gazing through the windscreen at the frontage. 'I loved going there after the evening classes with Neil and the others.'

'You don't drink alcohol,' protested Jason.

'I drink other things, orange juice and cola and so on. I occasionally have a glass of white wine. I just don't like beer and stuff.'

Isolde moved her gaze from the pub's front door to Jason, beside her. 'Are you meeting anyone, Jaz?'

'No,' said Jason resignedly, because it wouldn't have made any difference if he'd said that he was. 'Would you like to come in with me, Isolde? Just for one drink?'

'Oh, lovely!' exclaimed Isolde. 'I'll just drive round to the car park at the back.'

The Blackwoods went home and agreed it had been unfair of anyone to accuse Prue of spreading gossip. Gossip generally meant something untrue; but Prue had heard the news from Debbie Garley and it was Debbie's uncle had found the corpse. So it must be true, and that took it into the category of legitimate news. Henry had underlined to the others that they shouldn't start to speculate about any significance regarding the location and the Stewarts. There was nothing wrong with reporting facts.

Jenny Porter went home and telephoned everyone of her acquaintance who might not have heard the news. She informed them that the body recovered from the river had been found, you'll never guess, *at Glebe House*. Moreover, it was that of a young woman. Yes, Debbie Garley had said so and claimed her Uncle Wayne had found the corpse and then told Prue Blackwood, at the till. Yes, one of the tills at that awful eyesore of a new supermarket. Debbie worked on it, so she was able to tell every single shopper. People didn't need the Internet when they had Debbie Garley. The Garleys knew everyone's business. Jenny had put her name to the petition against the new store, but of course people only thought of their own interests. It ruined the approach to the village on that side. Yes! Glebe House where Neil Stewart and his wife live. Each person she informed put down the phone; and began to speculate like mad.

The Clavertons went home and told one another how sad it was and how it had spoiled everything somehow. Lucy thought the others had been very unkind about Dennis's idea of writing a letter to Neil. Perhaps they could write one anyway, later. Dennis said, yes, he'd think about it. Wasn't it his turn to make the cocoa?

Peter Posset washed up the mugs used by his visitors and wondered if there might be a play to be written around the event. When they knew how it turned out, of course. He thought it had been an excellent meeting.

Chapter 9

Tom Palmer, the pathologist, was a man of his word and had not wasted time. He phoned Jess early the following morning to come down to the mortuary.

'This is a strange one. There is a large bruise at the base of her skull and a suspicious wound just below her ribcage.'

'A blow at the back of the head, you say? Fatal?'

'Unlikely. Someone slugged her from behind and it would have dazed her, even rendered her unconscious. Most probably she would have fallen forward and, unless supported, down to the ground. The exact sequence of events to follow that I can't tell you. But she was stabbed from the front, by her assailant, or by a second one, using a long, thin, sharp weapon, not flat but rounded: something like a screwdriver, awl or skewer. It was thrust in below the breastbone and driven up into the heart. The entry wound is small but clear to see. Any bleeding was more likely to be internal, rather than gushing out through the puncture.'

'She was in the river. Could there be any possibility, despite the stab wound, that she drowned?'

'Highly unlikely. The weapon penetrated the heart. It would have ceased to function pretty quickly. I don't mean she would have died instantly, but we're talking minutes, perhaps only seconds.

There is nothing to indicate she was breathing at the time she entered the water.'

'How about the time of death?' Jess asked.

Tom grimaced. 'Always difficult to judge, as you know. In this case particularly so, because putting her into such very cold water was like putting her in a fridge. There was little sign of rigor. No trace of drugs, no indication of sexual activity previous to death. She'd had a meal of some sort earlier, no meat, only carbs and vegetable, and it was well on its way through the digestive tract. The body was initially observed in the river at nine in the morning, so let's say during the previous twelve hours.'

'None of this is very helpful, Tom!' Jess protested.

'Sorry, but I wouldn't wish to mislead you. Come on, Jess, you know how difficult it can be to be exact in these matters. Best thing you can do is to find someone who saw her alive the previous evening. Then we'd have a starting point. Show her picture round the Chinese restaurants and takeaways. What was in the gut looked like partly digested chow mein or stir fry, something like that.'

Jess sighed. 'Can you have her ready to be viewed? We're coming down there with someone who should be able to identify her. It's her father, but he's in gaol, and they're bringing him under guard.'

She heard Tom mutter something she didn't catch. Then, 'What's he in for?'

'GBH.'

'He's not likely to run amuck in the mortuary, is he?' asked Tom apprehensively.

'So we know she didn't just stumble into the river unaided,' Jess said. 'Someone deliberately killed her, having worked out exactly how to do it. Then that person dragged the body to the river – or conveyed it there somehow – and toppled her into the water. The river is in spate. It swept her away immediately. The murderer probably wanted to get rid of the body, or move it rapidly from the scene of the attack. The question really is why the killer wanted Courtney dead. She was just a young girl who worked in a pub. It might, possibly, have something to do with her father. He might have enemies who were seeking revenge. He's in gaol. They can't reach him. They could reach Courtney.'

'They couldn't reach him in gaol now, but he's due to be released soon. His imminent arrival back in her life worried Courtney, so Amy Fallon told you, Jess. So, if Higson was the man they wanted, why not just wait a few weeks longer? Then they could hit Higson himself.' Carter paused and frowned.

'There's a lot we need to know. How was a waitress, with a father in prison, able to afford a new car? Did Higson supply the cash from some reserves he has stashed away somewhere? Where is the car now? Where's her mobile?' He drummed his fingers on his desk.

'I don't know where the car is. The phone's probably at the bottom of the river.' Jess thought it was unlikely they'd find the mobile. The car, on the other hand, should turn up and soon.

'At least we know we're looking at murder.' Carter looked up. 'We'll have to take care how we tell Teddy Higson that. He's on his way from the prison. Handling it sensitively won't be easy with him, but we need to try. He may be a villain and violent; but he's a father who, if Amy Fallon is to be believed, is devoted to his daughter in his own way.' He caught Jess's eye. 'I'm the father of a daughter,' he said. 'I don't underestimate the effect of this on Higson one bit.'

'Yes,' said Teddy Higson hoarsely, 'that's my girl.' He raised his bloodshot gaze to stare at Jess. 'Who done it?' he rasped.

'We don't know yet what the full circumstances are that led to Courtney being in the river,' Jess told him. 'We'll do our very best to find out.'

Higson, as arranged, had been brought from prison under escort to identify the body. At first sight he appeared almost cube-shaped, as broad as he was tall, and, sideways on, thick with muscle and the beginnings of a paunch. He had a shaven skull; small, mean pouched eyes; and chipped front teeth. His neck was so thick it seemed to run down straight from his misshapen ears to his collarbones.

'You better 'ad! When *I* find out . . .' Tears trickled from his reddened eyelids, incongruous but real. He raised the thick forefinger of his tattooed right hand, and jabbed it at the police officers. 'She was my little princess,' he croaked.

'All right, Teddy,' said the prison officer who had accompanied him. 'Take it easy.' He sounded sympathetic, not for Higson himself, but for the man's genuine grief.

In all other circumstances, the officer's private opinion was that his charge was 'a nasty piece of work and violent with it'.

Certainly Teddy Higson was a frightening presence even in the mortuary. He was generally regarded with what he himself would have called 'respect'; and others would correctly have called fear. Even those who employed Higson, when he was on the outside, were nervous in his presence.

The mortuary assistant warily proffered a box of tissues, kept handy for such occasions, to Higson; who scooped out a handful with his massive paw, wiped them over his face, and dropped them on the floor.

'Wuz she raped?' he muttered.

'There's no evidence of that,' Carter said quietly.

'Drowned?' Suspicion oozed from Higson's voice. 'You're not going to stand there and tell me my little girl just fell in the river? I won't buy it. And don't go telling me she jumped in because she hadn't any reason for that! Besides, she wouldn't do anything so daft.'

Carter nodded. 'The pathologist considers that death was not caused by drowning.'

The guard looked at them in alarm and then at his charge. The viewing room was so still and quiet that not even the air seemed to move. This was Death's realm, and it had reached out and put its clammy fingers on them all. The mortuary assistant had removed himself as far away as he could and positioned himself by the door.

'What injuries 'as she got?' Higson asked abruptly and squinted at Carter. His voice had become flat and hard. He expected an answer.

'The cause of death appears to be by stabbing. I'm very sorry to tell you this.'

For the briefest moment they all feared, as Tom had expressed it earlier, that Higson would lose control, attack one or all of them, or just run amuck smashing up his surroundings. The guard with him murmured, 'Take it easy, Teddy!'

The wild look in Higson's eyes faded but the look that replaced it was chilling. 'How often?'

'Just the once, but fatally, I'm afraid.'

'Shiv? Knife blade?'

'The appearance of the wound doesn't suggest so. We haven't yet identified or found the weapon. Something else.'

'Get on wiv finding it, then!' Higson fixed his terrifying gaze on Jess before moving it slowly to back to Carter. 'I'll be waiting to hear some answers. My girl's death is down to someone. I wanna know 'oo!'

He turned away before either of them could reply.

'All right, then, Teddy?' asked the prison officer. 'Ready to go?'

Higson nodded but he wasn't quite ready yet. He addressed the body of his child. 'I'll get to the truth of this, Princess, don't you worry.'

'Leave it to us, Mr Higson,' Jess said quietly. 'Could I ask if you know the whereabouts of Courtney's mother, so that she can be informed?'

Higson swivelled his shining dome atop the tree-trunk neck and fixed his feral gaze on her. 'No,' he said.

With that he set off for the door, taking his attendant guard with him.

'If you ask me,' whispered the awed mortuary assistant, when Higson had gone, 'it's a good thing he's inside.'

During the afternoon the rain began to fall heavily again. The local news reported flooding in several areas. Wayne Garley arrived at Glebe House and stacked sandbags all along the rear of the property. He advised the Stewarts to move upstairs any valuable things like computers or televisions or anything else they didn't want damaged. When they expressed alarm, he reassured them that this was only a precaution.

'Water shouldn't get this far. But best to be prepared.' He squinted at them appraisingly. 'I've been told I gotta go to the inquest tomorrow morning,' he said. 'I gotta tell the coroner how I found her.'

'Yes, Wayne,' Beth told him, 'we've been notified, too, although we've been told that it's unlikely we'll be called to give evidence.'

'Funny business,' observed Wayne, and trudged away across the muddy expanse that had been their lawn.

Neil and Beth spent the rest of the day moving the entire contents of the study to a spare bedroom, together with anything else they could get up the stairs. The two leather sofas couldn't be shifted to safety, so they put bricks under the feet to raise them off the floor. Beth knew Neil was worried about the inquest in the morning. It didn't help that neither of them had ever attended such a thing. But when all this is over, she thought, I'm going to make it clear to him that moving here was a big mistake and we have to sell. She thrust to the back of her mind how long it had taken the executors of the late Mr Martin to sell the house before she and Neil came along.

Susie rang in the evening and asked, 'Are you flooded out? Shall we all be able to come for Christmas as planned?'

Beth told her of the steps they'd taken to prevent water getting into the house and said she was sure everything would be all right. She had not told Susie about the body in the river. Susie would ask any number of questions Beth couldn't answer. Perhaps, tomorrow, after the inquest, when there was some official ruling to report, she'd phone through and tell her sister all about it.

* * *

In the morning the heavy rain had lessened to a steady, cold, depressing drizzle. The coroner's court looked even less welcoming than usual, with a smell of damp coats in the air.

As Jess, accompanied by Sergeant Corcoran, entered, she was waylaid by Beth Stewart.

'There aren't very many people here,' she said.

'It will only last minutes,' Jess told her. 'It will be adjourned.'

'How about Neil and me, will we have to speak?'

Jess was trying to explain that would almost certainly be unnecessary and their being asked to attend was 'just in case', when Beth burst out, 'Good grief! Is that Wayne Garley?'

An imposing figure had entered. Clad in a good quality but obviously very old gabardine raincoat, far too long for today's fashions, and wearing an equally venerable trilby hat, Garley was coming towards them.

'He looks like he's walked out of one of those old Cold War spy stories,' whispered Beth.

Garley had reached them. He raised the trilby in greeting. 'I hope I'm not going to be kept here long. I got people ringing me up non-stop. They all wants sandbags put round their houses, or their garden furniture moved under cover. River's rising fast. But don't you worry, Mrs Stewart. You'll be all right. It's the pub that has got to worry.'

'Which pub is that?' asked Jess.

'The old Fisherman's Rest at Lower Weston,' he informed her. 'They've put down more sandbags, but their beer garden is already under water and I reckon if this keeps up, the water will get inside.'

Jess would have liked to ask more, but the coroner and his

clerk had arrived, together with a straggle of other people, some of them regulars at inquests, and clearly known to one another. At the very last moment Jess saw a tall man in a waxed jacket slip into the room and take up a discreet position at the very back. He took off his cap and she got a good look at his lean features and fairish hair. She had not met him before, but from Carter's description guessed this must be Graeme Murchison. He was, Carter had told her, the owner of the Fisherman's Rest. Via the manager, Gordon Fleming, Courtney had been Murchison's employee. Fleming himself wasn't here. Murchison had chosen to shed his anonymity and represent the pub himself.

Corcoran drew her attention back, indicating the coroner. He muttered, 'I don't know that guy. He's not the regular coroner.'

'Perhaps the regular one is sick – or called away.'

Proceedings were quickly under way and it was clear the coroner on the day, whoever he was, did not mean to hang about. Perhaps he had floodwater threatening his house.

Jess took the stand and told the court that the police had received information regarding a body in the river from a member of the public. She had gone to the location, together with an underwater search unit led by Sergeant Corcoran, but they had found nothing. A decision had been made, by herself and Sergeant Corcoran, to search further downstream. They had gone to Glebe House, the grounds of which were bordered by the river, to ask permission to check along that stretch of bank. On arrival, the owner had informed them that a body had just been discovered, wedged under a mooring platform at the bottom of the garden. It had just been found by someone delivering logs.

Now was Wayne Garley's big moment. He took the stand, imposing in his long raincoat, and, holding his trilby pressed to his chest as if paying his last respects, told the coroner how he'd found the body of a young woman and informed the house-owners. He'd hardly done this when the police turned up.

Had the police managed to discover the identity of the dead girl? asked the coroner.

Jess stepped up again and told the court that the body had been identified by her father as Courtney Higson, employed at the Fisherman's Rest as a waitress. Mr Higson had been brought under escort from prison to make the identification and was not present in the court at the moment.

So that only left Tom Palmer to state cause of death. The victim had not drowned. The large contusion at the back of the skull would almost certainly have caused loss of consciousness But it had not been fatal. The cause of death was mortal injury from a stabbing with a long thin weapon that had penetrated the heart. Subsequently, the body had been immersed in very cold water. Tests confirmed this as river water. As to the length of time she had been in the river, he ventured to suggest it had been more than twelve hours, but less than twenty-four. But he could not speak with any certainty as immersion in the river had resulted in the body being kept at a very low temperature; and this had confused the evidence. Toxicology tests were not yet complete, but so far there was no sign the deceased had taken drugs in any way, either prescribed or recreational.

The coroner said it appeared clear that this was a case of unlawful killing, and he would adjourn proceedings to enable the police to complete their inquiries. They would reconvene at a later date.

After that the room emptied with remarkable speed, Murchison the first to leave, so that only Jess, the Stewarts and Tom Palmer remained. The whole proceedings had taken just over twenty minutes.

'They didn't ask me to say anything,' Neil Stewart said. He sounded relieved but also a touch regretful.

How everyone likes a moment in the limelight, thought Jess. Aloud she said: 'The body was identified by a relative so it wasn't necessary for you to say you thought you knew her. You weren't sure, after all, were you?'

'Oh, no!' Neil replied quickly.

Tom Palmer approached their group and said cheerfully to Neil, 'I've read one of your books.'

Neil looked startled. 'Oh, have you? Right . . .' he mumbled.

'Bought it at the airport before a long flight. I enjoyed it.'

'Can I ask you something, Doctor?' Neil said suddenly. His wife looked at him in surprise.

'Sure, ask away,' said Tom.

'I'm not referring to this – er – case, you understand. I was just wondering . . . How difficult is it to tell if a person is alive or dead when he or she enters the water? Are there any obvious signs that you – as a pathologist – would look for?'

'Ah,' said Tom, scratching his mop of black hair, 'it's not that obvious. It depends on the case in question, of course. Generally, the presence of foam in the airways is taken as an indication that the person in question was alive on entering the water. But there can be other reasons for that. Stomach contents aren't always a guide. All kinds of silt and debris can find its way there without being actually swallowed. Sometimes there are external signs, like cadaveric spasm. I mean, if the drowning person clutched a piece of debris or vegetation in desperation. At the moment of death that clutching action can be frozen.'

Beth was heard to mutter quietly, 'I don't want to know this!'

Tom looked at Jess. 'It didn't happen in this case, anyway. She didn't drown. She was stabbed in the heart and it would have ceased to function adequately fairly quickly, certainly after a few minutes.' He looked back to Neil. 'OK?' he asked cheerfully.

'What, oh, yes, thank you,' Neil said.

His wife touched his arm. 'Come on,' she said impatiently, and he followed her away.

'Tom,' Jess asked him, 'before you go, have you time for a quick word with me, too?'

'Sure,' said Tom. 'Come and have a coffee.'

'What's the problem?' he asked a little later. Each equipped with a waxed carton of coffee from a dispenser, they had found a couple of chairs in the deserted waiting room.

'You have no further ideas about the nature of the weapon, I suppose?' Jess asked. 'You're not giving your evidence now, so I only need your guesses.'

Tom peered critically into his waxed carton. 'Sorry, I can only repeat what I told you originally. Something long, sharp, small in gauge, probably steel but any rigid material. The entry wound is tiny. The weapon managed, by luck rather than any skill, to miss the artery, so the bleeding was not as profuse as it might have been.'

Jess sighed.

'Cheer up,' said Tom encouragingly. 'If you're free this evening, come and have a curry with me somewhere.'

'From dead bodies to curry . . .' Jess said ruefully, pulling a face.

'Can't be helped,' said Tom matter-of-factly. 'It's my line of business. It does put people off. Come on, you're made of sturdy stuff. This morning's show hasn't put you off eating for the rest of the day, surely?'

'OK, I'll meet you at about seven fifteen at the place we ate at last time.' Jess eyed him. 'No news from Madison? Still in Australia, is she, on that research fellowship?' Madison either used to be, or still was (Jess wasn't clear), Tom's girlfriend. Her sudden decision to take up a research job offered on the other side of the world had understandably knocked a dent in Tom's self-confidence.

'Still there and not likely to return soon. Anyway, after an initial flurry of emails, I've not heard any more from her. I think the chapter's closed on that affair.'

'Sorry,' she consoled him. 'But if she's dedicated to her bugs and bacteria . . .'

'I accept she finds them more interesting than me,' said Tom. 'Don't feel you have to cheer me up. I'm over it. But I don't accept this horrible coffee. Let's go outside so that I can pour it away.'

Jess got back to work to find Dave Nugent had been busy at his computer. She had earlier passed the sergeant the address Fleming had given her for Courtney: Flat 5, Willow House, Rosetta Gardens estate. Now she found Dave looking pleased with his discoveries and keen to tell what he'd found out.

To begin with, there was the address, Rosetta Gardens. 'Sounds a nice place,' said Nugent, 'but it isn't.'

'I know where it is,' Jess said, 'it's a council estate on the outskirts of Weston St Ambrose. I don't know whose idea it was to build it there. I've never been there myself.'

'I have,' said Nugent glumly, 'and believe me, you don't want to go there unless you have to. I got in touch with the council housing department. The flat's not in Courtney Higson's name; the official tenant is her dad, Teddy.'

'Nice neighbour!' muttered Carter, who had wandered up to hear the news.

Nugent consulted his notes and gave them a brisk run-down of the rest of the information he'd gleaned. Higson and his family had been assigned the tenancy of the flat in Rosetta Gardens nearly fifteen years ago. The family then consisted of Mr and Mrs Higson and their four-year-old daughter. Mr Higson had not been in prison at the time, though he was known to have form. He'd been employed as a bouncer.

Eight years later, Mrs Higson had vanished from the scene. It was understood she had fled the matrimonial home; and was taking care her husband didn't find her. She did not take her daughter with her. Teddy's elderly mother moved in to look after her son and granddaughter. The older lady died two years later, when Courtney was fourteen.

Her father was in prison at the time of Courtney's grandmother's death and gained early release on compassionate grounds. He returned home to make arrangements for the funeral and take care of his child. Relationship of father and daughter had always been considered very good, so social services had not been concerned. But it had been made clear to Higson that should he return to prison, social services would take Courtney into care.

For two years, Higson had had no convictions. No one believed he had reformed, but he was being extra careful.

His prudence had only kept him out of gaol until just over a year ago, when his latest term of imprisonment had begun. Courtney, now eighteen and an adult, had been living at the flat alone. The rent was always paid on time. Teddy had made arrangements for that. 'Not a nice man at all,' observed a social worker who had known the family a long time, 'but a surprisingly good father. Well, on his own terms.'

Nugent laid aside his notes. 'That's about it, for now, sir.'

Carter and Jess retreated to Carter's office for consultation.

'Higson may be currently behind bars,' Carter said. 'But he will have contacts on the outside. We'll have to be very careful about any information we release or we're likely to find they get to potential suspects first. Besides which, he's due out in a couple of months' time, and is now likely to be released earlier on compassionate grounds. The last thing we need is Teddy Higson going berserk and dismembering anyone he thinks knows anything about her death. How did the inquest go, by the way?'

'Opened and adjourned, as expected. I think I saw Murchison there. It was a man who answered the description you gave me of a well-off country gent. He left at once at the end.'

'Did he?' Carter frowned. 'Perhaps Gordon Fleming had reported to him that one of the waitress had gone AWOL and couldn't be contacted. Murchison does own the pub, after all, and would want to know if one of the staff bobbed up in the river. I was at his house, asking him questions, too . . . Murchison has twigged that the Fisherman's Rest may turn out central to inquiries. What else happened?'

'Nothing, really. The only thing of interest was that Neil Stewart asked Tom, after we came out, how he could be sure she didn't drown. I think it was only a writer taking interest in some fact he might use one day. Tom had told him he'd read one of Stewart's books. We'll get on with interviewing all those who went to the Fisherman's Rest on the last evening of the course,' Jess continued. 'It's possible none of them had anything to do with it, or knows anything helpful. But quite a few of them, according to Neil Stewart, knew the girl by name.'

'It's likely a lot of people did,' Carter said. 'She was in regular contact with customers; probably she'd worked in other pubs or eateries. I think we ought to take a look at that flat in Rosetta Gardens. Send Stubbs to find a magistrate and get a warrant.'

Stubbs was able to find his magistrate and get a warrant in exemplary time. They set off to Rosetta Gardens, accompanied by a constable and a nervous young man from the housing department.

'Good grief . . .' Carter muttered when they arrived.

Weston St Ambrose was a small place and its inhabitants were largely financially secure and ultra-respectable. Rosetta Gardens was where it kept its less well-off and far less respectable. The estate was located a mile away, and had not been intended to be a dumping ground. It had been built towards the end of the sixties as an optimistic social experiment, a new community that would give hope to the socially disadvantaged. It consisted of four blocks of medium-rise flats, each bearing the name of a tree. Once smart and modern, they were now dated, weather-stained and depressing in aspect. They surrounded a litter-strewn patch of mud that might once have been grassed.

The young man from the council confirmed this. 'It was land-scaped when it was built. There was a kids' playground and everything. The first tenants were fine. But as the original ones gradually moved out, some rougher types came in; and it was all downhill after that. There are a few vulnerable people left and we try to keep an eye on them, fit security locks on their front doors and windows, things like that.' He looked round and sighed. 'Every other kid here has an ASBO.'

'Where are they all?' asked Carter, indicating the area and the absence of any visible life.

'Saw us arrive,' said the young man. 'They know I'm from the council and they know you—' He broke off in embarrassment and coughed.

'They know we're police,' Jess finished for him.

The Higson flat was on the second floor in the nearest block. The lift was working but the cabin stank. Cigarette butts and flattened chewing gum pellets littered the floor and someone in the recent past had vomited. They elected to walk up.

The council official watched glumly as the lock was forced. After the view of the lift, Jess wondered what the state of the Higson home would be like. But the interior of the flat, at first sight, was neat and tidy. The furniture was old and battered but clean. In stark contrast there was a spanking new computer in one corner of the sitting room; and the whole space was dominated by an enormous television set.

'No need to go to the cinema,' said the council representative. 'Just sit here in front of that! It's something, isn't it?' He sounded envious.

'We'll send someone for that computer,' Carter said. 'Get experts to look at it, see if she's got any emails of interest, what social websites she was on . . .'

There were three bedrooms but one was in use as a storage area. Various boxes and bulging black bin bags were strewn about the floor or stacked one upon the other.

'Worth taking a look at what's inside all those.' Jess indicated them. She prodded the nearest black plastic bag. 'Something soft, feels like clothing.'

Courtney's bedroom was painted pink: entirely pink. The walls and woodwork were pale rose; the curtains were a deeper pink velvety material. Over the duvet was thrown a carnation-pink ruched satin spread, sewn with an appliqué prancing pony. A group of soft toys, two teddy bears and a lion, propped one another up in the centre of it. There were posters of popular bands on the walls, and a row of Barbie dolls sat along the windowsill, watching the intruders with wide eyes. A second large television set stood at the end of the bed.

Courtney had liked clothes, particularly glittery ones. The built-in wardrobe was full of them. Some of them looked unworn. The kidney-shaped dressing table, hung with folds of pink silk, carried a jumble of make-up items and a painted wooden box that looked as though it might be Russian. The lid showed a scene of a beautiful maiden asleep and a mail-clad warrior leaning over her. A version of Sleeping Beauty? wondered Jess. That was how Higson had seen his daughter. She'd been his princess and he'd protected her not with a forest of thorns, but with his own menacing reputation.

Jess opened the little box. It contained Courtney's jewellery, mostly a mix of bangles and earrings of varying quality, together with some gold chains. Compared with the obviously cheap items, like the bangles, the chains appeared at least 18 carat, possibly more, and must have been expensive. Had the girl bought them? Someone whose idea of glamour was represented by the dolls and fancy bedspread, Jess decided, also the glittery garments in the wardrobe, would have gone for show, rather than value. More likely the gold items had come from another source, perhaps her father? If so, he might have bought them from a fence who'd received them as the result of a robbery. She closed the lid gently.

As she did so, Jess felt a great sadness wash over her. She thought Carter felt it too, and even the council official looked downcast.

'A kid,' said Carter softly, looking round him. 'Legally of age, with a dad in and out of gaol, and a mother who deserted years ago. But still a kid at heart. Yet someone hated her so much that a cold-blooded killer knocked her unconscious and then carefully stabbed her through the heart. She couldn't have been a threat. What on earth could she have done to earn such hatred?'

He turned to the council official. 'Higson is registered as the official tenant?'

The young man nodded. 'Never been behind with the rent once. They've looked after the place, no holes knocked in the walls, kitchen's clean, no festering rubbish. Never any complaints about him or his daughter from neighbours. Ideal tenants as far as we're concerned.'

Somehow, Jess wasn't surprised to hear that. Teddy, with all his many faults, had done his best to take care of his 'little princess' and provide her with a comfortable home. Courtney's wages from the pub hadn't paid for the monster TV or computer or expensive tat in her bedroom. But Teddy, if you had asked him, would have considered he had 'worked' hard to provide these comforts.

They left the constable on guard to await workmen sent by the council to secure the forced front door.

When they emerged from the building a few curious onlookers had appeared, mostly young. They clustered in a group, watching. As Jess walked towards them some melted away. The remaining ones stared at her in silent hostility.

'Any of you know the Higson family?' she asked.

They smirked. One of them nodded. 'The old man is well hard.'

Even Teddy Higson had his admirers.

'How about Courtney Higson?'

They nodded.

'Does Courtney have any friends around here?'

'What's she done?' asked one member of the group.

'How about boyfriends?' Jess ignored the question. They'd hear of Courtney's death soon enough. She was surprised the news hadn't reached them already. But Rosetta Gardens was like an eco-dome. It was its own world and contact with outside was limited, mostly, to the petty criminal.

They all shook their heads. 'No one pokes his nose in any Higson business,' one explained.

Teddy Higson was in gaol, but still cast his substantial shadow. What's more, sooner or later, he'd be back. Very likely, as Carter had said, his daughter's death would gain him early release; and his neighbours on the Rosetta Gardens estate would see him earlier than they expected.

Jess abandoned any attempt to learn anything and rejoined Carter and the council official.

'I've just been told,' Carter said to her, indicating the official as his source, 'that there are some lock-up garages behind the flats. Teddy Higson was assigned one of those. We'll take a look and see if Courtney's car is there.'

But the lock-up was windowless and padlocked. The official had no key to that.

'We'll break in,' said Carter to Jess.

The council official looked panic-stricken. 'Does the magistrate's warrant cover the lock-up too? Because, you know, this is council property and there is a limit to how much damage . . .'

Carter consulted the warrant. 'We'll get another one to cover the lock-up in the morning.' He glanced at his watch. 'Too late now.'

The early twilight had already cast its gloom over the scene. The council official was clearly not anxious to hang about Rosetta Gardens after dark.

'If you don't need me any longer . . .' he said. 'I'll get back and send out a couple of men to secure the door of the flat straight away, so that your constable can leave.'

Carter thanked him and he scuttled away.

As Carter and Jess were driving back, he said: 'Send Nugent down there tomorrow with help. The flat's got to be searched top to bottom by trained officers. That includes those bin bags in the spare room. As a priority, we need to find her purse and her mobile. We could pick up valuable information from it. A youngster like her, she must have used it all the time.' There was a short silence, then Carter added, more quietly, 'Millie's got one now, a mobile. I think she's too young.'

'They've all got them, sir.' Jess tried to sound reassuring.

He grunted. 'Any father worries about a daughter. It doesn't puzzle me, as it seems to puzzle others, that Teddy Higson worried about Courtney.'

'He probably thought everyone would be too scared of him to harm her,' Jess pointed out.

'Exactly,' said Carter. 'So we're looking for someone who didn't know about Higson, who had no idea her daddy was a full-time, kneecap-smashing, hard man. Someone, in other words, right outside Courtney's circle of friends.' He paused, then added quietly, 'We're looking for someone who appears absolutely respectable, Jess.'

They sat in silence for a moment.

'If we're looking for someone respectable, Ian,' Jess picked up his earlier words, 'then we've got practically the whole of Weston St Ambrose with the exception of the Rosetta Gardens estate on our list of possible suspects. We'd better start eliminating some of them. I suggest we make a start tomorrow with the writers' club.'

Dennis Claverton took a drink of hot sweet tea from the thermos provided by Lucy, to ward off the night air. He was conducting his own survey of the tawny owl population and its favoured hunting areas. Well wrapped up against the chill, and with a large golf umbrella at the ready should it begin to rain, he sat in his garden under the pale moon, listening and making notes by the light of a pencil torch. He'd already made a detailed and well-mapped sweep of the area around Weston St Ambrose and, over the last six months, gathered a lot of information concerning the location of the tawny owl population and its numbers. He was almost ready to write it up for an article he meant to submit to one of the nature magazines. You could understand, he thought, why people used to believe in spooks. The tawny owl was a denizen of the night. It uttered strange haunting cries; it materialised out of nowhere on almost silent wings. On several occasions, the patiently waiting Dennis had almost jumped out of his skin at its sudden appearance, the shrill squeak or scream of the prey and – when he'd switched on his torch and turned it in the direction of the predator – the momentary glare of savage shining eyes. You can get all the excitement you need in life, Dennis had informed Lucy, sitting out and waiting for that moment, a split second, when death swooped down out of the night. Lucy, he admitted, had seemed under-impressed. But that was because she worried that he'd catch a chill.

Jason Twilling was burning the midnight oil, too. He wanted to get on with his book, get it done. When he was in the world he'd created, he could blot out everything else: his father's grumbles, his mother's anxious inquiries, Courtney's smirk.

The Stewarts conducted a monosyllabic conversation over supper. Then Beth went to bed and Neil sat up until two in the morning, rattling the computer keys fruitlessly, wondering if he was ever going to get his present book finished.

Jess and Tom Palmer met up for the curry meal, as arranged, and spent a cheerful evening, mostly laughing at nothing very much.

'Do you reckon,' asked Jess, 'that the way we spend our working days has made us desperate to find something – anything – funny?

There's not a barrel of laughs in what I do, nor in your line of work.'

'Don't worry about it,' advised Tom. 'You and I have interesting jobs. We don't, either of us, see people at their best, I admit. But you've got to laugh at something . . . Shall we go somewhere else for a drink, after we've finished here?'

Chapter 10

Detective-Constable Sean Stubbs had a reputation for being very successful at interviewing elderly ladies. He found this more than a nuisance.

'Why me?' he asked plaintively the next morning, when told to go and interview a member of the Weston St Ambrose Writers' Club, by name Mrs Jennifer Porter. 'I always get that job. Can't Tracy Bennison go?'

'You'll manage fine,' said Dave Nugent to him. 'Old ladies like you. They make you tea and feed you biscuits and sponge cake. You can't go wrong.'

'I don't know where everyone gets that idea from,' grumbled Stubbs.

'Well-known fact. Off you go. I've got to get over to a magistrate, and then to the Rosetta Gardens estate with a couple of officers to search a flat, then break into a garage and search that. It's going to take the best part of the day.'

Stubbs took himself to Weston St Ambrose and, after some difficulty, found the home of Mrs Porter. To reach it meant following an alley running off the main road; and he wouldn't have found it at all but for a painted arrow on the wall announcing 'Clematis Cottage'. The alley entrance was so narrow he'd already walked past it twice. He wondered that anyone ever found the place; or if she ever got any visitors of more than usually generous build. He squeezed in and sidled awkwardly down it, like a crab stranded on the beach between two rocks. The back of his jacket scraped one wall and his nose was not very far from the other. Halfway along there appeared to be a bricked-up door in the wall he was facing. Stubbs paused to puzzle over this before continuing to the end of the alley, where he emerged into a small paved area, largely occupied by two refuse bins and some tubs containing miniature conifers. There was no sign of clematis, but a square of bare trellis showed where one such plant might have grown. Stubbs dusted himself down watched by a large grey and white cat, perched on top of one bin. It had long hair and large baleful yellow eyes; and it yowled at him as he knocked at the red-painted front door of a tiny brick cottage of the 'two up and two down' variety. He fancied the cat was probably calling a warning to whoever was in the cottage. Stranger approaches!

The lace curtain to the right of the door twitched and he had a glimpse of an unfriendly face before it disappeared. The cat jumped down from the bin and came to stand beside him, looking up at the door expectantly. It opened abruptly and a battle-axe of a woman stood before him. The cat slipped past her indoors.

The woman wore a baggy navy skirt, and matching navy hand-knitted jersey, with black tights and flat black lace-up shoes. Her hair was long, straggling and iron grey. She wore no make-up or jewellery. To Stubbs, with distant memories of his Catholic primary school, she resembled a modern nun, from one of those orders which have abandoned the traditional habit. She thrust forward untidy grey locks and fixed him with a stare that would curdle milk.

'Yes?' she said discouragingly. 'I don't buy at the door.'

'Mrs Porter?' Stubbs sounded determinedly cheerful. 'I'm not selling anything. I'm a police officer and I was wondering if you had a few minutes to spare me?' He produced his ID and held it before her nose.

She pushed her head even further forward, tortoise-like, and read it carefully before comparing the photo on it to the real thing.

'Very well,' she said. 'Come in.' Seldom could the invitation have sounded so discouraging.

She stepped back and Stubbs entered a dark hallway that, like the alley he'd passed through, was exceedingly narrow. The house owner promptly shut the front door and they were plunged into darkness. Somewhere in it lurked the cat. Wary of falling over it, Stubbs stood immobile and waited for directions.

'In there.' Mrs Porter's voice echoed grimly behind him. Her arm came out and a ghostly hand, large, square and more like a man's than a woman's, pointed at the dim outline of a door. Stubbs twisted the knob and opened it to find himself in a tiny sitting room, the one with the window where the curtain had twitched. The cat had disappeared.

'Sit down,' ordered the same unwelcoming voice at his shoulder.

He wasn't sure where to sit but took one of a pair of chintz-covered chairs. They, together with a small round table composed of a beaten brass tray on an oriental-looking stand, and a tall clock, pretty well filled the room. There was an old-fashioned gas fire in the hearth, but only half of it glowed red. On the shelf above the fireplace stood a row of photographs, all obviously taken years ago. In them, none of the subjects was smiling. If he was sure of anything, it was that he was unlikely to be offered any cake or tea here. He was relieved. He wanted to get out of this place as soon as he could.

Mrs Porter shut the door, imprisoning the pair of them in the suffocatingly tiny room, and took the other chintz armchair. She had been reading when he'd knocked at the front door and the volume lay face down but open on the arm of her chair. The jacket showed a pair of lovers gazing into one another's eyes. Blimey, thought Stubbs.

Mrs Porter sat with her knees apart and beetle-crusher shoes planted at forty-five degrees on the carpet, her large hands resting on her kneecaps.

'I dare say,' she boomed before he could begin with one of his prepared opening sentences, 'that you have come about the body.'

'Which body would that be, madam?' asked Stubbs politely.

She gave him a look that also recalled his younger schooldays. 'Do they not have minimum educational requirements for joining the police force? Which body should I mean? Is the place littered with them?'

'Er, no,' stammered Stubbs. 'You've obviously heard that a body has been recovered from the river not far from Weston St Ambrose.'

'A girl,' said Mrs Porter with a nod. 'It turned up at the Stewarts' house, in the river. Have you identified her?'

'Well, yes, Mrs Porter, we have. She has now been identified as Courtney Higson and she—'

Stubbs broke off as Mrs Porter leaned back in her chair, resting her head and staring up at the ceiling. 'Higson,' she said. 'Courtney Higson. Dear me.' For all the expression of regret she sounded highly satisfied.

'You know – knew – her?' Stubbs asked, unable to believe he'd turned up trumps right at the beginning of what had seemed an unpromising interview.

'I may have taught her, if it is the same one. But only briefly, I think. She came into the school the year before I retired. Dark-haired child. Problem family.' Mrs Porter sat upright and stared at Stubbs. 'How did she come to be in the river?'

'We, er, don't yet know, Mrs Porter. You said "problem family" . . .'

'Single parent. Not single mother, as is usually the case, but father raising the child alone. Mother had bunked off, I fancy. Unfortunately, father was a bad hat, so child looked after by granny. She was a pretty girl, I recall, and cheerful. Academically average, but polite. I can't tell you much else.'

She folded her large hands. 'Well, well, Courtney Higson,' she repeated.

'When did you last see her?' asked Stubbs, getting a grip on the situation and opening his notebook.

Mrs Porter stared dismissively at the notebook. 'When she was eleven or twelve years old.'

'You are a member of the Weston St Ambrose Writers' Club, I believe, Mrs Porter?'

'I am, but I don't know who told you that,' she retorted, flushing. She picked up the book on the arm of her chair, shut it, and placed it down on the brass table so that the romantic cover art couldn't be seen.

'And you also attended a creative writing course at the Elsworth College of Arts and Media recently. Neil Stewart, the writer, ran it.'

'Yes,' she said, squinting at him.

'On the last night of the course, you went with some other members of the club, who'd also attended the writing course, to have a meal at the Fisherman's Rest at Lower Weston.'

'You are well informed, Constable Stubbs.'

'Then,' said Stubbs, with a satisfying feeling of triumph, 'you would have seen Courtney Higson there. She was a waitress at your table.'

She looked as though he'd winded her. 'Good Lord!' she said at last. 'Are you sure?'

'Quite sure, madam.'

'I didn't recognise her!' Mrs Porter said brusquely. She sounded annoyed. 'I usually recognise pupils, even after a long period of time, and when they've grown up. But I didn't recognise Courtney. Of course, she was a little girl when I saw her in school. If I'd taught her as a teenager, I might have recognised her. But little girls can change quite a lot between the age of eleven in the entry class and sixth form. There was another young woman serving tables that night. The restaurant was very busy. Are you sure Courtney Higson served our table and not the other girl?'

'Yes, Mrs Porter, I'm surprised she didn't recognise *you*.'

Mrs Porter eyed him as if she suspected sarcasm. 'Well, either she didn't, or didn't notice me in the crowd. The place was packed out.'

'I believe some other members of your party recognised Courtney because they called her by name.' Stubbs smiled at her.

Mrs Porter looked down at her folded hands and meditated on the subject until Stubbs grew restless, and cleared his throat to remind her he was there.

She looked up. 'Yes,' she said. 'He did call the girl "Courtney". But I still did not connect her with Courtney Higson.'

'Who called the waitress by name, Courtney, Mrs Porter?' Stubbs asked.

She tossed back a lock of grey hair. 'Peter Posset,' she said firmly.

There came a yowl from the other side of the closed sitting-room door. Mrs Porter stood up. 'Monty wants to come in, too, and sit by the fire.' She went to open the door and the grey and white cat strolled in. Ignoring Stubbs, it made for the hearth and sat down facing the half-fire with its back to him.

Mrs Porter was still standing by the door, holding it open. Stubbs recognised that it was time for him to leave.

When he had negotiated the narrow alley back into the main road, he rang Inspector Campbell and summarised his findings. 'You did say keep in touch, ma'am,' he explained. 'The Porter woman says some geezer called Peter Posset called the girl by her name.'

'Then you'd better go and interview him next,' ordered her voice at the end of the connection. 'Hang on, I've got his address.' There was a pause and Jess Campbell returned. She read out Peter Posset's address and added, 'By the way, did Mrs Porter give you tea and biscuits?'

'You've got to be joking,' snapped Stubbs unwarily. 'Sorry, ma'am, I mean she didn't. She wasn't very welcoming at all.'

He had better luck on the refreshment front with Peter Posset.

'Indian or China, Constable?' asked Posset.

'Indian or China what?' asked Stubbs, caught unprepared.

'Tea, Constable.'

'Oh, well, um, Indian,' Stubbs told him. 'Thank you.'

'So few young people drink China tea these days,' said Posset with a sigh. 'Be with you in a tick, Constable. Make yourself comfortable. Just move my knitting from that chair. Try and keep it all together, will you? I lost a needle the other day and though I've looked everywhere, I haven't found it. I had to go out a buy another pair of needles in that gauge, specially. I expect the other one will turn up eventually . . .'

Stubbs turned and saw, on the seat of an armchair behind him, a large ball of oatmeal-coloured wool, a piece of worked knitting about six inches long and a set of sturdy knitting needles. He lifted the whole lot carefully and looked for somewhere to put it. After some deliberation, he set the work down on a Welsh dresser by the wall. He sat down in the seat where the knitting had been and waited with curiosity and some apprehension for the reappearance of the house owner.

Posset came back bearing a tray with two small teapots on it, teacups, and a miniature jug of milk.

'Shall I pour?' he asked. 'But please help yourself to milk if you take it.'

He sat down and leaned back, beaming at his visitor. 'Now then, young man, what can I do for you, eh?'

Stubbs's eye was taken by the striking design of bright green fir trees strung across the front of Posset's pullover. 'Do you, er, knit all your own pullovers, Mr Posset?'

'Oh, yes!' said Peter cheerfully. 'My grandmother taught me when I was very young. I keep to the same basic pattern, as you see, but vary the design on the front. I have one with reindeer on it and another with snowflakes.'

'Oh, right,' said Stubbs. 'I would like to ask you a couple of questions, sir, about a recent creative writing course you attended at the Elsworth College.'

'Excellent course,' said Posset. 'I recommend it to you, Constable, if another one comes along. Sign up for it, particularly if Neil Stewart is lecturing. We all learned a great deal. By "we" I am speaking in particular of the Weston St Ambrose Writers' Club. We all went along to Neil's course; and we all, I think I can speak for everyone, benefited by it.'

'Oh, yes, the writers' club, I was hoping speak to you about that,' Stubbs said quickly.

Posset's bushy eyebrows rose. 'Interested to join our number, Constable? We should be delighted to have you. I am the founder member of our little circle and we've been going now for four years.'

'I couldn't write anything,' said Stubbs unwisely.

Posset leaned forward. 'My dear boy, don't say such a thing! Have you tried? You would be surprised at what hidden talent you may have!'

'I'm too busy,' said Stubbs firmly. 'My wife and I have four-year-old twins.'

'Indeed?' Posset leaned back in his chair again. 'How very delightful.'

'On the last evening of the course,' Stubbs began again, sounding to his own ear rather desperate, 'the members of the writers' club, together with one other student on the course and the lecturer, Neil Stewart, all went out for a meal at the Fisherman's Rest in Lower Weston.'

'We did, indeed. An excellent hostelry, nothing fancy, but

everything very well cooked. All fresh ingredients. I recommend it. But perhaps you know it?'

'Not personally,' said Stubbs. 'Can I ask you if you remember whose idea it was to go there?'

Posset tapped his fingers and thought. 'Now, that is a very curious thing. I can't remember who suggested it.'

'You, perhaps, sir, as you know the place well?'

'I might have done,' conceded Posset. 'But I couldn't tell you for sure.'

'You are known there? And you know the staff?'

'They generally recognise me,' Posset agreed. 'I often go there for Sunday lunch. They do a very good roast and an excellent sticky toffee pudding.'

'The young woman who waited at your table, you knew her?'

Posset smoothed his luxuriant whiskers. 'May I ask the import of these questions, Constable?'

'Unfortunately,' Stubbs told him, 'the young woman in question is dead.'

There was a long silence. Posset's hand froze, resting on his sideburns. His florid complexion paled to very much the same oatmeal shade as his knitwear. 'Little Courtney?' he managed to say at last.

'I was told you addressed her by name, sir.'

'Who told you?' snapped Posset. 'I don't deny it. Why should I? I told you, I lunch there frequently on a Sunday and Courtney is often working there.' After another pause, he added, 'I only knew her first name, never her surname.'

'Her surname is Higson, sir, are you certain you haven't heard it before?'

138

Posset had recovered from his shock. He shook his head. 'Higson? No, no, I know of no Higsons. Well, since you tell me it was little Courtney's name, I appear to have known one Higson, albeit in a very superficial way. But I was unaware of her surname, as I told you.'

'You never met with Courtney outside of the visits to the pub for lunch, sir? By chance, perhaps, here in Weston St Ambrose?'

'No, never. Why should I?'

'Any reason at all, sir.'

Posset smiled at him. 'Young man, it is not my habit – it has never been my habit – to make assignations with young women.'

'Very well, sir,' said Stubbs woodenly.

'Constable,' Peter Posset said evenly, 'am I to understand from the roundabout method of cross-examination you employ that the young woman we are discussing is the same one as the dead girl taken from the river at Glebe House? I have, of course, heard about that.'

'Yes, sir.'

Posset expelled a long breath. 'That is very sad, both very sad and very shocking.' He passed a hand across his brow in theatrical fashion. 'Good heavens, drowned? She was little more than a child. Is it known how the tragedy came about?' He paused and waited for Stubbs's reply.

'Not drowned, sir, stabbed,' Stubbs informed him.

In the ensuing silence the whole room seemed to be holding its breath. Posset, in his cheerful pullover, seemed particularly incongruous. His face had become nearly as white as the whiskers surrounding it. He opened his mouth a couple of times and closed it without managing to speak. Eventually he recovered his composure well enough to croak, 'But you said she was in the river! If she was stabbed – dreadful thought – how did she get into the river?'

'That's what we're trying to establish, sir.'

'There is no doubt about her identity?'

'No, sir, none whatsoever. She has been identified by a close family member.'

'Then there can be no mistake.' Posset's face had returned to its normal colour. He seemed to have regained full control of his emotions. 'I wish I could be of help, Constable. Tell me, will you be talking to all the members of the writers' club?'

'Either I, or one of my colleagues, sir. I have already spoken to Mrs Porter.'

'Have you? I see. And could she tell you anything useful?'

'Mrs Porter taught Courtney briefly a long time ago.'

'Did she, indeed?' Posset frowned. 'I don't think Courtney greeted Jenny Porter, that evening at the Fisherman's Rest. But young people these days lack ordinary everyday civility.'

'I don't think either of them recognised the other, sir. Mrs Porter taught Courtney only briefly, several years ago, as I said.'

'Still, Jenny Porter normally has the proverbial memory of an elephant. Well, I'm afraid I can't contribute anything either. More tea, Constable?'

Stubbs recognised that, as on his earlier visit to Mrs Porter, he was being shown the door.

When he had left Peter Posset gathered up the tea things and took the tray out to his spotless kitchen. There he stood contemplating the cups for a few minutes before returning to his sitting room and picking up the phone.

'Peter here,' he said, when the person at the other end of the line answered. 'A police officer has just been here. He has informed me the girl who was taken from the river is, or was, Courtney, your Courtney at the Rest, no doubt about it. The worst of it is, my dear fellow, she didn't drown. The officer who was here told me. She had been stabbed and then thrown – or pushed – into the river. Oh, you have heard? Well, anyway, my sincere condolences, Gordon. Such a shock. You have no idea, I suppose, what she was doing down by the river?'

Constable Tracy Bennison had been assigned the interview with Jason Twilling. She found him, after a conversation with his landlady, at his place of work, a furniture warehouse. This meant asking for him; and that meant explaining that she was a police officer but no need to worry at all. It was a purely routine matter. By now, everyone working in the cavernous space with its smell of wood and varnish and a lot of dust, was watching with great interest.

'What did you have to come and see me here for?' demanded Jason crossly, when shown her ID. 'Couldn't you have come back tonight at my home address? Are you trying to lose me my job?'

'I'm afraid we don't have the time or manpower to keep going back and forth on the off-chance we'd find you at home,' Bennison told him with a cheerful smile.

'Well, I'm not talking to you in here with everyone else listening. We'll have to go outside to the unloading bay.'

It seemed a sensible idea in the circumstances, so Bennison

followed him through a side door into an open area. They were not alone. There was another worker there, surreptitiously smoking a cigarette. He looked alarmed as they emerged from the building and bolted back inside without being requested.

'Well?' asked Jason disagreeably. 'What do you want?'

'I believe you're a member of the Weston St Ambrose Writers' Club?' Bennison began.

'Don't tell me that comes under suspicious activities,' grumbled Jason. 'So what?'

Bennison explained that they were talking to everyone who had formed the party dining at the Fisherman's Rest on the last night of the recent creative writing course. As she spoke Jason's dissatisfaction, already manifest, grew.

'Sodding awful evening that was,' he said. 'Have you been there? Have you seen the prices on their menu?'

'Why did you go, if it's out of your pocket?' asked Bennison.

'I wasn't going to be the only one to drop out, was I?'

'Well, presumably you weren't the one who suggested that restaurant,' observed Bennison. 'Who did suggest it?'

'Blowed if I know. Probably old Posset – or it might have been Henry Blackwood.' Jason paused and frowned. 'Or one of the women, yes, I fancy it was one of the women. Probably Prue Blackwood – or Lucy Claverton. She and Dennis go there, too, I think. It might have been that old dragon, Mrs Porter . . .' Jason scowled. 'I can't remember for sure whose idea it was.'

'Did any of them address the waitress by name?'

'There were two of them,' said Jason promptly.

'Two people addressed her by name?'

'No, there were two waitresses. But the one who took the order was Courtney Higson. She said, "Hello, Jaz," so I had to say, "Hello Courtney."'

'You knew Courtney well?' Bennison controlled her eagerness as best she could.

'No, not well. I was at school with her. I was a year ahead of her but we sort of dated for a bit. Only while we were at school.'

'You never saw her later, after you both left school?'

'I must have passed her a couple of times in the street. I knew she worked sometimes at that posh pub because . . .' Jason paused and met Bennison's raised eyebrows, 'I don't know what all this has got to do with anything!'

'How did you know she worked at the Fisherman's Rest sometimes, if it was too expensive a place for you to go to?' persisted Bennison.

'If you must know, my car broke down one day out in the country. I had to walk home. On the way I passed the pub and I was thirsty so I went in for a beer. Courtney was there. I had to tell her the car had conked out on me. She thought it was funny.'

Jason eyed Bennison's notebook and the way she scribbled all this down. 'So what? Why am I being given the third degree about one rotten night out and someone I was at school with?'

'I'm sorry to have to tell you,' Bennison said sympathetically, 'Courtney Higson's dead body was taken from the river.'

Jason's face drained of all colour. He opened and closed his mouth a couple of times before he managed to croak, 'That dead girl, the one found in the river at the Stewarts' place, that's Courtney?'

'Yes, Mr Twilling. Cause of death was a stab wound to the

heart. The initial inquest has already been opened and adjourned so it will probably be in the next edition of the local paper.'

Jason uttered a squeak and crumpled to the ground in a faint.

'It wasn't my fault,' said Bennison defensively, when reporting this to Jess Campbell. 'He just passed out. I didn't think he'd do that or I'd have made sure he was sitting down already or something. I called an ambulance. But by the time it arrived, he'd come round and was sitting on the ground, crying his eyes out. Everyone in the warehouse had come running out. I was surrounded by a mob. It's an industrial estate and there are other warehouses there, building suppliers, that sort of thing. Word got round like lightning and nearly everyone working there shot out and rushed over. I thought I was going to be accused of police brutality. I nearly phoned for back-up. I didn't think I'd get away. But luckily they got distracted when Twilling was loaded into the ambulance. I jumped in the car and followed it as it drove off with him. He's OK, Twilling. They checked him over at A and E and said he was fine. He's gone home.'

'Don't worry, Tracy, I'm sure it was just shock made him pass out. I don't suppose at his age he's had much experience of violent death, certainly not among his old school friends,' Jess consoled her. 'How did you get on, Sean?'

'They ought to put a warning notice on that woman's front door,' said Stubbs gloomily. 'She's a retired teacher. She taught Courtney for one year only when Courtney was an eleven-year-old kid. That was just before Mrs Porter gave up teaching. That must have been a relief to everyone. She hadn't seen Courtney again and didn't recognise her at the pub. Or so she says. Oh,' Stubbs added, 'she did remember that Courtney's father was what she called "a bad hat". She couldn't remember who suggested they all go and eat at that pub.'

'What about Posset?'

'Barking, if you ask me. He drinks China tea and knits all his own pullovers to his own designs. He fussed about mislaying one of his knitting needles. He had to go out and buy another pair, apparently. Can you believe it? He also can't remember who suggested they eat at the Fisherman's Rest.'

'Jason thinks it might have been one of the women in the group,' Bennison put in. 'Apparently both the Blackwoods and the Clavertons go to eat there from time to time. But he can't remember exactly either.'

'Posset admits to addressing Courtney by name but says he never knew her surname. He only knew her as a waitress. I think we can believe that,' Stubbs said firmly. 'He suggested I join his writers' club. If I'd been there any longer, he'd have put his hand on my knee.'

'I need a sandwich and a pint,' said Ian Carter, when Jess relayed all this to him. He took a deep breath and took the plunge. 'Join me? We can review what we've learned.'

'Do you mean at the Fisherman's Rest?' Jess asked him suspiciously.

'Why not? They should be able to make a decent sandwich there.'

He set off before she could object further.

Chapter 11

The pub looked different in daylight, its long, mellow stone walls blending into the surrounding countryside. They could see now there was another entrance in addition to the one they'd used in the car park. This other entrance was bigger and fronted the roadside. It had Christmas trees in tubs, one either side of the wooden door case. Above the lintel was carved W + M 1691. Despite this, it was not in use and a small notice indicated patrons should enter from the car park.

The car park also looked different by daylight. There was a large wood store in the far corner and an entry into the gardens to the rear of the building. But this, too, was barred. A notice advised visitors that the gardens were closed due to recent rains. Jess and Carter walked over to the gate to inspect the reason for the warning.

Carter gave a low whistle. 'The river's really broken its banks here. It's nearly up to the back of the building! The water is halfway up those trestle tables at the far end, nearest where the river line ought to be.'

'They've stacked plenty of sandbags along the building.'

'They may need 'em!'

A harassed Gordon Fleming did not look particularly pleased to see them. By daylight, his pale complexion and lack of eyebrows

147

accentuated his facial resemblance to an egg on which some wag had drawn a cross face.

'If it's only a sandwich you want, I suggest you take a table in the bar area. Our bar menu is written up on a blackboard, over there.' His pale eyes rested on Jess. 'Amy's not here at the moment, if you wanted to see her again. She won't be in until tonight. If you want to talk to me again about Courtney, I can tell you again now I know absolutely nothing about her private life.'

'We're very sorry that Courtney Higson has now been publicly identified as the girl in the river. She did not, however, drown; she was stabbed.' Carter watched Fleming's face closely as he spoke. 'I expect you already know that. No doubt Graeme Murchison will have told you about the inquest.'

The cross expression faded from the egg face to be replaced by a defiant one. 'Yes, I've heard all about it from Graeme. He said he'd go and I didn't need to. But I still can't help. All I know is, I'm short of a waitress and it's very inconvenient.' Fractionally too late, Fleming added, 'I'm sorry about what's happened to her. Of course I am. But I can't ask Amy to work any more double shifts or she'll walk off and leave me with no one.'

'You will need to replace Courtney quickly, then,' observed Jess.

'Of course I'll have to replace her!' snapped Fleming. 'It won't be easy. You have absolutely no idea how difficult it is to find reliable staff. Have you decided on your sandwiches? Or would you prefer one of our wraps? Or we do a filled baguette and salad, that's popular.'

They settled for sandwiches and Fleming took himself off to relay their order to the kitchen.

'I wonder,' Jess said quietly, 'to what extent word of the dead girl's identity has already got round.'

'Not spread by Murchison, I think. OK, he told Gordon. But that's because Fleming runs the pub for him. If Murchison went round telling others, he'd be advertising his interest and thus his ownership. The news may have made a local radio station newscast. The inquest will be reported in the local rag. When's that due out?'

'Tomorrow, I think. Or that log man, Wayne Garley, could be spreading the word. He'll have told everyone what was said at the inquest.'

The only other table occupied in the bar was at the further end of the room and near the open log fire. The two men sitting at it were young and be-suited and looked as if they might have dropped by in the course of a business visit in the area. They had chosen sandwiches too and, as they ate, discussed something they could read on the screen of a laptop opened on the table before them. Jess and Ian made themselves comfortable in the bay window area where the pale winter sunlight brightened the interior.

'Originally,' Ian said quietly as he looked around at the horse brasses tacked along the wooden beams and antique agricultural implements fixed to the walls, 'I'd have said that the visit of the writers' club to this pub, with Stewart and Murchison tagging along, was largely coincidental to our investigations. I've still got a few doubts about Stewart's account. Had he really only seen the girl once during a visit here, yet was able to identify her from a brief glimpse as she was taken dripping wet from the river? Why didn't he say so at once? OK, he was shocked. But there's Murchison as well. He's hiding something but I don't know what it is. He owns this place and so he knew Courtney and the other girl, but he leaves the hiring of staff to Fleming.

'In addition to all that, I'm not happy about that writers' club. Some of them have more of a history with Courtney than you might think. These are respectable people with an interest in literature and in writing. What should there be to connect any of them with the daughter of a thug like Teddy Higson, a girl who worked in a gastro-pub, as I believe they call this sort of place? Yet, of the three members interviewed so far, one dated the girl during their schooldays. He reacted dramatically when told of her death. Another one taught her briefly eight years ago. Mrs Porter seems to have good recall of Courtney's circumstances, her villain of a father and so on, but denies recognising her here. Oh, and Courtney didn't address *her* by name or appear to recognise a former teacher. The pub was crowded, I admit. But was there some old quarrel that led to each of them ignoring the other?'

'I'm not being catty here,' Jess said, 'but perhaps Courtney didn't bother to suss out the women. Perhaps she was only interested in the men.'

'Point taken. Well, Posset is a regular. He admits he knew Courtney by sight and, he stresses, as a waitress only. None of them admits to remembering who suggested they all eat there. Collective amnesia on the part of a group of people who otherwise appear to have very good recall is very odd. Coincidence only goes so far before it becomes interesting. I'm getting very interested in the Weston St Ambrose Writers' Club.'

'Before he passed out, Jason Twilling told Bennison that he thinks one of the women in the party suggested they all come here for that end-of-course dinner. Both the Blackwoods and

the Clavertons also use the Fisherman's Rest.' Jess added thoughtfully, 'If that's the case, wouldn't they know Courtney, even if only
as a waitress?'

'We'll divide those interviews between us,' Carter decided. 'I'll
take the Blackwoods and you can take the Clavertons.'

Jess nodded. 'That leaves Isolde Evans, the supply teacher. She
won't have taught Courtney. She's too young. But I'll call by her
flat and see if she's home. I would send Tracy Bennison but
her confidence has suffered a knock from having Twilling collapse
at her feet.'

'If that's the worst thing that ever happens to her in her police
career, she'll be lucky,' said Carter unfeelingly.

Jess looked round the bar. 'I'm sorry Amy Fallon's not here. I
think we need to speak to her again. We mustn't forget Courtney's
mystery boyfriend. Amy is so certain he existed, and she thinks
he might have been married.'

'I'm not forgetting him,' Carter told her. 'That's a familiar
scenario. The secret girlfriend suddenly wants to be the public
woman seen around with him. He's afraid the wife will find out
. . . That's ended in murder before now.'

'On the other hand, the secrecy appears to have been Courtney's
idea,' Jess argued. 'She was afraid her father would interfere and
break up the affair. Perhaps she was so worried about her father
that she tried to break off the relationship ahead of Teddy's reappearance; and the mystery boyfriend didn't like that. Amy told
me that Courtney spoke once of having to tell the man she mightn't
be able to see him for a while. Perhaps she did just that and he
decided that if he couldn't have her, no one else would. We've
met that situation before, too.'

She fell silent as a young man in a white jacket and houndstooth check cotton trousers appeared from the direction of the kitchen and bore down on them with two wooden platters.

'Ham and pickle!' he announced, 'and tuna. Whose is the tuna?'

Jess owned up to the tuna and he placed the wooden platter before her with a flourish. The sandwiches were tastefully arranged and came with a side salad and crisps.

'And the ham!' declared the young man putting the other platter before Ian Carter. He then lowered his voice and added in a stage whisper, 'You're the police!'

'We are,' agreed Carter, 'but just taking our lunch break.'

'I love a mystery,' said the young man confidentially. 'I watch all the TV series.' He frowned. 'Of course, in real life it's not the *same*, is it? The dead girl really is poor Courtney? You know, I still can't get my head round it. I don't care how many times I'm told. It's just so – so unexpected and no one can think of any reason.'

'Yes, the dead girl has been identified as Courtney Higson,' said Carter. 'Where did you learn the news? Did Fleming tell you, after the inquest?'

But the young man looked puzzled. 'No, no one said anything about the inquest. Mr Fleming didn't go to it. If he knew, he didn't tell us. But one of your guys went to see Mr Posset, didn't he? Mr Posset phoned Gordon to express his condolences, as she worked here. After that, Gordon came and told us all. Oh . . .' He placed his hand theatrically over his heart. 'I can't tell you how the news affected me. A cold shiver ran all over me. It was like a ghost had materialised and stood by me. Do you think it could have been poor Courtney?'

'No,' said Carter curtly.

The young man sniffed. 'Well, Mr Posset told Gordon she was stabbed, and then the killer put her in the river. We were all very shocked. It does make you wonder, doesn't it? You don't know who's out there.' He shuddered.

Carter said coolly: 'We're continuing with our inquiries. We're interested to know Courtney's movements over the couple of days prior to the discovery of her body. If you know anything about that, or you hear anything, get in touch, won't you?'

The sous-chef looked dissatisfied with this response. 'I would, if I could, but I don't know a thing. I never talked to her much. I'm in the kitchen nearly all the time and Courtney would just come in to collect an order and take it out to the restaurant. It's still very strange, isn't it? I don't just mean the stabbing, that's horrible enough, but then the killer put her in the river. The weather's been terrible, so much rain. All along the river the bank is a dreadful mess. She wouldn't go walking down there, no one would, for no reason. If you ask me,' he lowered his voice, 'she was lured.'

'Lured?' Jess asked. 'Who lured her?'

'Well, I don't know, do I?' he retorted; and left them to their meal.

'Lots of feverish speculation,' Jess commented, 'and very little fact. So now we know that, after Murchison told Fleming about Courtney's identity being established at the inquest, Fleming didn't pass it on to his other staff. They learned about it only after Peter Posset's call.'

'I told you what I think.' Carter glanced towards the bar to make sure Fleming wasn't within earshot. 'That has to do with

Murchison not wanting it to be general knowledge that he owns this place. Perhaps the other staff don't even know that he does!'

'My guess,' murmured Jess, 'is that Fleming was scared out of his wits at the idea of one of the staff being murdered. He just didn't have the guts to tell the others. Perhaps he thought they'd quit, *en masse*. He knew word would get round eventually, so he just waited until he had to say something to them.'

Carter was glowering at his wooden platter. 'What's wrong with a proper plate?' He removed the toothpick securing a gherkin to the topmost of his ham sandwiches and contemplated it.

'It looks attractive like this,' Jess countered. She picked up a triangle of tuna on wholemeal bread. 'You know, I was just thinking what Stubbs told us about his interview with Peter Posset. Posset knits all his own sweaters and is working on one at the moment. Tom Palmer suggested that Courtney was stabbed with a long thin weapon, like a screwdriver or an awl. How about a well-sharpened, larger-gauge knitting needle? Posset says he's lost one.'

'Hm,' said her companion. He made a stabbing motion upwards with the toothpick. 'It would take some strength and determination. That brings us back to motive. Who on earth would be driven to that extent to kill a girl like Courtney?'

They ate in silence for a minute or two, then Carter said, 'Actually, Jess, I wanted a word about something else. I know that it's extremely inconvenient for me to take a day's leave at a moment like this, but . . .'

'But you want to go and see Millie in her school play,' Jess said.

'Yes, Millie asked me.'

'Of course you must go; and we can manage fine. When is it?'

'Tomorrow,' he admitted. 'I tried to ring Sophie but she was at her keep-fit class. She hasn't rung back so I'll text her today and confirm I'll be there.'

'What about – um – her present husband? Will he be there too?'

'Rodney? No idea. Probably not, if I am.'

This isn't my business, thought Jess in some exasperation. It's not my concern in any way. But she asked, 'Everything is OK, is it? With Sophie?'

'As far as I know. Although . . .' He hesitated. 'If it isn't, I'll probably find out sooner or later. If there is a problem in Sophie's life, she doesn't tolerate it for long. She's a great fixer – of her own troubles, that is. I don't think she ever considers the possibility that other people might have anything to worry about.'

'Well, it's really no problem if you want to go to the pantomime,' Jess told him briskly. She shouldn't have asked him if everything was all right. He was glowering at what was left of his lunch. Work came to the rescue.

'If we talk to the Blackwoods and the Clavertons this afternoon, that will be the writers' club dealt with.' She paused and pushed away her platter. 'It's not as though we have dozens of other leads to follow up. I hope that by tomorrow the technical boys will have got into Courtney's computer and will have found something to give us an idea where to look.'

'Charlie?' Graeme Murchison paused at the edge of the clearing where the shack stood. Smoke spiralled upward out of the improvised chimney, showing that the old man had lit the wood-burning metal stove he used to heat his home.

155

The two dogs, Max and Prince, were sniffing round the area eagerly. Perhaps the old chap had been setting rabbit snares again and the bodies of his victims were hanging up somewhere nearby. Murchison walked over to the shack and rapped at the door. There was no reply so he pushed it open. Smoke billowed out. One of these days the old man would be found asphyxiated, he thought. Inside the shack, as his eyes adjusted to the gloom, he made out the bed with its neatly folded sleeping bag and the home-made table bearing various utensils that constituted Charlie's kitchen unit. But of the old man himself there was no sign.

Murchison went back outside, grateful for the fresh air. He drew in a deep lungful. As he did, the dogs began to bark. Something had attracted their attention in the spindly trees and dense undergrowth on the far side of the clearing. They would know if Charlie approached. This was something or someone else who was coming.

He called the dogs to heel. They came obediently but they longed to go and investigate. Max crouched by his feet, nose lifted to scent the air, and the younger dog, Prince, stood ready to bound forward. Murchison reached out and touched the dog's head to reassure him. The wood was clearly marked all round the boundary with signs saying it was private, but people still came through from time to time. Sometimes it was walkers, occasionally gypsies. Murchison didn't mind the gypsies, nor did Charlie. The walkers were a different kettle of fish. They knew they were trespassing and could, on occasion, be quite truculent if challenged. Charlie, if he saw walkers, would descend on them in rage and drive them off. Charlie might be old and small, but he still presented a formidable opponent when waving a strong stick and yelling. The gypsies, occasional visitors, knew Charlie and he knew them. Generally they called by his shack to let him know they were about. If any of them encountered Murchison they were shy and called him 'sir' because they knew he owned the land. He let them pass through unimpeded.

But there were others, too, neither gypsies nor walkers, who prowled around the outskirts of the house after dark. He suspected they came through the wood to reach the house, although there was a track running off the road up the side of the garden wall before it petered out in fields. Occasionally, in the mornings, Murchison had found fresh strange tyre tracks there. As he'd explained to that chap Carter, there were those who saw in the Old Manor a likely target for burglary. Someone watched the place, but he'd be ready, if they came.

Now he heard it, too, the crack of twigs and rustle of disturbed bushes. Max scrambled to his feet and growled.

'Show yourself!' Murchison called across the clearing. 'The dogs won't harm you but they're nervous if they can't see you.'

There was a movement among the trees and a slender figure appeared, pushing a way forward. It was a girl, with long hair, wearing jeans and a bomber jacket, and carrying a plastic super-market bag. For a second he almost thought . . . Then he recognised her.

'Amy!' he exclaimed. 'Your grandfather's not here. I don't know where he is.'

She came towards him, swinging the bulging plastic carrier. 'Mum sent me up here with his groceries,' she said. 'I'll leave them inside.'

The dogs relaxed, too, now that he had. Besides, they had recognised her scent. After a sniff at her jeans, tails wagged, and Max pushed his snout into her hand.

'I don't have anything for you!' she said indulgently to him, lifting the plastic carrier out of the way.

She walked past Murchison and went into the shack. After a moment, she came back without the plastic bag. 'He'll find it,' she said. Her eyes scrutinised his face in a way that struck him as the look wildlife gave you, sizing you up, not sure whether to proceed or turn and flee. 'Police came talking to me,' she said casually.

'Yes, someone came and talked to me, as well.'

'About Courtney,' Amy said. She broke off her scrutiny of him to stare at the back of one of her hands. Her nails were lacquered purple and one had chipped badly. 'Look at that,' she said crossly. 'I did that coming through those trees. I'll have to put another coat over that before tonight when I go to work.'

Carter had not mentioned Courtney when he'd called at the house that evening, Murchison thought. Now he found that odd – or canny. His visitor had talked about any number of things: the dogs, the creative writing course. For his part, Murchison had told the superintendent about his break with Barbara and how he'd returned from New York to make a new life here. They had spoken about the Fisherman's Rest and Murchison had admitted to owning it. Now that he thought about it, he'd told Carter a good deal about himself, too bloody much. Had he appeared nervous? But he hadn't told Carter . . .

'They're there again,' Amy said.

For a moment he didn't follow and raised his eyebrows.

Impatiently, she said, 'The cops, they're at the Rest again, right now. I saw them arrive as I left our house to come here and find Granddad. The same two, the tall bloke and the woman with the red hair.'

'Really?' Murchison said more easily than came naturally to him.

'Yeah, I bet they want to talk about Courtney again. She was the one they found in the river over by Neil Stewart's place.' Her round, slightly protuberant, gooseberry eyes, with their elusive wild creature's stare, fixed him again. 'Old Posset rang the pub with the news. Gordon already knew but he hadn't told us because he was so shaken, he said. He's in a rotten mood. How did you find out? Did you go to that inquest? It was you told Gordon, wasn't it?'

Murchison said nothing. The dogs had sensed his mood and moved closer to him, protectively. Max whined.

Amy had probably not expected him to admit his presence at the inquest and thought she'd gained an advantage.

'She was identified by a close family member, Mr Posset said. The cops had told him that, so it's right. That'll be her dad, I expect, who identified her. I don't think Courtney had any other family. The cops said Courtney was stabbed.'

Max whined again. Murchison asked, trying to control the sudden quaver in his voice, 'Has anyone on the staff got any ideas about that?'

'No. They don't know how she got into the river. Malcolm, that's the cook's boyfriend, calls himself the sous-chef, he's got any number of nutty theories, but that's because he reads whodunits. I wonder,' said Amy artlessly, 'if they'll let Courtney's dad out of gaol, now she's dead, let him go home. He's a right hard case, is Teddy. Courtney, she was his princess, that's what he called her. If he got hold of anyone who took a fancy to Courtney, he'd cut up really rough. I bet,' she added, giving him a slightly mocking sideways glance, 'Teddy Higson doesn't know about you and Courtney. I bet the cops don't know, either. Oh, it's all right . . .' She peered earnestly into his face. 'I won't tell.'

Murchison knew he'd paled. But he wasn't going to let the little bitch see she'd rattled him. 'There's nothing for you to tell anyone, Amy,' he said calmly.

'The woman cop asked me, when she came the other night, if I knew who Courtney's boyfriend was. I said I didn't know, that she hadn't told anyone. But she did tell me. You were having an affair with her.'

The sudden and unexpected use of that favourite tabloid word 'affair', combined with shock, made Murchison laugh. Amy hadn't expected laughter and scowled at him.

'Well, you were,' she said stubbornly. 'You were having it off with Courtney all the time she worked at the Rest.'

'Perhaps Courtney wasn't telling you the truth, Amy,' Murchison said quietly. 'She was fantasising, trying to impress you, or just having you on.'

'Sure, it's the truth. She used to sneak into your garden the back way, through that little gate my granddad uses, and come to see you.' Amy glanced back at the shed. 'That's no place for an old bloke like my granddad to live,' she said. 'He should have more comforts at his time of life. But he's got no money, no more have I – or my mum and dad. We could all do with being a bit more comfortable.'

'Amy,' said Murchison in the same quiet way, 'are you trying to blackmail me?'

Perhaps this conversation wasn't now going the way Amy had anticipated and his quiet manner rattled her. She blinked. 'Course not, I'm just being a friend. I won't tell the cops about you – nor tell Teddy when he comes home, like a friend wouldn't tell. But I can't be your friend if you're not mine, can I? I'm not black-mailing you or anything like that. I just think you could help my granddad – and my family. My granddad's useful to you. He looks after those dogs there for you and keeps an eye on your place when you're away. You don't pay him anything. You let him live here . . .' Amy nodded towards the shack. 'But it's not fit for any human to live in. I bet the council wouldn't like him living in these woods. They'd put a stop to it. You've got to have planning permission or something like that.'

'I happen to know, Amy,' Murchison told her, 'that officially your grandfather resides with your parents in your cottage. That is his address on the electoral roll and in all places where his address is listed.'

'He doesn't like it with us,' said Amy. 'Mum makes him take off his boots when he comes indoors and she won't let him sit on the best chairs in his old trousers. He likes pottering about here. He can do what he likes.'

'Then it seems to me your grandfather and I have a mutually agreeable arrangement and you ought not to interfere with it. Also, you'd like to keep your job, I dare say.'

'Gordon employs me!' she snapped, reddening.

'And Gordon will sack you if I tell him to do it. Incidentally, the police are aware that your grandfather stays overnight in the hut. I told Superintendent Carter about that. So, you see, Amy, it really isn't in your interest to make trouble for me. Trouble for me means trouble for you and your grandfather.' Murchison leaned forward and she stepped back hastily. 'Don't try and get money out of me, Amy. It won't work and really, it's very, very unwise.'

Chapter 12

Ian Carter sought out the Blackwoods that afternoon, after he and Jess returned from the Fisherman's Rest. He found them inspecting their sodden garden and overflowing miniature pond.

'All this rain,' said Henry with a sigh. 'I bet you a pound to a penny, come the summer, we'll be told there's a water shortage and we have to conserve the stuff. Right now, it's "water, water, everywhere . . ." like the poem. Of course, we're fortunate here. We won't be flooded. Properties near the river will be most at risk.'

'I understand,' said Carter, 'that the beer garden of the Fisherman's Rest is already under water.'

'Oh, dear,' said Prue. 'I hope it doesn't get into the building. They redecorated right through only last year.'

'You know the place well?' Carter asked them.

'Oh, we've always liked going there, haven't we, Henry?'

'It's very reliable,' Henry gave his support. 'The vegetables are always fresh, the meat top quality, and it's always well cooked and presented.'

'Was it you, perhaps, who suggested the writers' club and Neil Stewart go there after the last lecture of the creative writing course at the Arts and Media College?'

They looked surprised at the question, consulted one another, and shook their heads in unison.

163

'I wouldn't have liked to,' confessed Henry, 'because the prices have got so steep and people like young Jason can't have much spare cash. It passed into new ownership last year. That's when the redecorating was done – and the prices went up. To pay for all the refurbishment, I suppose.'

'Oh, do you know who owns it?' Carter asked them casually.

They shook their heads. 'I've always supposed,' Henry suggested, 'it must be one of the big chains, a brewery or something like that. I'm sure that chap Fleming is only the manager.' He frowned. 'But there's not much in the way of advertising around the place, which you'd expect if a brewery owned it, or a restaurant chain.'

So they didn't know Murchison owned it, and it wasn't Carter's place to tell them.

'How about the staff? Did that all change when the pub changed hands?'

'Oh, entirely. Gordon Fleming came in as manager. I think they got a new chef. The waitresses were new. Local girls, I suppose.'

'Do you know either of them personally?'

The Blackwoods looked at one another. 'I wouldn't say that,' said Prue doubtfully. They returned their joint gaze to Carter, clearly wondering why he was asking all this.

'I'm very sorry to tell you,' he said, 'but the young woman whose body was taken from the river near here recently has been identified as one of the waitresses at the pub. Her name is Courtney Higson.'

They shook their heads sorrowfully but expressed no particular surprise at the name.

Henry said cautiously, 'Well, we had heard . . . that is, Prue shops at the supermarket where Denise Garley works. Her uncle is Wayne Garley. That's where we first heard about the body being found at Glebe House. Then, when we went shopping there again, Denise told us her uncle had been to the inquest and the dead girl was Courtney Higson and she had been a waitress at the Fisherman's Rest. That was truly very shocking to hear.'

'Oh, dear,' murmured Prue and shuddered. 'Oh, I don't think we'll be going there again, at least not for a long time. I think I do sort of remember the girl. I didn't know her name then but I remember she served us. To think that now she's drowned. How awful.'

'I'm afraid she didn't drown, Mrs Blackwood. She was stabbed before she went into the river.'

Carter was surprised Denise hadn't added that detail, but perhaps the rest of the queue at the checkout had been restless and she hadn't had time.

Prue gasped. Henry put his arm round his wife's shoulders. 'This is truly dreadful news, Superintendent Carter, but we can't help you, really we can't.'

'You mean,' Prue asked shakily, 'there's a murderer about?'

'We're not near the river,' Dennis Claverton explained to Jess. 'But there is a brook that feeds into the river, and runs along the bottom of our garden. I'm keeping an eye on it. It's certainly more full than usual and running very fast.'

Lucy brought coffee. Both Clavertons appeared pleased to see Jess, which surprised her. She could only suppose they didn't get many visitors. They were remarkably alike, small in build with wispy greying hair. Their mildly inquiring expressions, Jess suspected, were habitual.

They agreed readily that they went to the Fisherman's Rest from time to time. They liked it because it carried a vegetarian menu and Lucy was not an eater of meat.

'I never have been,' she assured Jess earnestly, 'not since I was a very young girl.'

'I don't eat much . . .' Dennis murmured defensively. He leaned forward to Jess. 'And only white meat. I always cook it myself. I wouldn't consider it fair to ask Lucy to do it for me.'

When they were asked, Lucy admitted they had recognised the waitress on the evening when they'd gone there with the writers' club and dear Neil Stewart, such an inspiring man . . . And that other man came too, what was his name, Dennis? Oh, yes, Murchison. Lucy had to confess she had found Murchison rather difficult. Difficult to talk to, she meant. He didn't volunteer anything during discussions or ask any questions, and he wasn't writing anything himself. It made you wonder why he'd come along to the creative writing course.

Oh, the waitress, yes, they knew her by sight because she had worked there for quite a while, since new owners took on the pub. They didn't know who owned it now. Denise Garley had been telling every shopper in the supermarket the identity of the dead girl and that she was the waitress. Lucy hadn't wanted to believe her at first, because Denise could be, well, a tiny bit unreliable. But Denise had been adamant, because her uncle, Wayne Garley, had been called upon to speak at the inquest the day before. Apparently it hadn't been a full inquest. It had been adjourned. Was that normal? Oh, to allow the police to complete their investigations.

'I thought,' said Lucy doubtfully, 'that the coroner returned a verdict of murder by persons unknown? That's what happens in the whodunits I've read. I've got loads of them over there.' She pointed at a bookshelf full of battered paperbacks. 'I like Margery Allingham, Agatha Christie and others writing about that time. I don't like the modern books so much because they're so violent. Of course, murder is violent but we don't need to have it all spelled out, do we?'

Jess broke into this run-down of Lucy's tastes in mysteries to say, 'The coroner doesn't return that verdict any more, hasn't done so for a long time.'

'What a pity,' said Lucy. 'It must have been so dramatic when he did.'

The result of all this was that neither Dennis nor Lucy could recall ever being told what the waitress's name was. She hadn't worn a name badge.

'Sometimes they do, don't they?' Lucy appealed jointly to her husband and to Jess, for confirmation.

Dennis said he'd been in places where the girls had worn badges, but it would probably be seen as a bit downmarket for the Fisherman's Rest. He did not think either he or his wife had suggested their party went there that evening, to celebrate the end of the writing course. They might have done. 'What do you think, Lucy?'

Lucy couldn't remember, honestly, she couldn't. She pressed more shortbread biscuits and coffee on Jess.

The delay in getting away from the Clavertons' meant that the early twilight was fast gathering by the time Jess found Isolde Evans's address at just after five p.m. The dull orange glow of the streetlight already gleamed on the roof of a little silver smart car parked outside the door of the thirties-built villa. Jess was encouraged to hope Isolde was at home. There were two house bells, downstairs and upstairs flats. Isolde was the upstairs resident. Jess pressed the buzzer and waited. After a while her ear caught the sound of someone noisily descending wooden stairs and coming towards her. Jess took out her identification and held it up ready.

'Oh, police . . .' said the young woman who opened the door, peering at the identity wallet. 'Oh, dear, I don't know anything that would interest the *police*.' She blinked at Jess like some sort of poor-sighted animal unexpectedly driven from its burrow.

'Miss Evans? Just a brief chat, if you've got a few minutes.' Jess smiled reassuringly.

Isolde seemed happy with that and invited her inside. Jess followed her along the uncarpeted, parquet-floored hall, and up the stairs, which were also uncarpeted and varnished dark brown. No wonder she had heard Isolde coming. The two of them making their way upstairs sounded like a stampede. It must inconvenience the dwellers in the downstairs flat, but that was in darkness so at the moment they weren't in.

Isolde had left the door to her flat open and they went straight in. 'This way,' she directed her visitor.

It was, she informed Jess as she ushered her into the living room, a good thing Jess had not come earlier. Isolde was currently holding down a post at a school some distance away, as substitute for a teacher unexpectedly hospitalised.

'And I've only just got back home,' she explained.

Jess wondered if that was why the flat was so cold. If Isolde was out all day, she might well economise by not switching on the heating until she got home. The only sign of it now was a convector heater over by the wall. The waves of warmed air it sent out did little to dispel the chill. Isolde herself was well wrapped up against it. She wore a long shapeless cardigan over a garment that resembled a middle-European folk costume, and black ankle boots. She also wore fingerless mittens on her hands, and a red crocheted cloche hat pulled down over her ears. The general effect was striking because she was a tall young woman. Jess couldn't help but be fascinated by the single long braid of reddish brown hair hanging down Isolde's spine to her waist. How did she manage to plait it so neatly?

'I'll make us a cup of tea,' offered Isolde, who obviously had no intention of taking off the mittens or hat. 'Just make yourself at home.'

She disappeared and could be heard rattling crockery in her kitchenette. Jess, already awash with coffee from the Clavertons, did not really want tea, but Isolde's absence gave her the opportunity to study the room. Originally this would have been the main bedroom of the villa. The room itself was made a little larger by a bay window. A window seat had been built around the recess, covered in garishly coloured cushions. The ceiling was high, with a central carved rose from which was suspended an art deco light fitting that might even be original. There were bookcases and fixed bookshelves everywhere. Jess began to look at some of the titles, wondering if Isolde, like Lucy, was a fan of Golden Age mysteries. But it was quickly apparent that Isolde was an avid reader of romantic fiction, both modern and past. Jess was still looking at the books when Isolde came back, carrying two mugs of tea.

'The schools break up for Christmas at the end of next week,' she said, as she put the mugs down on a small round table. 'I'm really going to be glad of the break. The children I'm teaching at the moment are hard work. They're not especially naughty, but they are very . . .' Isolde searched for the word she wanted. 'Active,' she said. 'It's because I'm not the regular teacher and they take liberties, you know. There is a teaching assistant but, honestly, she isn't really a *help*. I suspect she likes to see me struggle. But only another week! Then I'll have a bit of time to concentrate on my book. I've got stuck in the middle and I'm tired in the evening when I've been teaching all day. So to have some real time to think it through will be great.'

'Is this the kind of book you write?' Jess asked, indicating the bookcase.

'Oh, yes!' Isolde beamed at her. 'People think it must be easy to write romantic fiction but it's terribly difficult. I've never been published but I don't give up hope. That's where belonging to the writers' club is so helpful. One doesn't feel, you know, *alone*.'

'Did you find Neil Stewart's creative writing course helpful, too?'

'Wonderful!' Isolde declared. They had both taken seats now and Isolde sat hunched forward, her mittened hands clasping the mug of hot tea.

Jess was doing the same thing. Any source of heat was welcome. The chill in the room was beginning to seep into her. It was like sitting in a fridge. Besides the convector heater, there seemed to be nothing to warm the place up. She touched a nearby radiator but it was stone cold. She thought she was disguising her discomfort well but, obviously, not well enough.

'I'm sorry it's not very warm in here,' apologised Isolde. 'But

I'm out all day so it really doesn't make any sense to heat an empty flat, does it?'

'No, of course not. I – er – leave the thermostat on very low when I go to work.'

'Oh, I haven't got that sort of heating. Well, there are radiators.' Isolde indicated the one Jess had investigated. 'But, you see, I just can't afford to run central heating. The convectors are really good. I switch on that one over there when I come in, and the one in the bedroom on just before I go to bed. Of course, I don't leave the bedroom one running all night! I switch it off when I get into bed. I've got a hot water bottle,' she concluded.

'You must have a great imagination,' said Jess, leading Isolde away from any further details of the inadequate heating arrangements. 'I couldn't write a thing.'

'Oh, but you could, you know!' Isolde assured her. 'You must have confidence and you must believe!'

'Believe you will be published one day?'

'Oh, yes, that, too,' Isolde said, 'but above all you must believe in what you write.'

'I see . . .' said Jess doubtfully. 'But you make up your stories, don't you?'

'Oh, plots, yes, of course. But the characters you create have to be real to you, the writer. How could you persuade any reader to believe in them if the writer doesn't?'

That seemed logical enough, but Jess still had a quibble. 'All the passion stuff, meeting someone and falling instantly in love, and the rest of it – it's not like real life, though, is it?'

'But of course it is!' Isolde grew animated and her eyes sparkled behind her spectacle lenses. Her pale cheeks flushed. 'People have

171

always fallen in love! It's the most powerful and enduring emotion of them all. Think of all the great love affairs in history! Antony and Cleopatra! Napoleon and Josephine!'

'They didn't end up very happily, though, did they?' Jess was still playing devil's advocate.

Isolde leaned forward again. 'Because other people misled them!' she said firmly. 'They made the wrong choices. If Napoleon had stayed married to Josephine, his life would have been quite different. He wouldn't have ended up all lonely on that island.' Isolde sighed. 'And Elizabeth Taylor – I mean Cleopatra – wouldn't have had to hide in that tomb and have Richard Burton – I mean Antony – hoisted up to her on a plank. I know that's the film version, but it's only what happened really in history, isn't it?'

It was one of those unanswerable arguments and Jess didn't try and answer it. She also felt vaguely ashamed of trying to undermine Isolde's confidence.

She turned to asking, as she'd intended when she came here, about the dinner at the Fisherman's Rest.

'Oh, yes, our last evening of the course.' Isolde looked wistful. 'I was so sorry when it ended. We wanted to show dear Neil our appreciation so we took him out to dinner. I don't know who suggested the Fisherman's Rest. I don't go out to restaurants much, so I'm no good at suggesting places to eat. But the others knew it. It's a very popular eating place.'

'I don't think Jason Twilling eats there regularly,' murmured Jess, mindful of how he had complained to Bennison about the prices.

'Well, Jaz might not,' conceded Isolde. 'It's a bit pricey. But I'm sure all the others do.'

'Do you remember the waitress that night?'

'There were two of them,' said Isolde. 'One was busy with the other tables. The one who came to our table had an over-familiar manner. She *ogled* Neil Stewart. I'd have thought the Fisherman's Rest expected its staff to behave more professionally. She was a very tarty sort of girl.'

'Did any of the group address the waitress by name?'

'They might have done,' said Isolde vaguely. 'But I really can't remember.'

'Are you sure? How about Mr Twilling?'

'Jaz? Oh, yes, I think he knew her. But he didn't look very pleased to see her.' Isolde stared into her emptied mug. Then she looked up and asked unexpectedly, 'Is she the girl in the river? Is that why you're asking all these questions?'

'Yes,' Jess said quietly. 'The body has been identified by a family member.'

Isolde became thoughtful, staring at the steam rising from her mug. 'Oh, dear,' she said.

'Not a nice business,' Jess agreed.

Isolde looked up and said suddenly with deep conviction, 'Then I shouldn't have criticised her, as I did just now, to you. I said she was forward and tarty and so on. But one shouldn't speak ill of the dead. If I'd known she was the girl they found in the river, I wouldn't have done.'

'You hadn't heard any rumour about the identity of the dead girl?'

The long braid of hair had fallen forward over Isolde's shoulder and she began to twist it absently round her finger. 'No . . . I've been away from Weston St Ambrose all day, as I told you. What was her name, anyway?'

Jess told her.

'Oh,' said Isolde vaguely. 'I didn't catch what Jaz called her when he said hello to her. He sort of mumbled. I just got the impression, you know, that he knew her.' She brightened and leaned forward. 'Jaz is very talented, you know. He's a really good writer. He and I went for a drink together at the Black Horse after the last meeting of the writers' club and he told me all about his book.' She sipped her tea. 'And I told him all about mine.'

Nugent returned at the end of the day from Rosetta Gardens and brought with him four large cardboard boxes, containing sealed multi-packs of cigarettes, and the black plastic bin bags seen by Jess and Carter.

'This is all the stuff in the spare room at the flat,' he informed them. 'The bags have got clothing in them, just jumble, weird, really old-fashioned. These are the boxes and all of them contain cigarettes.'

'Well, the cigarettes appear to be smuggled goods,' said Carter. 'We don't know who brought them into the country or why they were in that flat. Perhaps just being stored there temporarily, as a favour. Pass them all to Customs and Excise. They can look into that. What do you mean, the clothes are weird?'

Jess had opened one of the bags and took out a folded cardigan of considerable age and wear, but clean. There were cheap skirts and blouses, again old and well worn, but clean and ironed. Another bag yielded several nightgowns and underwear of a practical sort. Last of all, a bag yielded up a winter coat and several pairs of misshapen shoes. Everything smelled fusty.

'Why would anyone keep all that rubbish?' asked Stubbs.

Jess said quietly, 'I know what it all is. These are Courtney's grandmother's things. When she died, none of it was thrown away. It was all laundered and folded neatly and kept as a sort of link or memento.'

'I can't imagine a kid like Courtney doing that,' said Nugent. 'Youngsters hate anything old-fashioned.'

'No, but Teddy Higson would. He'd keep his mum's stuff.'

'A thug like him?' protested Nugent.

'Oh, yes,' Carter told him, 'a thug but devoted to his old mum. He kept the lot.'

He thought: and now there's a strong possibility Higson will keep Courtney's bedroom untouched, all her Barbie dolls and pop star posters, everything. It was hard to feel any sympathy for someone like him, devoid of any pity for his own victims. But, with the loss of his only child, Higson's one remaining link to anything outside the world of violence and crime had been snapped. It was frightening to think of Higson roaming the world a free man, angry, grieving, vengeful and inarticulate, ready to strike out at anything for any reason.

'Nothing of interest to us in the flat?' he said aloud.

Nugent shook his head. 'Clean as a whistle. We conducted a thorough search. But we found her car in the lock-up.'

'What about car keys?'

'That's the funny thing,' said Nugent. 'We searched high and low for those, but we couldn't find them.'

'So,' said Carter with a sigh, 'we're back where we started. Why on earth would anyone want Courtney Higson dead? But someone did.'

175

'Random killing?' suggested Jess without much conviction. 'Nutter roaming about looking for a victim?'

'Such a person would leave Courtney where she fell, where she was stabbed. We need to find out where that was. If it was on the riverbank, then what on earth was Courtney doing there at a time when the rain has made the area a morass? It increasingly looks as if she was killed elsewhere and transported to the river. The murderer took the trouble to put her in the river – and ran the risk of being seen doing it. Perhaps the killer hoped the body would sink. Or that it would float away, taken by the strong current, and not turn up until it was miles away – if at all. That it lodged under the Stewarts' landing stage was pure bad luck for them and for the murderer.'

Chapter 13

'Rodney not coming?'

'Not tonight, he was able to come along yesterday afternoon to the dress rehearsal, so he has seen it.'

Carter and his ex-wife stood facing one another in the brightly lit foyer of their daughter's school, the following late afternoon. Around them, in a buzz of excitement, surged other parents and assorted children. The younger pupils had obviously been set to illustrate the forthcoming attraction of *Mother Goose*, and their multi-coloured crayoned efforts decorated the walls. Treble voices filled the air. Along with sounds and sights, schools have their own particular smell, thought Carter. Now, in wintertime, it was a mix of wet coats, Wellington boots, paper in all its forms and the vegetables served at lunchtime in the cafeteria.

'You look well, Sophie,' he said politely.

Privately, he thought she looked stressed out and unhappy. Surely that wasn't just because he was there? She'd lost weight since they'd last met. Perhaps that was due to the keep-fit classes. Her long fair hair was brushed back from her face and secured with a bandeau. There were dark shadows under her large, normally expressive blue eyes. Tonight that vivacity was gone. Yet she was still a very attractive woman.

177

'We ought to go to the hall,' she said impatiently, 'or we won't get good seats.'

She didn't wait for his reply but turned and walked briskly down the foyer towards the far end. Carter could do nothing but follow her, dodging a mother with a buggy and a pair of tussling little boys. He caught up with Sophie just as she turned right, and found himself in the hall that was tonight's theatre, filled with rows of plastic chairs.

'There!' said Sophie, pointing, and dived towards two unoccupied chairs near the front.

Carter was just about to sit down when a woman accosted Sophie, and he was obliged to stand up again as Sophie introduced him.

'Millie's father.'

The woman smiled brightly at him. 'Really nice to meet you, Mr Carter.'

Carter smiled back and nodded wordlessly.

'It should be a really fun evening,' said the woman. 'The children have worked so hard.'

'Yes, so Millie said . . .'

'So glad you could make it!' the woman rolled over his reply and, to his relief, moved away.

'Who was she?' he asked Sophie.

'Miss Waterton, Millie's teacher, I did say!' Sophie snapped.

'Sorry, I didn't catch it. She wrote the words, right?'

But Sophie was already talking to someone else. Carter subsided on to the plastic chair. It was both too small and unyielding and pressed into his back, mid-spine. He found himself wondering how long the show would last. Then, looking down, he saw

178

Sophie's capacious bag on the floor by his feet and, poking out of it, MacTavish, the Scottish bear that accompanied Millie everywhere.

'I see MacTavish is here,' he said to Sophie when she sat down beside him.

'I had to bring him. He's a mascot. Millie thinks everything will be all right if MacTavish is standing by.'

There was a rare fleeting moment in which Carter's gaze met Sophie's; and the worry and hope that parents wrap round a child like a blanket was shared between them. Then it was gone.

'She'll grow out of it,' said Sophie and the words went through Carter like a knife.

Despite the discomfort, and the baby who began to wail, the fidgeting audience, the man with the cough, and the grandma on his right who sucked extra-strong mints all the way through, it was indeed 'a fun evening'. Millie, in her gosling costume, jumped up and down in the dance, flapping her paper wings with enormous enthusiasm, if less elegance. She had spotted him with her mother and kept grinning at them. Carter grinned back.

When it was all over and the audience had streamed back into the foyer, they were offered instant coffee in waxed paper cups organised by a group of cheerful volunteers, and even Sophie looked relaxed. Millie joined them, out of costume now, red-faced and elated.

'It was great,' said Carter sincerely, hugging her, 'and you were the best of the bunch.'

Millie accepted this compliment as her due and skipped off to speak to a friend.

Sophie drew a deep breath. 'Do you want to come back to the

house for a proper coffee, or a drink, or anything? Say "hi" to Rodney?' She consulted her wristwatch before he could reply. 'It's getting late so I'll be getting Millie off to bed as soon as we get indoors. She's tired.'

Millie, in the background, was still hopping around with no visible lack of energy. But Carter took the hint.

'I'd love to, but I've got a long drive back – and work tomorrow. I'll say goodbye in the car park.'

She couldn't disguise her relief. 'Oh, fine, just as you wish. Whatever suits you.'

No, he snarled inwardly, *whatever suits you*!

Without warning, and not looking at him but across the area towards Millie, she said, 'I suppose it's another murder or something gruesome.'

'Yes, as it happens, it is a murder case.'

She hunched her shoulders and made no further comment.

So he said goodbye to them both in the cold, dark car park, surrounded by voices and engine sounds, and where it was beginning to rain again. Nevertheless, before they parted, he managed to ask out of earshot of Millie, 'Is everything all right, Sophie?'

'Absolutely fine!' she retaliated in a tone that blocked any further inquiry.

Millie clung to him and whispered in his ear, 'I'm really glad you came.'

'Of course I came, sweetheart, it's lovely to see you.'

'You ought to have brought Jess,' she told him, adding sternly: 'Bring her next time!'

He didn't know whether Sophie heard that or not. She gave no sign.

He drove homewards, the raindrops spotting the windscreen and the wipers swishing back and forth to dislodge them. There won't be so many more occasions like that one, he thought. I'm missing all her growing up and turning into a young woman. Even if Sophie and I were still married, I should miss so much because of work.

Teddy Higson had missed his daughter growing up because he'd been in and out of gaol. But we make our own prison bars, thought Carter. He drove on through the night back to his empty flat and self-assembled furniture, a tin of soup, some toast and a brandy nightcap.

The members of the writers' club, with the exception of Jason Twilling and Isolde Evans, had met 'in conclave' as Peter Posset jocularly called it.

'Although there is indeed nothing amusing about the situation.'

'A murderer,' said Lucy dolefully, 'a murderer in our quiet little community.'

'You did suggest, Dennis,' Peter went on, 'the last time we met, that we write a letter of support to Neil Stewart. It didn't seem appropriate at the time because the inquest had not been opened on the dead girl, and we didn't know then who she was. But we know now, so perhaps we could write a letter after all.'

'I don't know, Peter,' said Henry Blackwood. 'It might read as if we were assuring him we thought he had nothing to do with it, whatever others might say.'

'Has anyone said he had anything to do with it?' demanded Jenny Porter. 'I haven't heard so.'

'If it were worded tactfully,' said Peter, 'it shouldn't appear like that.'

'I would, of course, consult with you all before I sent any letter,' said Dennis.

Posset rubbed his whiskers. 'Ah, well, Dennis, we all know you are a gifted poet. But this calls for something rather more – well – formal. I was going to suggest that I draft something and then, of course, consult with you all.'

'Why you?' asked Lucy, bridling. 'Dennis can do it perfectly well and it was his idea!'

'I am quite happy to let Peter do it,' said Dennis meekly.

'It should be a joint effort,' said Henry. 'If Peter drafts a letter, we can meet and discuss it. How long will it take you, Peter?'

'Oh, not long. I've already put together some ideas.'

Lucy gasped and her pale face turned a dull red.

'I'll get on to it immediately and we don't need to meet, do we? I'll email you my draft and you can email back to me with your comments.'

'Honestly, Dennis!' said Lucy, when they got home. 'The nerve of it! It was your idea. You shouldn't have let him get away with it, you know.'

'I really don't mind, dear,' said Dennis. 'I'm concentrating on getting the last data together for my owl survey.'

Lucy leaned forward. 'Dennis, I know how much the survey means to you but just now, with a murderer roaming around, I don't like you being out there at night on your own.'

'I'm quite all right, dear, honestly. I don't go very far.'

'And I don't like being left on my own at night,' Lucy added.

'It's only for another couple of nights,' he told her. 'Really, I'm almost done.'

The dogs began barking just after midnight. Murchison swore and got out of bed feeling the resentment of one who had not long retired and just fallen into the deep first sleep of the night. He stubbed his toe as he made his way to the window. He had not switched on a light because it was easier to look out with no light behind him. But, when he reached the curtains and pulled them aside, he was poorly rewarded. Clouds sailed like funeral barges across the indigo of the sky. Without the moon to illuminate it, the garden was just a well of inky darkness. But at least the rain had stopped for a while.

The dogs started up again, Max first. He could pick up the older dog's deep tone. Then Prince joined in at a higher pitch. He should perhaps go out and investigate but he didn't fancy wandering about out there with a torch, at the mercy of unseen obstacles and – should there be an intruder – someone who would see him with his beacon torch, while he could not see them. To be honest, he didn't think an intruder had breached the security of the grounds. The dogs, if there had been a real and present danger, would be hysterical by now. Instead they barked on and off, pausing to listen between flurries of bellicosity. The danger, if any, was distant: over there somewhere, beyond the high dry stone wall.

He decided to let it be. If anyone had been hanging around, intending to break in, the dogs would have put the interloper off by now. He let the curtain fall back into place and returned to bed. But not, now, back to sleep. He found himself wondering if Charlie were all right, out there in the woods. The visit from Amy – silly little bitch with her clumsy attempt to get a pay-off from him – had nevertheless disturbed him. He ought to give serious thought to the wisdom of allowing the old man to continue living in the shack. Goodness knew how old Charlie was. He was as gnarled and brown as an old tree stump. But he clung to his home in the woods and only returned to the bosom of his not particularly loving family when the winter weather was really severe. Recent rains alone hadn't driven him to seek refuge in their cottage. If it turned to snow, that might force him out. To deprive Charlie of his beloved abode would hit the old fellow hard. But if he were to be found dead on his narrow cot one morning, it would take some explaining to the authorities. Murchison might find himself censured.

The dogs had quietened now. The nocturnal prowler had gone and Murchison no longer had to fight off the responsibility of investigating. He knew that occasionally a fox found its way into the gardens at night. Either it squeezed through the bars of the gate or it had scraped a tunnel under the stone wall. Perhaps this night's intruder had been Reynard. Even as he thought this, his ear seemed to catch the distant sound of an engine. He could be wrong about that.

He should, perhaps, have taken the opportunity of the visit from that police chap, Carter, to explain that this sort of disturbance had been going on for about three months. But what more could he have said, that he had not said at the time? What could the police do?

Beth lay awake. It had stopped raining, thank goodness. Lettie had told her it wasn't always like this in the winter hereabouts.

On the other hand, Lettie had added elliptically, 'we can get a fair drop'.

Of course, it would be raining in London, too. But city rain flowed into drains and was carried away out of sight. Pavements dried in the air and wind. But here all around Glebe House was mud. Walking to the gate had become a slippery obstacle course. The garden was out of bounds. She had not tried to walk down to the river's edge and the mooring again. The wooden platform had finally collapsed after the attentions of the police team and, come summer, Wayne would come and drag the remains out and take them away. Always supposing, of course, the river didn't carry the wreckage away first. Come summer . . . It was hard to believe it ever would.

Neil had had a phone call that evening and taken it in the bedroom he'd turned into a temporary office, with his computer and files. He'd spoken for some time with the caller but he hadn't mentioned it to her when he rejoined her in the next room. They had made a sitting room of another of the spare bedrooms and installed the television there with the books and DVDs from downstairs. When the family all arrived for Christmas, as planned, it would complicate things. Perhaps she should ring round and put them off. But Wayne had assured them the sandbags he'd brought were only a precaution, just as moving the television and other stuff upstairs was a precaution. Water shouldn't come into the house. If it hadn't, by Christmas, they would need to move everything back down there again.

Her ear caught a change in the pattern of Neil's breathing. She asked, 'Are you awake?'

He didn't answer at once but eventually she heard, 'Yes,' muttered from the pillows.

'Who rang you this evening?'

The pause before answering was even longer. 'Jack.'

'Jack Calloway? What did he want?'

'Cop came to see him.'

'From here? One of the officers investigating that girl?'

'No, a guy from the Met. But he came because the coppers here had asked him to check out my story – about meeting Jack and going for a drink. They checked me out, just like you said they would.'

'Silly sods!' said Beth angrily, sitting up.

Neil sat up beside her. 'No, they were just doing their job, being thorough. It's like you said. I identified that girl but I couldn't really explain how I was able to do so. She was just a waitress I'd seen one evening a couple of weeks before. She'd been alive then, all bright and competent, scribbling down our order; made up with lipstick and eyeliner, fluttering long eyelashes at all the blokes. Not a bit how she looked coming out of the river, dripping wet hair, white-faced, and dead as a doornail. Jack confirmed my story, of course. But he was mad with curiosity and wanted me to tell him what it was all about.'

'What did you tell him?'

'What happened: how Wayne found the body in the water. How I'd thought I'd recognised her and gave a name to the cops. Or half a name and the place she worked. That's it, isn't it?' After a moment, Neil added, 'I told him it was a murder inquiry, that's why the police were checking everything. Jack will spread the word, you know how he is: a real old gossip. It's a blasted nuisance. The next thing you know, my agent will be on the phone about it. I was wrong to tell the police I thought I knew her.'

'No, you weren't wrong!' Beth protested. 'You had to tell them who you thought the poor girl was. We didn't know then it would be murder. It could have been accidental, she could have just – just stumbled and fallen in.'

'Well, she didn't, did she? We know that now. And by this time tomorrow night, everyone who knows us in London will know that a murder victim was stretched out on our back lawn, after being found wrapped round our mooring platform.' Neil turned towards her and asked with a fury she'd never heard from him before, 'Do you know what that idiot, Jack Calloway, said?'

'No, you didn't even tell me he rang!'

'I didn't tell you,' Neil leaned towards her and his anger seemed to radiate in waves, sweeping over her. 'I didn't tell you because Jack said, "Never mind, old chap, you'll get your name in the redtops! No such thing as bad publicity, eh?"'

Chapter 14

In the morning, Murchison took the dogs out for their run and made for the woods. He'd check on Charlie, who was still on his mind. He walked up the track that ran alongside the outer wall of the gardens, and led towards the tangle of trees. There were new tyre tracks. They only led a short distance into the lane; then it appeared the driver had reversed out again. So some blighter *had* been out here, parked up on this lonely muddy lane, during last night. What the devil for? Or was it just a case of secret love, seeking a quiet spot? Secret love . . . He pushed away the memories.

Charlie was at home. The dogs bounded forward, tails wagging, as the old man emerged from his shack. He was wearing an aged army greatcoat, secured round the waist with a wide leather strap that looked as if it might once have formed part of a harness. His woolly hat was pulled down over his ears and his brown, whiskery face crinkled into a smile of welcome.

'You come just at the right time,' he told Murchison. 'I've just brewed up.'

Inside the shack was surprisingly warm. Charlie bustled about at his ramshackle kitchen unit and came forward with a two mugs of dark brown liquid.

'Here you are, a drop of proper tea!'

189

Murchison put his hand in his pocket and produced a half-bottle of whisky.

'Ah!' said Charlie, eyes gleaming in appreciation, 'That'll do it!' He unscrewed the cap and splashed a generous tot into each mug. 'I can give you a biscuit, if you want one!' he offered. 'I got two packets of chocolate digestives. My granddaughter brought 'em yesterday when she brought my groceries. I like a chocolate digestive.'

'I saw Amy here yesterday when I called,' Murchison told him.

'She's telling me,' said Charlie, as he raised his mug in salute, 'that she's got a boyfriend. She reckons they're going to get engaged. I told her, she wants to take her time and think about it.'

'Good advice,' said Murchison. The tea was so hot he couldn't drink it. Charlie must have a fireproof lining to his throat.

'She was telling me about that other girl they had working over at the Rest.'

'Oh?' Murchison raised his eyebrows.

'They took her out of the river, but she didn't drown. They reckon she was murdered, stabbed. That right?' Charlie paused in slurping his tea for confirmation of the facts.

'That's right, Charlie. The police are investigating.'

Charlie got up and went to fetch the biscuits. 'I know,' he said, rustling the wrapping paper and extracting one. 'I know you were friendly, like, with that lass. But I reckon as that's your business and nothing the police need know.'

'Thank you, Charlie. You might have a word with Amy about that.'

'I'll talk to her. She'll understand.' Charlie munched away, scattering crumbs far and wide. 'The only trouble with chocolate digestives is, you can't dunk them. The chocolate melts. If you want to dunk a biscuit, you need ginger ones.'

'I'll remember to bring some, next time.'

'It wasn't me as told my granddaughter about that lass using the garden gate to visit you. Amy saw her for herself, slipping out that way, when she was coming back from visiting me one Monday. Those girls don't work on a Monday. She did tell me at the time what she'd seen, and I told her to keep her lip buttoned. But they got no sense these youngsters, none of them.'

Charlie drank noisily for a moment or two. 'I heard them dogs of yours setting up a shout last night,' he said, in a complete change of subject. 'Sound carries on the night air. I was outside, anyway.'

'In the middle of the night, what for?' Murchison asked him.

'Just poking around the place,' mumbled Charlie. 'I don't sleep much. The old owl was out hunting. I heard him hooting. I reckon he caught something right outside here. I heard the squeal and the rustle in the leaves. I felt the air move, as his wings swept by over my head. I got good ears. Nothing wrong with my hearing.'

'Did you hear anything else, Charlie?'

'There was a car. Not a big old job like you drive, something smaller. I heard it just after the dogs quietened down. Could've been coming from the pub.'

'Charlie,' Murchison sought to phrase his next words carefully. 'I am a little concerned about you, out here this time of year.'

'I'm just fine and dandy!' snapped Charlie.

'OK, but it might not be a good idea to wander round at night. If you like, I could leave one of the dogs here, with you.'

'No need,' said Charlie. 'Likely the other dog'll pine; and the wild creatures won't come near if they think a dog's about the place.'

'If you think you hear anything unusual, come and let me know,' Murchison told him.

Charlie squinted at him. 'You got someone hanging round your place at night?'

'Probably only foxes. There might be a courting couple park up in the lane.'

'They got no business!' declared Charlie. 'It's like them walkers. I tell them, they got no business!'

Courtney's computer had yielded up its secrets.

'Printout of her outgoing emails,' said Nugent, placing a list before Jess. 'She sent an awful lot to this fellow. She had a very affectionate nature, I reckon, if they're anything to go by!'

'Well, well,' said Carter, a few minutes later. 'Time to call on Mr Murchison again, I think. You'd better come along, Jess. It should prove interesting.'

'How did the pantomime go?' Jess asked him as they drove out to Lower Weston.

'Very well indeed.'

'Millie happy with it?'

'Ecstatic. My ex-wife seemed a bit down in the mouth. Probably because I was there.'

They were approaching the walls of the Old Manor. Suddenly they saw a figure emerge from the lane leading to the woods, a man in a crumpled Barbour, attended by the two muddy German shepherd dogs.

'And here,' added Carter, 'is Squire Murchison himself!'

They drew up and Murchison stooped down by the car. 'Coming to see me?' He looked tired and sounded wary. Beside him, the dogs flanked their owner protectively and studied the newcomers with alert, inquiring expressions.

'If you've got a moment.' Carter indicated Jess. 'This is Inspector Campbell.'

'I know,' said Murchison shortly. 'I saw you at the inquest, Inspector. Hold on. I'll open the gate for you and put the dogs in their pen. I've just taken them for a run in the woods. They'll settle.'

In the vestibule, Murchison shrugged off his Barbour and held out a hand for his visitors' coats. 'There's no open fire lit today. The heating is going full blast and you'll be too warm sitting around in those. You wouldn't mind just slipping off your shoes, would you? Because the cleaning company has only just been.'

Beside him, Carter heard Jess give a little gasp and forestalled any protest she might have been about to make by saying, 'Yes, of course!' and taking off his shoes, hoping and praying he hadn't 'spud' in his socks.

Murchison disappeared briefly into a cloakroom just off the hall with all the coats.

Jess hissed, 'What's he playing at?'

'Mind games,' murmured Carter.

Murchison was back, leading his visitors to the same drawing room where Carter had talked with him before. Their host had, Carter noted, acquired some leather slip-ons while in the cloakroom, so that Carter and Jess had to pad after him, disadvantaged by the loss of their shoes. He could feel Jess, beside him, simmering with resentment.

However when they entered the drawing room he heard her gasp again, this time with surprise and delight. Seeing the room now by daylight, Carter, too, could appreciate its dimensions and how light and bright it was. The pale blues and greens of the upholstery and the subtle pattern of the carpets invited a more civilised and gentle conversation than the one they were about to conduct. As they took seats in the comfortable chairs, he caught Jess's eye. She grimaced and waggled her toes in their socks.

'What can I do for you both?' Murchison spoke to both, but kept his eyes on Carter.

'Perhaps,' Carter told him, 'we could begin with what you haven't done. You have not come forward with information regarding a murder victim. Courtney Higson? You know we're looking into her death.'

Murchison put up a token resistance. 'What could I tell you? Gordon hired her to work at the Fisherman's Rest.'

'You could have told us,' Jess forced her way resolutely into the conversation, 'that you were the boyfriend she was so anxious to keep a secret.'

Murchison turned his head to stare at her thoughtfully. 'Has Amy been talking to you?'

'Amy Fallon?' Jess frowned.

'She tried to get money out of me yesterday, for her silence. I told her there was no chance.'

'Not Amy,' Jess told him, 'Courtney's computer. She sent you a lot of very friendly emails.'

'I did wonder if you'd check her computer.' Murchison sighed. 'I didn't tell you about my friendship with Courtney when I heard she'd been identified as the girl in the river, I admit. That was partly because I was shocked and distressed, and partly because it's irrelevant to your inquiries.'

'I think we should be allowed to judge the relevance,' Carter told him.

'It wasn't only my idea to keep our friendship a secret! It was hers, too. It suited her.' Murchison knew his carefully contrived grip on the visit was slipping and began to sound irritated.

'Did she tell you why it suited her?' Now it was Carter in charge.

Murchison shrugged. 'She didn't want the others at the Rest to know, I suppose. Didn't want them prying or teasing her. She wanted it to be private. I like to keep my personal business private, too. I told you, Superintendent Carter, that I don't broadcast my ownership of the Rest for the same reason. It concerns no one but me. I dare say Gordon may have had his suspicions about Courtney and me, but I'd made him manager of the Fisherman's Rest. He wouldn't rock that boat.'

'Mr Murchison,' Jess said quietly, 'we'd like you to tell us about your relationship with Courtney.'

'Would you, indeed?' snapped Murchison.

'We appreciate you think of it as a private matter. But we are investigating a murder. At times like this we have to intrude on people's private grief and ask all manner of questions.'

Murchison slapped the arms of the Queen Anne-style chair he sat in. 'Very well. On your previous visit here, Superintendent, I told you that I'd been in a relatively long-term relationship in

New York. It finished in a way I found particularly humiliating at the time. One morning, it was a Sunday, I got up first and I was standing by the breakfast bar in our flat, making the coffee, when Barbara appeared and said, quite casually, "Time to call it a day, Graeme, don't you think?"

'I must have looked surprised because I wasn't expecting it, or not just like that. I made some stupid crack about surely, my coffee wasn't that bad! Playing for time while I worked out how to respond, really.'

'"Come on, Graeme; don't let us fall out over this. We're adults. We've had some good moments. It's simply time to move on. This relationship's been fun but it's not going anywhere. It's stale." I think it was then I realised she'd met someone else. She'd probably been two-timing me with him for months.'

Carter thought that there was something dismally familiar about the story. Sophie had suggested they part in the same off-hand way, so sure he'd understand and agree: so anxious that there should not be any unseemly rows, for Millie's sake. But this time he did not remark on it to Murchison.

'So, when I got back here to the UK, I wasn't keen to rush into any new relationship. I'd burned my fingers, if you like, and I intended to keep them well out of the fire. But, once I'd got settled here, I was lonely. I missed female company. I'd met Courtney because she worked at the Rest.'

Unwisely, Jess began, 'I wouldn't have thought—'

Murchison interrupted. 'Wouldn't you? I dare say not. But that's because you don't know how it was between Courtney and me. I was extremely fond of her. No, I wasn't "in love" with her, much less was I "besotted" by her. If this gets into the press, I dare say I'll be able to read that I was both. But spare me the journalese now. There was no intention of any permanency in the relationship. I wasn't seeking to replace Barbara. I've explained to you. I didn't want to do that. Courtney was just what I needed and I repeat, I became very fond of her.'

He was aware of the expressions on their faces and continued angrily, 'Yes, I know I'm old enough to have been her father!' He sank back, his hands on the arms of his chair, and spoke more quietly, his tone reminiscent. 'She was so full of life and so – uncomplicated. She was an innocent in her way, despite a tough background. The first time she ever came in here . . .' He indicated the room. 'She went round and round, looking at everything with such an expression of awe on her face, and asking questions all the time. The silver, for example, over there in that cabinet, that fascinated her. "What's this? What's it for?" I told her some of it was Georgian, but she didn't know really what that meant. When she discovered it meant some pieces were three hundred years old, she was fascinated. She didn't understand hallmarks. I explained them. She listened like a child following a story, and she remembered it all, mopped up the information. It was the same with the paintings, and when she saw the old books in the library, well . . . "The paper feels funny," she said of some of the oldest ones. I told her that was because it was rag-based. "What's that funny letter like an ƒ?" I said, no, not an ƒ, it's an s.'

'It sounds as if you were making her your Eliza Doolittle,' Jess said. She was unimpressed by what she found herself thinking was a load of tripe.

Murchison turned his gaze to her, his grey eyes sharp. 'It may sound that way to you, Inspector Campbell, but that's not how it was. She was not a project I'd undertaken. I didn't want to change her. I liked her as she was. She made me feel – happy. Happiness is a rare commodity. It deserves to be prized.'

Jess was silent and Carter glanced at her.

'I took her on outings, to places away from this immediate area where we'd be unlikely to be spotted, and which I thought might interest her. We went to a craft fair once. There was a stall there with a lot of imported stuff, mostly Russian. There was one box she liked because of the picture on it.'

Jess said, 'A princess asleep and a knight or warrior, stooping over her. It's in her bedroom at her flat. She kept her jewellery in it.'

'So, you've seen it. Do you know what the picture represents?' When Jess shook her head, Murchison explained, 'It's the story of Ruslan and Ludmila. They are betrothed but she is kidnapped by magic and he sets out to find her. After many adventures when she is returned to her father, the Prince of Kiev, she cannot be wakened until Ruslan arrives and does so. Courtney thought the box was beautiful. She liked it even more when I told her the story, so I bought it for her.'

'Are you telling us there was no sex involved in this relationship?' Jess's scepticism bubbled over. Hell's teeth, she'd seen the flat in Rosetta Gardens and its drab surroundings. No wonder Courtney had been dazzled when she came into this elegant home. It must have appeared as a palace to her. Murchison was making the whole sordid episode sound like a Russian fairy tale. Not while I'm around, chum! she thought angrily.

'Of course there was!' Murchison sounded exasperated. 'I didn't seduce her. I wasn't the first man she'd ever had sex with. She liked sex. The things I bought her weren't payment! I wanted to make her happy, because she made me happy.'

'What things?' Jess asked. 'What did you buy her other than the trinket box?'

'Oh, clothes and so on.' Murchison smiled ruefully. 'She had terrible taste. She loved anything shiny, like a magpie. But who was I to try and change it? I bought her what she liked. If that was a pair of hoop earrings the size of saucers, so what?'

Carter broke in gently, 'She was wearing one gold-coloured hoop earring when she was taken from the water. The other was probably lost in the river.'

Murchison looked away from them across the room. When he looked back he said, voice and face expressionless, 'If you examine the earring you have, you'll find it *is* gold.'

'Did you buy her car, the Mini Cooper?' Carter's tone was still mild.

'Yes. I told her, if anyone asked how she financed it, to say she'd borrowed the money from a relative.'

Carter heaved a sigh. 'You were running a lot of risks. Someone that young can be unpredictable. And it's hoping far too much that they will keep their mouths shut indefinitely!'

Murchison absorbed Carter's exasperation, as he'd earlier dealt with Jess's disapproval. When he spoke, he sounded defiant. 'I suppose so. I took what I thought were sensible precautions to avoid others knowing about us. Courtney did the same. I did realise that eventually it would become known. We couldn't keep it quiet for ever.' After a moment he added quietly, 'I didn't kill her, either to prevent her blabbing or for any other reason. I can't imagine why anyone would do something so senseless and wicked.'

In the quiet moment that followed, the ticking of a longcase clock on the far side of the room seemed unnaturally loud.

'Mr Murchison,' Jess said briskly, 'We need to establish Courtney's movements on her last day, whom she met, where she went . . .' She was watching Murchison's face as she spoke and saw the look of pain in his eyes before he was able to disguise it. 'Did you meet up with her on that Monday? The restaurant at the Fisherman's Rest is closed on Mondays and both girls are free.'

'Yes. We went into Cheltenham. We had lunch and wandered round the place.' Murchison gestured vaguely.

'Where did you lunch?'

'It was a Chinese restaurant. I've got the bill somewhere. I'll look it out for you.'

'I'm sorry to have to ask,' Jess said. 'What was Courtney wearing? Do you recall?'

'Oh, jeans and a leather-look jacket with fake fur panels in it. I remember that jacket because I thought it – awful, if you must know. But Courtney was very proud of it.' He sounded sad.

'Those are not the garments she was wearing when she was taken from the river.'

'We came back to Weston St Ambrose about six in the evening, or a little before. I dropped her off near that dreadful estate where she lived. The plan was that she'd drive out here later – to this house. We'd – we'd spend the night together. She must have changed her clothes. She would do, I think. Anyway, she didn't wear the hoop earrings when we were in Cheltenham. I expected her back here about ten. She didn't turn up. I tried to contact her but only got her voice mail. If you check her phone, you'll find my messages on it.'

'We don't have her phone at the moment.'

Murchison frowned. 'She always had it with her. Glued to it.'

'How would she get here from her home?' Jess asked him.

'She'd drive. She'd park up in the lane alongside the house. Then she'd walk round to the garden gate at the rear of the property and let herself in. She had a key.'

'This would be identical to the key Charlie Fallon has? How many examples of this key exist?'

'Three,' Murchison said promptly. 'As you say, Charlie has one, I have one and – and Courtney had the third. It will be on her key ring.'

Jess told him, 'That's another thing we don't have, her key ring.'

Murchison looked alarmed for the first time.

'You say,' Carter took up the questioning, 'that you knew she'd had a tough upbringing. Does that mean she told you about her father?'

Murchison raised his eyebrows. 'I gathered he was some sort of petty crook and not around.'

'Teddy Higson is a violent thug and currently in prison. Despite his many failings, he was – and remains – devoted to his daughter. He's due for release soon. You may have trouble with him, if he finds out about your relationship with Courtney. He was possessive about her and didn't like any of her boyfriends. I dread to think what he'd make of you. Also he has equally violent associates. We'll keep you informed. But he'll be making his own inquiries, I'm sure, by unorthodox means.'

'Indeed?' Murchison considered the information. 'Well, I'll cross that bridge when I get to it.'

'You should bear in mind,' Carter warned him, 'that if the killer has her keys, then he has the key to the garden gate of this property. I suggest that's not a problem you can leave until you get to it.'

'I'll have a new lock fitted immediately.' Murchison's worried look returned. 'People do sometimes hang around here at night, making the dogs bark. I was confident they couldn't get into the gardens. But now, yes, of course, I'll seek out a locksmith straight away.'

'One last thing,' Carter said to him. 'Do you have a key to the flat in Rosetta Gardens, where Courtney lived?'

Murchison looked surprised. 'No, why should I? It's not the sort of place I'd fancy hanging around.'

'But you went there occasionally?'

'If I picked up Courtney from home,' Murchison told them. 'I waited nearby. There's a lay-by on the main road. Nothing would have induced me to park my Range Rover there even for a few minutes. I would have returned either to find it vandalised – or missing altogether.'

'You'd never been in the flat?'

'No,' Murchison said firmly. 'Never.'

'One room was used as a storage space. Among other things it contained several large sealed multi-packs of cigarettes, almost certainly smuggled into the country from the Continent.'

Murchison looked startled. 'Good grief! You're not going to accuse me of being a cigarette smuggler? Look here, even if I were – and I stress that I am not! Even if I were, as I say, I wouldn't store anything at Rosetta Gardens.'

'Can you think of anyone who might?' Jess took up the questioning.

'No! I don't know the names of all the people Courtney knew.' He paused and concluded quietly, 'I'm beginning to think I didn't know anything much about Courtney at all. I suppose I could have asked her more about herself. But I wasn't interested in anything she didn't want to tell me. Perhaps I just didn't want to know.'

'And she didn't want to tell you,' said Jess.

'Probably!' Murchison's gaze was directly towards the window and the nodding branches of the winter-bare trees. 'Our relationship, Courtney's and mine, was a fragile thing. In my heart, I always knew it. I suppose my problem was that I stopped my brain absorbing just how easily it could fall apart.'

As the gates of the Old Manor closed behind them, Carter said, 'No, he didn't kill her, not for my money.'

'Blooming cheek of him to make us take off our shoes. He does spout a load of rubbish. Calling his relationship with Courtney a "fragile thing" and rabbiting on about Russian princesses. If he saw her as Ludmila, who did he think he was? Ruslan? He's no gallant knight. He's a sophisticated version of the traditional dirty old man!'

Carter, suppressing a chuckle, said, 'Calm down, Jess!'

'Well . . .' Jess thrust her hands into her jacket pockets. 'He annoyed me.' In a more reasoned tone, she added, 'When you spoke about that missing garden gate key, he looked shaken.'

Carter nodded. 'He should be. He mentioned to me he suspected people were hanging round, casing the house, he thought, for a possible burglary. But now we ought to consider it might be one person, someone who was jealous of his relationship with Courtney. Damn stupid!'

'His relationship with Courtney?' Jess twitched an eyebrow. 'You do agree with me, then?'

'Yes, of course. Even if he didn't know about Teddy Higson, it was the hell of a risk. Bear in mind that it doesn't mean Teddy didn't know about him. He couldn't watch over his daughter himself from prison. But he might have asked one of his friends to keep an eye on her.'

'Then, wouldn't it be Murchison who was pulled out of the river? If this hypothetical minder reported back to Higson in gaol?'

Carter sighed, 'Yes, you're right. Higson's sole purpose would be to keep his princess safe. It was still daft of Murchison to get involved with the girl: the sort of really stupid thing that an otherwise intelligent man might do. He knows about art and antiques and gracious living . . . but he was in completely unknown territory when he took up with Courtney Higson. He didn't want another relationship with a sophisticated high-flyer like the Barbara he talked of. She'd let him down badly and hurt his pride. So, what does he do? He goes to the other extreme and, in doing so, right off the spectrum!'

'Do you think I needled him unnecessarily? Even if he did ask us to take off our shoes,' Jess asked. 'You gave me a couple of funny looks.'

'No, we were just playing a toned-down version of "good cop, bad cop". I wasn't aware I was giving you funny looks. Your socks were perfectly respectable. So, for once, were mine. Not even a small hole in the toe.'

'My imagination, then.' Jess looked down the road in the direction of the Fisherman's Rest. 'I think we ought to have a word with Amy Fallon. She lied to me. She knew the identity of Courtney's boyfriend and spun me a real yarn.'

'According to Murchison, she's also tried her hand at a little amateur blackmail. We'll both have a word with her.'

But Amy was not at the pub. Gordon suggested they try to find her at home. Accordingly, they crossed the road and knocked at the door of the end cottage.

The door was opened by Amy herself, in an off-duty garb of skinny jeans, ending clumsily in fashionable Ugg boots, and a sweater patterned with hearts, the bulky sleeves pushed up above her elbows. Her long hair was now twisted up into a knot on the top of her head and secured there with a large tortoiseshell clip. The expression on her face, when she saw who stood there, was comical in its dismay. Her round gooseberry eyes almost bulged.

'Hello, Amy,' said Jess. 'I think we need to talk again.'

'What about?' Amy cast a nervous glance back over her shoulder towards the sound of pots being rattled. 'My mum's in the kitchen. You can't talk to me while she's here. She'll want to know everything you say.'

'Then we'll walk down the road a little way and find somewhere to chat,' Jess suggested.

Amy scowled. But she reached for an anorak hanging on a peg on the wall. As she dragged it on, she called out, 'Just going over to the Rest, Mum, to check something with Gordon.' Then she shut the front door quickly before her mother could appear.

The three of them walked away from the row of cottages and the pub and stopped when they had turned a bend in the road.

'I get the impression, Amy, that you lie easily,' Jess said.

Amy flushed. 'That's not true! You've got no right to say that!'

'I've got reason. You told me you had no idea who Courtney's man friend was. But you knew, didn't you, that it was Graeme Murchison? You tried to get money from him for keeping silent.'

Amy flushed scarlet. 'That's not true! He's—' She saw the quizzical look on Jess's face and her mouth snapped shut. After a moment she said, 'I didn't ask him for a lot of money, not enough to make it proper blackmail. I just suggested he could help us a bit, me and my family, to show his appreciation.'

'Appreciation for what?'

'For not telling you about him and Courtney,' Amy said sullenly.

'It was a very silly thing to do, Amy, and could have got you into a lot of trouble.'

Amy glowered at them. 'Why am I the one in trouble? What about him, Murchison? He's old. He'd no business hanging around Courtney.'

Carter murmured, 'Sometimes age has nothing to do with it, isn't that what they say?'

'You tell me,' said Amy, with a derisive look at him. 'I wouldn't know. I don't go out with old blokes.'

'Do you know if Courtney confided in anyone else at all about her friendship with Murchison?'

Amy shrugged. 'Don't know, don't think so. I told you last time; she was scared her dad would find out. That's why she told me; she was worried and wanted to talk about it. He'd be coming home soon, coming out of prison, and she was dead scared. She thought—' Amy stopped.

'Go on, Amy,' Jess encouraged.

'Look,' said Amy earnestly, 'I can't win, can I? If you think I'm lying, I'm in trouble. If I tell you something I'm not sure about, then I might be lying and not meaning to, and still be in trouble with you lot. You get what I mean?'

'I get what you mean, Amy. What is it you're not sure about?'

Amy shuffled about and dragged her anorak more tightly about her. The wind was sharp here and carried on it the promise of yet more rain. Behind them the bare branches of the trees creaked and groaned.

'Courtney wasn't sure but she fancied someone spied on them, on her and Murchison. Sometimes, when she spent the night at his place, those dogs of his would start barking like mad because they knew someone was prowling round. Not inside the gardens, mind you, but outside on the other side of the wall. Once she got up to go to the bathroom and she went to the front of the house, upstairs, and looked out down the drive towards the gates. There was someone standing there, she said. Standing there and looking through them at the house. It wasn't someone walking home from the pub. It was too late for that, after midnight. She couldn't tell anything about the person she saw, it was just a dark outline, but it was someone. She went and woke Murchison and told him to come quick and look. But by the time he got to the window, whoever it was had gone. He reckoned she'd imagined it. But she was sure. She thought perhaps her dad had arranged to have her watched. He's real bad news, Teddy Higson.'

Jess exchanged glances with Carter. 'All right, Amy. If you remember anything else, anything at all, call me. I'll give you a number, here . . .' Jess scribbled on a page of her notebook. 'Call this number and ask to be connected with Inspector Campbell.'

Amy took the paper, stuffed it into the pocket of her anorak, and asked sulkily, 'Can I go now?'

They told her she could, and she turned and ran back the way they'd come, a gangling figure with matchstick legs terminating in clumsy boots. There was something both comical and oddly sinister about the sight.

Chapter 15

Carter put down the phone, sighed, and went to find Jess Campbell.

'They released Teddy Higson at six thirty this morning. Don't ask me where he is now. He's meant to be returning to the flat in Rosetta Gardens. He's also supposed to report to the police station nearest to his home. That means he's roaming around out there, ostensibly arranging for his daughter's funeral, and unofficially on the path of anyone he thinks knows anything about her death.'

'Are you going to warn Murchison?'

'We'll have to let him know. Send Nugent out to Rosetta Gardens to find out if Higson's been seen there.' Carter stared out of the window, scowling. 'I just wish I knew where he is as of this precise moment!'

Teddy Higson placed his pint of beer on the table with the slow deliberation of a man who hasn't had a pint for many months. The bar area wasn't large, the ceiling low, its beams blackened, its brown walls decorated with advertisements for various lagers, the tops of its wooden tables stained with overlapping rings marking where a generation or more of beer glasses had rested. The fruit machine in the corner struck a garish note of colour and twinkling lights. Nobody played.

The lunchtime clientele of the Black Horse chatted and drank; and did its best to ignore the corner table where Higson presided, his mean little eyes sweeping the room and resting, from time to time, on the street door.

That door opened to admit a newcomer who looked around, and made his way to Higson's table. The whole bar fell silent and then everyone started talking at once, too loudly. One or two drinkers decided that they had to get back to work, or home, or elsewhere fast. The others also remembered pressing engagements.

Higson looked across the emptied room and ordered the nervous barman, 'Bring us a couple of these!' He pointed at his own glass.

When the beer had arrived, Higson added, 'Why don't you go outside and have a smoke, eh? Anyone else come along, you tell them, the bar's closed for ten minutes, right?'

'Right!' said the barman and exited quickly into the street, leaving Higson and his guest alone.

The guest raised his glass in salute. 'Good to see you back, Teddy. Sorry about your girl.'

'Yeah. You were there when she was found, a little bird tells me.'

'I was delivering a load of logs to a punter out at Glebe House,' said Wayne Garley. 'Name of Stewart. He's a writer, you know, books. The river's burst its banks all the way along there. I went down to take a look and saw . . .' He hesitated. 'It gave me a nasty shock, I can tell you. There was – there she was, wedged under a sort of wooden platform they've got there, for tying up a boat, you know? Only, they don't have a boat. The landing stage is pretty rickety but it was enough to catch her.'

'You recognise her?'

Garley shook his head. 'She was face down. Then the police arrived, some of them by car and another lot – underwater search unit – by boat. They'd already had a report of a body in the river, further up. But by the time they got to the original spot, the current had swept her down to where I found her. The divers brought her out and put her on the lawn.'

'You recognise her then?' Suppressed pain echoed in Higson's voice, together with a simmering anger.

Garley heard it. He leaned forward. 'If I'd recognised her, Teddy, I'd have got word to you, straight off. I swear it. No, I didn't. I wasn't close enough, for one thing. The police were crowding round her, for another. The woman copper, she was bending right over her. Then another of them, a sergeant, came and wanted me to make a statement – I went with him and done that, and I went home.'

Higson sipped his beer. 'How come, do you reckon, they found out it was my Courtney? Someone must've given them the idea. They was at that place where she worked, the Fisherman's Rest, ain't it? They were there, asking about her.'

Garley nodded. 'I don't drink there. Poncey sort of place.'

'Yeah? Well, the kid who worked with her, Amy, she spread the word around that the cops had been there, that same evening, asking about Courtney. Amy told your brother's girl, Denise, ain't it? Works at the new supermarket? She told Denise all about it. The cops'd talked to her and the manager. Amy told them, Courtney hadn't turned up for work that day. Manager told them the same thing.'

'You've spoken to our Denise?' Garley's voice sharpened.

'I'm back in the flat, Rosetta Gardens; I needed some stuff, tea, bread, so on. So I called in there right after I got back, and your Denise was on the till. Everyone in Weston St Ambrose,' said Higson with an unexpected, and unwelcome, smile, 'knows that if you want to know what's going on here, you ask a Garley. I asked her. Now I'm asking you.'

'Can't tell you any more, Teddy,' Wayne said, looking apprehensive. 'If I could, I would. I'll keep my ear to the ground.'

'You do that. See, I've been working out a sort of timetable, right? Someone reports a body in the river. Police get there but it's floated away. You find the body – my girl's body – stuck under this jetty or whatever, at this Glebe House. Police turn up. They take her out of the river. They don't know who she is at that time. You don't tell them it's Courtney, or might be. So,' Higson stared into his empty glass. 'Someone told them to ask at the Fisherman's Rest, if not you, then someone else. What I want to know from you, Wayne, is – was there anyone else there, when they took her out of the water? Anyone one who could have got a look at her and tipped off the cops?'

'No! Well, Mr and Mrs Stewart were standing by, the ones who own the house. They're not local. They come down from London.'

'He's the writer, you said?'

'That's him.'

'Old guy?'

'About forty or forty-two. Nice-looking wife.' Garley swallowed. 'Can't see how either of them could have tipped the cops off. They both looked like they were going to throw up. Never seen a dead body, likely. Well, not like that, anyway.'

'Upset, were they? Dear me,' said Higson. 'What a shame.'

He stood up. 'See you around, Wayne.'

After he'd left, the barman edged his way back into the pub. 'OK, Wayne?' he asked.

'Gimme another drink,' said Garley. 'I need it.'

'Can you believe it?'

Beth looked up and saw her husband standing in the doorway, brandishing a piece of paper. 'Believe what?'

'This!'

'What is it? Calm down, for goodness' sake.'

Neil drew a deep breath. 'The secretary, as he terms himself, of the Weston St Ambrose Writers' Club – that is to say, Posset – has written on behalf of the members, to express their support. He sympathises with the unfortunate incident, as he calls it, regarding the discovery of a body floating at the bottom of my garden, and hopes that we are both recovering from the shock and distress.'

Beth considered the information, 'I dare say he means well.'

'*Means well . . .*' Neil spluttered and had to wait a moment before he could continue. 'I told you this would happen. People assume, because that girl's body came to rest under our landing stage, that we – I – that I am somehow involved in her death!'

'That's not what he says, Neil,' she pointed out.

'It's what he implies! I shouldn't have told the cops I knew her. I should have kept my mouth shut! I shouldn't even have told you.' He glared at his wife, 'Then you wouldn't have insisted I tell the police!'

'Hey! Don't blame me! You know you had to tell them.'

'When this is over,' Neil muttered, 'we're going back to

London. You'd think, wouldn't you, that living quietly in the countryside, you'd have some privacy? But no, all they do round here is watch one another and take an unhealthy interest in what their neighbours are doing.'

'I didn't want to come here in the first place!' Beth yelled at him, suppressed anger and resentment welling up.

'Why didn't you say so?' he shouted back.

'Because you were so damn keen and – and I was upset about losing my job and I thought—' Beth jumped up and went to the window, her back turned to him and looking out towards the garden and the expanse of water that was the river. 'Neil . . .' she said, much more quietly, but uneasily.

'You should have said so!' he was continuing the argument, 'You—'

'Shut up, Neil! There's a man in the garden. An odd-looking man. He's as broad as he's tall and looks a bit of a thug. But he's carrying a bunch of flowers.'

He came to join her, 'Where?'

She pointed. 'Down there, near the landing stage. He's just standing there, staring at the water and – and that's a beautiful bouquet he's gripping.'

'Would you credit it?' her husband gasped. 'First I get a letter of support from Peter Posset that all but accuses me of being involved in that girl's death. Now we get ghoulish sightseers!' Neil straightened up and said grimly, 'I'm taking care of this right now!'

There was rain in the air yet again. Beneath his feet the sodden lawn squelched and oozed brackish water as Neil strode towards the figure standing at the river's edge. The man did not turn although he must have been aware someone approached. He seemed as immovable as a rock, standing there in a black leather jacket, clasping an expensive bouquet, the bright, hot-house blooms seeming incongruous in the setting.

Neil felt a twinge of doubt, but cleared his throat and said loudly, 'Can I help you?'

The man turned slowly and studied Neil, head to toe, with small expressionless eyes. Then he spoke.

'This the place?'

Neil clung to the resolve that had brought him marching out here. Damn it, it was his garden! The man was a trespasser. 'If you mean, is this the place where the young woman's body was found in the water, yes, it is. But this is private property, you know. We don't encourage sightseers. I'm sure you mean to show respect . . .'

It was as if he'd not spoken. The visitor said, 'Caught up under that bit of rotten jetty, was she?'

'Yes,' Neil admitted. Perhaps it would be best just to let the man set down his bouquet and, with luck, leave.

'You found her?'

'No . . . someone else. But he came and told us and we – we came out here. Then the police arrived.'

The man turned back and stooped to set the bouquet carefully on the ground. 'There you go, Princess,' he said.

Something occurred to Neil that he told himself ought to have occurred to him before. 'Did you know her?' He'd meant to sound sympathetic but was aware he only sounded awkward.

'She was my little girl,' said the man, staring down at the flowers. 'She was my princess.'

215

'You – you're her father?' Neil remembered that, during the adjourned inquest, it had been mentioned that the dead girl's father had identified the body, but had not been present on that day in the court because he was in prison. 'I thought you—' he blurted and stopped.

'Early release on humanitarian grounds, family tragedy,' said the visitor expressionlessly.

'Oh, yes, well, I'm very sorry for your loss. If you'd come to the house first . . .'

The man stopped staring down at the bouquet and turned to face Neil. 'What I want to know,' he said, 'is 'oo identified her.'

'I thought you . . .' Neil babbled.

'Don't mess me about, sunshine,' said the visitor, the warning all the more frightening for being so quietly spoken. 'I made the official identification – next of kin. But before that, the police had gone to the pub where she worked, asking questions. So someone had already pointed them in that direction. Who told them, the girl they found here –' he gestured towards the submerged mooring – 'that she was someone who worked up at the Fisherman's Rest? It wasn't Wayne Garley – I asked him already. So, was it you?'

'I – I only told them I thought . . . I wasn't sure.'

'Neil?' Beth's voice came from behind them.

'You tell your wife,' said the visitor, without looking towards Beth, 'to go on back indoors, make herself a cuppa or something.'

'It's all right, Beth,' Neil said obediently. 'You can go back into the house. This is Mr Higson, the – er – father of the girl found here. We're just talking. Go on, go indoors. You'll catch cold out here. It's starting to rain.'

Beth withdrew reluctantly.

When she'd gone, Higson asked, 'How come you knew my girl?'

'I didn't know her!' Neil said desperately. 'I went to the Fisherman's Rest three or so weeks ago with a – a group of other people for a meal. She was the waitress. Several of the others were regulars at the pub. They knew her. They spoke to her by name. When I saw – when the divers put her down on the lawn here, I saw her face and I thought – though I wasn't sure, honestly. I didn't say anything to the police there and then. But I told my wife later and she said I ought to tell them. So – I did. I told them I wasn't certain. That time at the pub was the only time I ever saw her, I swear!'

'There's a nice little car in my lock-up,' Higson told him. 'Mini Cooper, new. You buy that for her?'

'Buy? Good grief, no! I didn't know her, Mr Higson!'

'Lot of new clobber hanging in her wardrobe,' Higson continued. 'Big new telly, computer, all sorts of stuff cost a bundle. You know anything about any of it?'

'No! This is ridiculous.' Neil saw his visitor's face darken and added hastily, 'No, I don't mean it's ridiculous for you to want to know; it's natural. I mean, it makes no sense to think I'd know anything about any of it.'

'All right,' said Higson, to Neil's relief. But the relief was short-lived. 'These other people who were with you at the pub, the ones who knew my girl? I want their names.'

'Beth Stewart has just phoned in a panic.' Jess put her head through Carter's door some twenty minutes after their return from Lower

Weston. 'Teddy Higson is out at Glebe House! I'm on my way now.'

'I'll come with you.' Carter jumped up and grabbed his coat.

But by the time they reached Glebe House, the unwelcome visitor had left. The Stewarts were pathetically pleased to see them.

'He was the most scary bloke I'd ever met!' Neil told them fervently.

'Did he threaten you?' Carter asked him sharply.

'No, no, he didn't – that is, not directly. In a way it was touching. He'd brought flowers to put down there.' Neil pointed in the direction of the river. 'To leave at the place she'd been found. If it had stopped at that, it would have been fine – a bit of a shock but well, nothing sinister. But then he started asking questions. He wanted to know who had told the police the dead girl might be Courtney; and that she worked at the Fisherman's Rest. I had to admit I'd told you. He was the sort of bloke you don't refuse to answer. Then he wanted to know how well I knew his "princess" as he called her. I had a bit of a job persuading him I hadn't known her at all, only seen her at the pub that night. That I only knew her name because others in the party knew her and spoke to her by name. I think I managed to get him to believe me. But he wanted . . .' Neil paused and glanced at Beth. 'Look, he wanted the names of all the others who'd been with me at the Rest that evening. I know I ought not to have given them to him, but, well, like I said, he wasn't the sort you say no to.'

'Did he say anything else?' Jess asked him.

'He talked about a lot of expensive new things in the flat where his daughter lived. He wanted to know who bought them for her, but I couldn't tell him. He said she owned a car, a Mini Cooper, and he wanted to know who bought her that. Honestly, he's like a – like one of those dogs who don't let go when they've got hold of something.'

'But he let go of you, eventually, figuratively speaking?' Jess asked. 'He didn't physically assault you or make any threats?'

'Well, no, but he didn't need to, did he?'

'It was what we expected,' Carter muttered as they left the house. 'Teddy is making his own inquiries!'

'We can warn him off.' Jess considered her own words. 'Well, we can try. We can't blame him for wanting to know what happened to her, and so long as he doesn't actually make any direct threats or assault anyone . . . But we can tell him to leave the investigating to us.' She paused and glanced at the roadside. 'This isn't the way back. Where are we going?'

'The Old Manor. I did warn Murchison that Higson might be out soon and could be trouble. I think we should re-enforce the warning. You heard the questions he asked Stewart, about the car and other expensive items in the flat. Higson knows someone bought them for his daughter and he means to find out who.'

But no one answered their call at the gates of the Old Manor except for the two dogs. They ran up and pushed their noses inquiringly between the bars.

'He's either not answering, or he's taken off and left the dogs loose to make sure no one gets on to the property in his absence,' Carter said. 'We'll try again later.'

Worried, Jess asked, 'You don't think he's done a bunk? Taken fright and run for it?'

'Always possible but I don't think so. He's left his pets. Damn Higson! He's like a fox in a henhouse. Everyone will be flapping around and looking for a hidey-hole.'

Chapter 16

'Oh, Isolde,' said Jason unenthusiastically. 'Um, come in . . .'

He could hardly refuse to invite her inside. It was now pouring with rain and when he'd opened the front door that evening it had been to find a drenched figure, long skirt wrapped around her ankles, and holding a newspaper above her head. Nor was he surprised to see her. That policewoman had visited him at work again. (Much joshing from his workmates and cries of 'She must fancy you, Jaz!') No, DC Bennison had brought the news that Courtney's father was home and free – and might contact all members of the writers' club.

'What on earth for?' Jason had demanded of Tracy Bennison. 'What has any of us got to do with Courtney's death? How would he know who belongs to the writers' club, anyway?'

Apparently, Higson had gained that information from that prize prat, Neil Stewart. What could you expect? fumed Jason inwardly.

'Hurry up!' he urged his waterlogged visitor now. 'The rain's coming indoors!'

Isolde stumbled into the narrow hall from the darkness of the stormy night like, thought the exasperated Jason, a character in a Victorian novel. Her long hair was not plaited tonight but clinging about her face and shoulders. She wore her usual long skirts and those peculiar mittens without full fingers, only the lower halves. It wouldn't surprise him to hear her cry out, '*Heathcliff!*' But she zoned in on him instead.

'Oh, Jaz!' wailed Isolde. 'Isn't it awful? And I've stepped into a puddle, a really deep one, it went right over my ankle boots.'

He didn't know if by 'awful' she meant the weather, stepping into a puddle, or the likelihood of being contacted by Teddy Higson. He presumed the police had warned her, as well as the rest of them. Possibly she meant a combination of all three, so he said, 'Yes, lousy evening. Come into the kitchen. My landlady's out and it's the warmest room in the house. You can get dry.'

In the kitchen, she divested herself of her outer garment, a long knitted cardigan, a woollen scarf, and her boots. Jason put the gas oven on low, set the boots on a shelf and left them to dry out with the oven door open. They looked like a pair of small dead animals, side by side, being slow-roasted for a mediaeval dinner. He boiled the kettle and made them both a mug of instant coffee, then prepared for Isolde's tale of woe.

'Oh, Jaz!' moaned Isolde again, hands clasping the mug, and peering at him pathetically between wet strands of hair, 'Oh, Jaz, isn't it just dreadful? I'm terrified, honestly, absolutely terrified!'

'What for?' asked Jason, knowing the answer but feeling obliged to ask. He'd probably be stuck with her the entire evening. That was the trouble with Isolde. You always felt so damn sorry for her.

'The police came and told me that girl's, Courtney Higson's, father is out of prison and he's going round all the members of the writers' club and asking if they know anything about her death. He's a very dangerous man! I don't know why they let him out. I don't know what I'll do if he comes to my place.'

'Oh, he's all right,' said Jason in a half-hearted attempt to calm her down. 'He looks scary and he's been in and out of prison for years. But he isn't going to attack you, Isolde. Why on earth should he?'

'You *know* him?' Isolde goggled at him over her coffee.

'I've met him – years ago. It was when I was at school with Courtney and we dated for a bit.'

'I thought you knew her, that evening,' said Isolde. 'You know, when we all went to the Fisherman's Rest.'

'*Used* to know her! I told you, we dated for a bit when we were kids. Then, one evening, we'd arranged to meet up and go to a party. When I turned up, there was Courtney waiting as usual, but she didn't wave or anything. I thought she looked a bit fed-up – and then I saw she had this caveman with her.'

'Caveman?' gasped Isolde.

'That's what he looked like to me, then, all low forehead and long arms. Turned out he was her dad. "Don't worry, son," he said to me. "You don't have any reason to be scared of me unless there's something I don't know!" Courtney just stood there looking at her feet and shuffling about. He went on to say he was just "checking me out", because he took a lot of interest in his daughter's friends and where she went in her spare time. He told me to bring his little girl back home by half past ten – I ask you! We were going to a party and things wouldn't get going until then! But I promised, because I didn't have any choice. Then off he went, saying to Courtney, "Have a good time, Princess!" And Courtney said, "Yes, Dad."

'We didn't have any kind of a time at all, having to leave at ten to get back to her place in Rosetta Gardens by half past. It put a downer on our relationship, too. I didn't date her any more after that. I told her, "Look, I can do without your old man putting the frighteners on me." She said, "That's all right, he always does that. Don't take any notice." But well, I was the one he would come looking for, wasn't I?'

'I see,' said Isolde thoughtfully. 'It must have been scary.'

At that point a curious smell began to waft through the kitchen, originating in the oven. Isolde screeched, 'My boots!'

Jason reached in to pull out the smouldering footwear and they burned his fingers so he swore and dropped them. While he and Isolde were trying to cool them down by putting them into the vegetable tray at the bottom of the fridge, the front doorbell rang again.

'Your landlady?' whispered Isolde.

'Course not, unless she's forgotten her key.'

'*Him*?' gasped Isolde, grabbing Jason's arm.

'Pull yourself together, Isolde!' he ordered, detaching himself from her grip. 'Just sit there and wait. I'll go and see.'

But it was Teddy Higson. As soon as Jason opened the door, the space was filled by a hulking figure. The street light was behind the visitor and his features in the shadow, but a well-remembered voice said, 'Hello, sonny, don't I know you?'

At Higson's appearance in the kitchen, looming over Jason, Isolde let out a shriek, jumped up, and spilled coffee over the floor.

Higson looked at Jason. 'What's the matter with her?'

'You startled her,' said Jason. 'Honestly, Isolde, did you have to make such a mess? Hang on, I'll find a cloth.'

'Oh, right?' Higson studied the quivering Isolde. 'She belong to this group that writes books?'

'That's right,' said Jason from the floor where he was mopping up coffee. 'This is Teddy Higson, Isolde, he's Courtney's father.'

'Yes, I'm Isolde Evans,' stammered Isolde and held out her hand. 'How – how do you do, Mr Higson.'

'My little girl's dead,' said Higson to her. 'How do you think I am? Finish up doing that, can't you?' This was addressed to Jason.

Jason obediently stood up and put the cloth on the draining board.

'You used to be my girl's boyfriend,' growled Higson.

'Years ago,' Jason reminded him, 'when we were at school. I was really upset when I heard what had happened, of course.'

'Oh, yes, Mr Higson,' said Isolde timidly, 'it must be a dreadful thing for you. You have my most sincere condolences.'

'Accepted,' said Higson to her. He turned his attention back to Jason. 'You hadn't been dating her more recently than that?'

'Courtney? No!' Jason told him. 'Look, since we were at school, I've hardly seen Courtney.'

'You saw her not that long ago at the pub where she worked, though, didn't you? The Fisherman's Rest? You was there with the rest of that lot what writes books.'

'Well, I saw her *there*, that night we all went out for a meal. We all saw her, didn't we, Isolde?'

'Yes,' whispered Isolde, 'only I didn't know her name.'

'You never see Courtney anywhere else, around the place?' Higson was concentrating on Jason.

'No, well, occasionally, over the years. I'd pass her in the street. We might stop and exchange a couple of words. That's all.'

'Never see her with anyone, a bloke?'

'No, honestly!'

'Still going to those parties you used to like so much?'

'I was sixteen then!' howled Jason. 'I don't go out much at all now and never to parties! I spend all my spare time writing.'

'What? A book is that, then?' asked Higson.

'Fantasy adventure,' Jason told him. 'It's about—'

Higson was not really interested in the subject of Jason's book. 'They had someone come to the prison, adult education, getting people to write stories and such. I never bothered with it.'

'Jaz's book is awfully good,' Isolde told him. 'I'm writing a romantic novel.'

Higson's glance at Isolde did not disguise what he thought of that. 'What I want both of you to do is keep your ears open, right?' he ordered them. 'You hear anything about Courtney's friends, specially boyfriends, you come and tell me, straight off, right? You, Jaz, ain't it? You know where I live.'

'Well, if you're still in Rosetta Gardens,' said Jason, congratulating himself on avoiding the trap of appearing up-to-date about Courtney's address.

'That's right, Rosetta Gardens.' Higson frowned. 'You been cooking something, burned it?'

'Oh no,' said Isolde earnestly, 'that's my boots. We put them in the oven and they got singed. But it's all right, they're in the fridge now.'

Higson, when he left the house, sought shelter from the rain under the hood of a bus stop, and took out a notebook and pencil. He consulted the list of names he'd obtained from Neil Stewart. Carefully he crossed out Jason's name. 'Not him,' he muttered, 'too dopey.' He moved down the list and put a line through Isolde's name. 'And not the batty bird in the long dress.'

* * *

It had stopped raining at last. Murchison had become so accustomed to the sound of it pattering on the windowpanes at night that it seemed odd to be without its background noise. He had turned off all the indoor lights, but not undressed or gone to bed, although it was now past midnight. He was waiting. He knew his nocturnal visitor would come. Whoever it was, and whatever brought him, Murchison had had enough. The unknown person was playing with him, a sick game. He no longer believed it was anything so straightforward as intent to burgle. He pressed his mobile phone and it flashed up the time: a quarter to one. It would be about now. This was when the prowler usually came, circling the outer walls of the garden. Tonight he would find out who it was.

Max heard the prowler first, as he always did, and began his deep throaty bark. Prince joined in. Murchison stood up and picked up the heavy-duty flashlight he had ready. He opened a side door and slipped out of the house.

The security light picked him up and briefly illuminated him before he gained the darkness of the garden. That could not be helped. He made his way to the kennel and released the dogs from their pen. They knew the hunt was up and whined their excitement. Murchison led them to the garden door in the rear wall.

Earlier that day, after the departure of the police, he'd driven into town and arranged for a locksmith to come out at once and change the lock. When Carter had warned him that the original key, Courtney's copy, might be in the hands of the murderer, Murchison had realised how lackadaisical he'd been. It was something he should have thought of for himself, at once. But there were probably a hundred and one things he should have thought of when he set out on his friendship with Courtney. Sitting here, behind the high walls surrounding the gardens, he'd felt himself in charge of his personal kingdom. He could do as he wanted, go where he wanted, and sleep with anyone he fancied. He'd fancied Courtney and, in a crazy moment, had acted on an impulse.

The police clearly thought him stupid. The whole thing, as adults would have warned him when he was a child, was 'bound to end in tears'. In fact, it had ended in murder and who was to say the cops weren't going to try and pin that on him?

The new lock mechanism meshed smoothly and the door opened with the faintest of sounds. Murchison had oiled the hinges and they didn't make their usual creak of protest. He ordered the dogs to silence and they began a slow circuit of the walls. Just here, right to the rear of the property, was an open area that had originally been the paddock for the horses on which the Victorian and Georgian owners had depended for sport and mobility. Now it was overgrown, dotted with self-set blackberry bushes, the grass buried beneath weeds. He'd never tried to do anything about tidying it up, persuading himself it was a wildlife meadow. On the further side was the woodland that surrounded the house on three sides, and eventually would invade the meadow, too. The trees rustled and groaned as they swayed in the night breezes. Large wings flapped overhead and something pale swooped across the moonlit sky, and dropped down in the centre of the meadow. There was a frightened squeak and the owl was up and away, his prey in his beak. Prince, overcome with youthful eagerness, bounced forward with a yelp and he had to call him back in a low voice. But the sound of the dog and Murchison's order were magnified on the night air – and it was enough. Just around the corner of the tall wall, on the track to the woods, an engine started up.

Murchison swore and blundered forward, stumbling over roots and stones in the moonlight. The dogs raced ahead, giving tongue now that the quarry was in flight. But they were too late. All they saw was the gleam of a car's rear lights as it turned out of the track on to the road and sped off towards Weston St Ambrose.

He had missed his chance. Murchison swore again and called to the dogs to come back. But, normally so obedient, this time they didn't. He switched on the flashlight and shone its powerful beam ahead of him down the track. The dogs had found something and were snuffling round it. It was a heap, to one side of the track. Max lifted his head and howled.

The sound reverberated around, bouncing off the high garden wall, and was sucked away into the trees on the other side of the track. Murchison ran to the spot. Huddled immobile on the ground was a figure. He knew, from the dogs' behaviour, who it would be, even before he shone down the torch and saw the old coat and muddy boots. When he hunkered down and stretched out a trembling hand, he touched hair sticky with blood.

'Charlie,' he whispered in horror. 'Oh, my God, Charlie . . .'

Chapter 17

'I've just come from the hospital,' Jess said.

'How is he?' asked Graeme Murchison. He looked and sounded uncharacteristically nervous.

'In a coma, but hanging on,' she told him. 'The medical opinion is out on the likelihood of his recovery. He's eighty years old and, although clearly in a good state of health before the attack, it's going to be hard for him to pull through this.'

'I had thought,' Murchison muttered, 'of going to visit him, but I suppose there's little point in that if he's unconscious. It's just . . .' He let the words tail off.

'His family are there at the moment. Quite a crowd,' Jess added, 'his son, Harry Fallon, with his wife, their daughter, Amy, and Amy's boyfriend. I understand a married daughter, Harry's sister, is on her way from Herefordshire and expected late this afternoon.'

They were sitting in Murchison's elegant drawing room. For Jess, no setting could appear less appropriate.

'Gordon Fleming rang me to let me know. Amy told him.' Perhaps Murchison also found their surroundings incongruous. He leaned his head against the back of his chair and stared up at the white-painted moulded ceiling.

Jess found herself doing the same and gazing at the frieze that ran around it. It was classical in theme, naked putti dragging carts laden with grapes and greenery, nymphs in floating draperies, the grinning faces of satyrs peering through vine leaves. Perhaps the mid-Georgian artist who had designed it had done so after a heavy drinking bout, or had been at the opium.

'Amy explained she wouldn't be coming in to work today because of what's happened to her grandfather. Now he's got no waitresses; the river is threatening to rise even more; Saturday night is always busy and tomorrow he expects good trade at lunchtime – if he's not flooded out. He's going spare, poor old Gordon. He's been ringing round everyone he knows. He hopes some woman who used to work at another place he ran, a few years ago, will come and fill in until things get back to normal.' Murchison shut his eyes briefly. 'Things never are going to be normal again, are they?'

'That's what murder does,' Jess told him, trying not to sound irritated. 'It knocks the world out of kilter for everyone, even if only marginally involved. As for family and friends of the victim, well, their world has changed forever. Charlie isn't dead and this isn't yet a murder investigation. But it could become one at any minute. It's a miracle he is still alive; and there is the real possibility this is connected with the death of Courtney Higson.'

'How?' asked Murchison dully.

'I don't know!' Jess had come here with the intention of keeping her cool and not letting herself be irritated by Murchison. But he annoyed her just by sitting there and looking sorry for himself. She heard herself saying sharply, 'There is a lot we don't yet know. But Courtney was your girlfriend. She worked at a pub you owned. You kept both of these connections secret. Sadly, secrets have a way of working their way to the surface, Mr Murchison. Anything involving you is of interest to our investigations. If someone's been staking out your house, we want to know why. If that mystery watcher turns violent and attacks an old man, finding out why becomes urgent.'

Murchison winced. He must have expected someone to come and talk to him about the attack on Charlie. But he'd also clearly hoped to see Carter, greeting her arrival with, 'Oh, Inspector Campbell? On your own?'

'It's Saturday and you wouldn't normally see me,' Jess had retorted. 'But we're short-handed and I'm giving up my weekend.'

So that Ian Carter could enjoy his! He had appeared at Jess's door quite late, around nine the previous evening, with apologies and explanations. He had rung his ex-wife and arranged to drive down and see his daughter again over the weekend, even though he'd seen Millie so recently at the school panto.

'Something's not right down there,' he'd said, sitting on Jess's sofa and nursing the glass of the inferior white wine she'd managed to find in the fridge. 'It's been on my mind since I spoke to Sophie that evening at the school. Something is worrying her. I've told her I'm coming down for the weekend. I've booked a hotel room nearby, so as not to inconvenience them, her and Rodney, that is.'

'I'll be on call,' said Jess. 'If anything crops up, I'm sure I can handle it. I don't have any weekend plans.'

Some chance, she thought mutinously. All the same if I had, I suppose!

'Thanks for understanding,' he'd told her.

That, of course, was before someone had knocked Charlie

Fallon cold in the early hours of this morning, necessitating ambulance, police and general mayhem around Murchison's place. Goodbye to any thought of a quiet weekend off, time to recuperate, do all those jobs around the flat that seem so trivial and manage to pile up into a mountain to scale. Even a chance to do a serious food shop in order not to expire from lack of basic supplies – and put something in the fridge to replace the out-of-date packet of beefburgers. Perhaps substitute something drinkable for that opened bottle of terrible white wine. It had not escaped her that Carter had left unfinished the glass she'd poured for him the previous evening. After he'd left, she'd tipped what remained of the contents down the sink.

Instead had come the early apologetic call from Dave Nugent who, in the continued absence of Phil Morton, had been on call that weekend. Dave clearly believed that if he was to be disturbed then someone senior could be also. So here I am, she thought ruefully.

It didn't help to know she must look a mess. She'd showered in a hurry with no time to do more with her wet hair than towel it semi-dry and brush it into what she'd hoped was some sort of style, letting it dry as she drove to the hospital.

Doing what I'm supposed to do. This is the career I chose. I like to think I'm capable at it. All this she'd told herself in an attempt to turn up the burner under her mood. But she still thought she probably looked like something a cat dragged in at dawn. Police work was all too frequently a dirty job, dealing with the mess and misery inflicted by greed, viciousness and vice. It was as Tom Palmer had said at the recent meal in the curry house. They didn't see people at their best.

From the busy hospital she had come to this blue and grey Georgian room. It contrasted horribly in her memory with the image of the old man, his head swathed in bandages, his arm attached to a drip and a variety of other support technology, surrounded by weeping relatives. Attacks on the very young and the very old were always particularly sickening. All police officers hate them. You have to overcome natural revulsion, the burning anger, the desire to make someone pay; and keep a cool head, ask the questions, note the answers, check out the details. Routine, on these occasions, is a saviour of an officer's sanity.

Jess was aware that Murchison was watching her moodily. Now he spoke, startling her. 'You disapprove of me, don't you?' he said.

'I'm the neutral corner,' Jess said resentfully. 'I represent the law. You know, that blindfolded woman holding the scales of Justice? That's me.'

She knew she wasn't sounding very professional, but, as far as she was concerned, this sorry saga had come about because of Murchison and his impulse to take up with Courtney Higson. Stupid man! she thought. How on earth did he think that little romance was going to end? How long did he imagine it would last? He would have become bored with Courtney and then what? Drop her? Take an unsophisticated teenager from a run-down housing estate like Rosetta Gardens and show her all of this . . . Jess glanced around the room again. And then say, fine, that's it, off you go. Don't bother me any more? Apart from the callousness, even the cruelty of it, the risk to himself, to her, to anyone involved in any way was immense. It now seemed Charlie Fallon might be the latest person to suffer harm because of it.

'You're not a lump of stone, you're a human being.' Murchison had leaned forward in his chair, set for an argument. He had been watching her face, on which her thoughts had obviously been clearly written. 'Of course you bloody disapprove! All right, I was stupid. I was selfish. I was using Courtney, if you want to call it that, and making her a kind of hobby. No, not my Eliza Doolittle, as you accused me before of doing! I had no aspirations or wish to prove a point. That would at least be an excuse. I have no excuse. I was a lonely, middle-aged man with too much time on his hands and a wounded ego from a failed love affair. I was looking for something impossible – a relationship without strings. There is no such thing, is there?'

'I suppose,' said Jess, 'the sex industry would say that's what they offer.'

He uttered a hiss of annoyance and briefly buried his head in his hands. When he looked up, he said: 'You really don't understand, do you? I can't explain it.' After a moment, he went on, 'I shouldn't have left Charlie in that shack. He wanted to be there, and was happy there. But I knew he wasn't safe. People were prowling round the place. I knew it, even if I didn't actually see them. What the hell . . .' He swept his hand through the air as if brushing away any difficulty. 'If we all of us always made the right decisions, the world would be a wonderful place, wouldn't it?'

'Can we talk about last night?' Jess was not going to be dragged any further down some metaphysical path. 'You'd previously told Superintendent Carter that you suspected the house was being cased at night, from the lane, with a view to burglary.' She pointed through the windows towards the distant treetops.

'That's what I thought at the time. I also thought it could be a courting couple. My mistake was to tell Charlie. He has always been keen to defend my property from those he thought had no right to trespass on it. Obviously he decided to keep watch last night – and disturbed whoever it was. The blighter struck out and knocked the old fellow out cold, and escaped. I was out there with the dogs on the same errand, hoping to catch the snooper, but all I saw were a vehicle's disappearing tail-lights. The dogs found poor old Charlie.'

Defensively, Murchison added, 'He was a poacher in his younger years. He knew his way around woodland at night as well as he did by day. Yes, it was risky letting him stay there at night. I even offered to leave one of the dogs with him but he refused. He was an eccentric and obstinate. He did his own thing. I respected that.'

Murchison paused. 'I'm talking about him in the past tense. But he's not dead yet. I suppose, I'm bracing myself for his death. I shall always feel responsible.'

You *are* responsible! Jess wanted to snap, but she had herself under control now. Adopting the blandest police tone she could, a real Policewoman Plod, she told him, 'Apart from urging you to maintain vigilance, perhaps put a few more security lights up – on the external side of the garden wall, for example, where the lane runs alongside it, so that anyone parking there would trigger the lighting – well, I don't know that we could have done much. We don't have the manpower to provide a private watchman service.'

Jess broke off as Murchison jumped up and walked to the window, gazing out with a grim expression. 'All right, every damn thing I've done, every decision I've made, has been wrong! Either that, or I've failed to do the obvious. Yes, I could have hired a private security outfit to patrol at night . . . but I didn't.'

Jess didn't answer. Murchison swung round to face her. 'It's long past lunchtime,' he said unexpectedly. 'I was thinking of going over to the pub. I need to see what the situation is with the flooding. Join me in a sandwich?' He pulled a wry expression. 'You can carry on questioning me, or lecturing me on my failures, if you want.'

'I think I'm about done for the moment,' Jess told him. 'But I could do with a break. I should tell you, were you thinking of treating me, that I can't accept any hospitality. That would be quite out of order.'

'Far be it from me to seek to bribe an officer of the law with a packet of crisps and a bacon butty,' he told her gravely.

The last of the lunchtime diners were driving away as they arrived. As one car passed them, Jess saw that the driver bore a striking resemblance to Peter Posset, as described by Nugent. The death of a waitress he'd known had not put him off lunching there.

Now the interior of the Fisherman's Rest was deserted and, apart from a muted clattering from the kitchens, quiet.

'I was about to call you,' Gordon Fleming informed Murchison. He looked even more doleful than previously. 'We've managed this lunchtime, but may not be able to open the restaurant tonight. The water's right at the back door. I've warned Cathy. She's the woman I told you about, the replacement waitress. I don't think she'll be needed. I have contact numbers for tonight's bookings. I'll phone them and put them off.'

If he'd been surprised to see Jess with Murchison, he did not show it. Jess thought that probably Fleming didn't care about the progress of any investigation or the attack on Charlie Fallon, or anything other than the situation at the Fisherman's Rest. No waitresses, water at his back door, his business under threat, it was enough to cope with, without murder and violent attack.

'Fair enough, try not to worry too much, Gordon,' Murchison consoled him. 'All right for us to have sandwiches or something?' He indicated Jess. 'Inspector Campbell is anxious you should know she is not my guest and will be paying for her meal.'

'Yes, you can have a sandwich, that's not a problem,' Fleming told them. 'What sort do you want?'

'Poor old Gordon,' said Murchison when he had left them. 'We are insured, of course, as far as the building is concerned. But loss of business, that's something else.'

'Does he live on the premises?' Jess asked.

'Yes, he's got a flat upstairs. He may yet find himself marooned in it, but the water shouldn't reach it. If we are flooded, the utilities will be out of action, however, so he might not want to stay there.'

'I should tell you,' Jess said, 'that Teddy Higson has visited the Stewarts and also spoken to at least two members of the writers' club. So keep an eye open for him. He still doesn't know about you and Courtney, or so we believe, but he may find out.'

'I realise that. It seems to me that keeping secrets is not an easy thing around here,' Murchison raised his pint in salutation. 'To your success, Inspector Campbell. May it come soon. I have had just about as much as I can stand of this.'

Jess realised that he meant exactly what he said. She ought to be easier on him. Murchison having a nervous breakdown wouldn't help.

Gordon was back, reduced to serving food himself in the absence of his waitresses. He put down their sandwiches and said moodily, 'Would you believe it? Chef's just noticed that one of the items is missing from the display case, round the corner there, on the way to the toilets.' Gordon pointed towards a corridor leading off the bar-room marked out by a wooden placard reading *Toilets*.

'What sort of item?' asked Murchison wearily. His manager's minor problems were clearly of no interest to him just at the moment.

'One of the tools,' said Gordon, indicating the variety of agricultural and other implements fixed to the walls by way of décor. 'Not a big one, so no one noticed until just now.'

'Which one?' Murchison was trying to summon up interest.

'The saddler's awl,' said Gordon.

Jess froze with her sandwich halfway to her mouth, 'A what?' she asked sharply.

Gordon stared at her resentfully. 'Awl,' he said. 'A sort of pointed steel punch, to make holes in leather, if you want to stitch harness together. Some light-fingered sod has taken it out of the display case. Sandwich all right?'

Jess ate her sandwich far too quickly for easy digestion. Her mind was buzzing with the new possibility. Was it possible her interrupted Saturday and visit to Lower Weston might have resulted in a clue to the nature of the murder weapon? Saddler's awl . . . Hadn't she suggested to Carter that the weapon might have been a knitting needle? A saddler's tool would be that much stronger, inflexible and probably quite sharp. More and more, it was appearing that Courtney's death was connected with her place of work.

She left Murchison discussing the beer garden situation with Fleming, and hurried into the car park. Before she could leave, however, the slam of a car door further away caught her ear. She looked up and saw a vehicle parked across the road outside the Fallons' cottage. Amy had just got out, together with the boyfriend Jess had seen with the family at the hospital earlier. Jess hesitated. She should go and ask if there was any more news of Charlie's condition.

Neither Amy nor the boyfriend looked pleased to see her. The boyfriend, now that Jess had time to take a proper look at him, had an expression of sullen hostility she suspected was permanent. She'd come across enough young men of his type. They bore the world a grudge, often had little control of their temper, and tended to get into fights. She supposed she ought to ask his name.

Amy performed a reluctant introduction. 'This is Hedley Morris. He's my fiancé.'

Amy wore no engagement ring but Hedley didn't appear prepared to argue about his status. He just glowered silently at Jess. She made a mental note to ask Nugent to check if he was anywhere in police records.

'How was your grandfather when you left the hospital, Amy?'

'Just the same. My Auntie Sheila's turned up and she's there now with my mum and dad.'

'It'd be all the same to your lot if the poor old devil was dead,' said Hedley unexpectedly.

241

'We take all attacks on the old very seriously indeed, Mr Morris.'

'Murderer roaming about, ain't there? You want to do something about that sharpish before someone else gets knocked on the head.' He thrust forward his own shaven skull.

Jess asked quietly, 'Are you suggesting the same person who killed Courtney Higson also attacked Mr Fallon? Do you have reason for thinking that?'

Hedley gestured at his surroundings. 'Look at Little Weston. It's a dump, innit? Never anything happens here. Or never used to. You got a ruddy maniac running around and you ought to be doing something about it. Come on, Amy,' he added without a pause, turning away from Jess.

She let them go indoors without seeking to detain them any further. She would have liked to ask Amy if any one had ever expressed any threat to any member of her family, or if they were on bad terms with anyone generally. But she realised that when Hedley was with Amy, Hedley did the talking.

Peter Posset had arrived home from his visit to the Fisherman's Rest. He'd enjoyed his lunch, even if the menu had been sadly reduced owing to circumstances. But the salmon fish pie had been good. He was feeling relaxed and ready for a little drop of something as a *digestif*, after which he would settle down to watch some sport on the television. It was as he was deciding between a splash of Grand Marnier and a *soupçon* of Tia Maria that his doorbell rang. When he opened it he had, as he described afterwards, a very nasty shock.

A burly figure in a sheepskin coat stood there, glowering at him. He had small mean eyes fixed on Posset. Peter's mind was telling him to shut the door at once and, probably, phone the police. But he couldn't move, any more than some hapless victim frozen before a stoat.

'You run the writers' club, right?' said this person without any preamble.

It wasn't a question. It was a statement of fact and Peter could not deny it. 'Er, yes,' he stammered. 'May I ask . . .?'

To his fears was added another horrible thought. I do hope this dreadful-looking man doesn't want to join us!

'My name is Higson,' growled the visitor. 'You knew my little girl.'

'Little girl?' Peter was bewildered for a moment. 'Oh, young Courtney! Er, yes, I only knew her as a waitress at the Fisherman's Rest. I was shocked, terribly shocked, when I heard the news.'

'You've just been down there, eating your dinner.' Higson rolled over Posset's words. 'I saw you. I followed you back here.'

'My – er – lunch, yes . . . I didn't see you in there.' The idea of being followed by this thug made him want to throw up his recent meal.

'Mind if we have a chat?' said Higson, and despite the way it was phrased, this was not a question. He stepped forward.

Posset automatically, though unwillingly, stepped back to allow him access. He didn't want this ghastly man in his house. But he could hardly wrestle with him to keep him out.

Higson walked past him, still uninvited, and went into the sitting room. Peter dithered over whether to shut the front door, imprisoning him with the visitor, or leave it open as a means of escape. Reluctantly, he shut the door and followed the unwelcome guest into the sitting room.

Higson was looking around. His gaze fell on the knitting and derision flickered in his mean eyes. He continued to survey his surroundings. Reaching, in due course, Posset's modest collection of liqueurs, tastefully arranged on a silver tray on the sideboard, the derision flickered again.

'Would, er, you like a drink?' faltered Peter. 'I haven't any beer. I do have whisky . . .'

'No,' said his visitor.

Peter was relieved. If Higson settled in, drink in hand, who knew how long he might stay.

'I've been watching that pub,' said Higson. 'My girl worked there and the way I see it, what happened to her has something to do with her working there, see?'

'Oh, yes, I do see,' Peter assured him. 'But I can't . . .'

'You're a regular, ain't you? You must see what's going on. You see anyone chatting up my Courtney?' Higson leaned forward. 'She was a beautiful girl.'

'Oh, yes, she was!' agreed Peter. Then, lest this should be misconstrued, he blundered on with: 'Although I myself . . . I mean, of course, I agree she was extremely attractive, but I personally . . .'

Higson hissed impatiently. 'Don't waste my time. I've got your number. What I want to know is, if you saw any man in particular talking to Courtney, or act, like, specially friendly with her?'

Afterwards, when telling the tale to others, Posset would assure his hearers that he had been on the verge of demanding Higson leave his house. But he had felt obliged to listen to a man who, after all, was grief-stricken and deserving of sympathy, no matter how uncouth he was. His listeners well understood that Peter would never have summoned up the courage and, even if he had, it would have been a waste of breath.

'Honestly, Mr Higson,' Peter told his visitor, 'I can't say I ever did. Perhaps you should talk to Amy Fallon. She is the other girl working there. Although she isn't there today.'

'Yeah,' said Higson thoughtfully. 'I put her on my list.'

Incongruously, there ran through Posset's brain a fragment of Gilbert and Sullivan. He forced it away but it remained tinkling at the corner of his consciousness, trying to get back in. *I've got a little list . . . and they never would be missed . . .*

'Only,' he babbled, 'you couldn't speak to her today. She's not working today. There was an attack last night on her grandfather, in the woods. The manager told me.'

'What?' Higson's eyes, like a couple of shiny black marbles, gleamed at Posset. 'Where?'

'In the woods near Lower Weston, just on the edge of the place. He, er, old Mr Fallon lives there, in a hut. He's some sort of gamekeeper for Mr Murchison who owns the land and the big house there. But last night, as I understand it, someone attacked the poor old fellow and now he's in hospital and all his family is there with him.'

'Poacher got him?' asked Higson, still watching Posset closely.

'I, er, have no idea. No one knows yet. It happened in the middle of the night, I understand.'

'I see . . .' said Higson thoughtfully. He took out a small notepad and, watched by the fascinated Posset, carefully made a note. 'Right, I'll look into that, and all. And if you remember anything . . .'

'I'll let you know,' promised Peter, and never had any promise in his life been made more fervently.

'That's it. Rosetta Gardens estate, that's where I live.'

I'm not surprised to hear it, thought Peter. But, to his enormous relief, his visitor had done with him. He pushed the notebook back in the pocket of the sheepskin coat, turned and walked out of the room, down the little hallway, then with a slam of the front door was gone.

Peter tottered to his drinks tray, but he'd given up the idea of a liqueur. He poured himself a very large whisky.

'You've taken a chill, Dennis,' said Lucy Claverton fretfully. 'I warned you about going out at night, sitting around in the garden and all over the place, and in this damp, cold weather. I know how keen you are to finish the owl survey, but ruining your health doing it is nonsense.'

'I'm all right, really,' her husband protested. 'Lacking sleep, perhaps, but otherwise in good shape.'

'I can see for myself that you aren't. You're all huddled up there by the fire and miserable. You are not, Dennis, going out again tonight. I don't care what you say. If you are ill, I am the one who will have to look after you.'

'I will have to go out this afternoon,' he told her. 'Just for a little while.'

'Those owls . . .' began Lucy.

Dennis avoided her gaze. 'There's just something I need to check at the library – it's to do with the owls, I admit. The library's open today. It's only in business on certain days, as you know, now that volunteers staff it. It'll be closed until next Tuesday. So, if I don't go today, I'll have to wait. I'll just pop out for a short time. I won't be gone more than an hour, if that.' Placatingly he added, 'If there's anything you need me to bring in, let me know. I can drop by that supermarket place.'

'No,' said Lucy, 'stay away from there, Dennis. That awful Garley girl might be on the till again. We can go and do our usual shop on Monday.'

'All right, dear,' said Dennis meekly.

Chapter 18

During all this time, Ian Carter, oblivious of the developments at Lower Weston, had arrived on Saturday in time to take Millie to lunch at a pizza restaurant. It was a crowded place, full of parents and children, and the noise they generated, together with the scrape of chairs on the tiled floor and snatches of canned music, assaulted his ears. The tables were set as close together as possible, to accommodate the maximum number of customers. Every time the woman behind him moved, the back of her chair banged against the back of Carter's and sent painful tremors up his spine. None of this bothered Millie who, fizzing with excitement at his unexpected extra visit, enjoyed a large wheel of baked dough topped with gooey cheese, dried-out slices of sausage and bits of frazzled bacon. Carter faced the only non-flour-based item on the menu, the salad. Even that came with garlic bread.

She'd insisted on bringing along MacTavish, the stuffed bear, but she did not, today, constantly refer to his opinions. Any conversation with his daughter was usually conducted with MacTavish as a kind of interpreter. The bear's head, crowned with its tartan tam o'shanter, stuck out of a little pink backpack. Carter fancied MacTavish had a discomfited look on his face and his beady eyes fixed Carter with more than usual resentment. But that Millie might no longer feel a need to channel her side of conversation with him through the bear was progress.

Silently, Carter telegraphed to MacTavish now, 'She won't need either of us one day, old chap. We both know it.'

He'd returned them both to her home in the afternoon and was now, in the late afternoon gloom, walking with her mother in the damp surrounds of a local park. They almost had the place to themselves. There were no mothers with infants or old men sitting on the benches gossiping, no youngsters fooling about in the bushes. Millie and MacTavish were watching television. Rodney was in his home office engaged on paperwork ('always something to catch up on, Ian! No rest for the wicked, eh?'). Sophie, muffled in a quilted jacket, paced alongside him, her eyes on the ground. Time and opportunity to grasp the nettle.

'All right, Soph,' Carter said to her. 'What's wrong?'

'You know,' she snapped, 'you always sound as if you're interrogating a suspect!'

'Can't be helped, I'm afraid.' A remark like hers would once have needled him. Now he'd long found the easiest way to deal with Sophie's petulance was to accept it as normal conversation.

'I – Rodney and I – have been intending for us to get together for a discussion, but you rather caught us on the hop, suddenly phoning up and announcing you were coming today. We—' Sophie began after a moment or two, only to break off in mid-sentence.

A large woman in a tracksuit had lumbered by them, followed by the only dog walker in sight, a thin, worried-looking man with a very large, confident-looking dog.

'Good evening,' said the dog walker. The jogger didn't have enough breath to exchange greetings.

When both were out of sight, Sophie began again. 'The thing is, we – Rodney and I – are making plans for the future.'

She paused and cast him a sideways glance, waiting for some comment.

'And?' was all he said.

'Rodney has a friend who's selling his house in France. It's in the Rhone valley, not far from Lyon. It's a lovely place, not exactly rural, but in a small community, couple of shops and so on. Good communications through Lyon with the rest of France and internationally via its airport—'

'Sophie,' Carter interrupted, 'You sound like a travel brochure or an estate agent. Get to the point, can you?'

'We're thinking of selling up and going to live there,' said Sophie abruptly.

The large woman was coming back and puffed past them again.

'I thought the world of big business couldn't operate without Rodney's presence?'

I'm being petty, thought Carter, but this is one heck of a bombshell.

Sophie had flushed. 'People used to need to meet face to face. Now he can reach anyone at the touch of a button. As I was saying before you so rudely interrupted, communications are good from Lyon. You can fly direct from there to Heathrow. He could come back for a visit if he needed to.'

'I see, and what would you do with yourself all day, while Rodney is jet-setting around, sewing up the latest deal, and what about Millie?' Carter could hear himself building up a head of steam.

Sophie let out a hiss but remained doggedly calm. 'It's not

finalised, of course, but I think I have a part-time job lined up in Lyon, at one of the museums. I used to work in restoring antiques, if you remember. I am qualified for the job.'

'I repeat, where does Millie fit into all of this? And, if I might mention it, my own contact with my daughter?'

Sophie stopped and whirled to face him, her hands thrust deep into the pockets of the quilted jacket. 'They do have excellent schools in Lyon. However, since Millie has to go up to another school in September next year anyway, we were considering sending her to boarding school here. I think she'd like that, once she settled in.'

'You've discussed it with her?' Carter had told himself, once he'd seen how things were going, that he was not going to lose his temper. No matter how provoking Sophie might be, he would keep his cool. It was getting more difficult by the second.

'Not directly,' said Sophie. 'I wanted to talk to you first.'

'And when, exactly, were you planning to do this? Coming here this weekend was my idea, not yours, as you've pointed out. You said nothing at the pantomime.'

'Oh, for goodness' sake, Ian! The panto evening was hardly a suitable place or time. Of course I was going to speak to you soon! Look, if Millie goes to boarding school, you'll have even more opportunity to see her, won't you? Because she can come to you for half-term, things like that.'

'How very convenient for you and Rodney. So, Millie gets dumped at boarding school, you and he fly off to a luxury home on the Rhone, and I stay here and pick up the pieces. Oh, aren't boarding school fees rather expensive? Who's going to pick up the tab for those?'

Sophie's pale face now flooded with an ugly tide of red. 'I knew you'd be like this! No wonder I put off talking to you! Look, I would contribute what I could to the fees. That's why I'd be taking the job in Lyon. But you're her father, after all. You can't expect Rodney—'

'I don't expect, want or need anything from that wheeler-dealer you've hitched yourself to! I don't give a damn what you do or where you go. But I do care about Millie. She is not going to suffer because of some selfish impulse on your part.'

Carter's suppressed anger had leached out into his voice. He'd kept the volume quiet but he couldn't keep out the fury; and the result made Sophie step back, the red tide receding and leaving her face ashen.

'I'm not in the interview room and I won't be bullied!' she managed.

'You're not the victim here, Soph!'

Her voice shaking, Sophie stood her ground. 'Nor is Millie. She's growing up, Ian! You have to think about her future!'

He wanted to shout that no, Sophie was thinking about her own future. But it was useless arguing with his ex-wife. It had been like this during their marriage. Sophie would decide privately what she wanted to do. She'd make all the arrangements, to suit herself, and present him with a *fait accompli*. Then, when he raised any objection, he was the one being awkward and uncooperative. The pattern was a familiar one.

'Nothing changes, does it, Soph?' he heard himself say, sounding resigned.

She didn't answer for several minutes, during which time they paced round the small lake, clogged with weed and inhabited by a few miserable-looking ducks. Then she said, also quietly, 'No, Ian, nothing ever does. You think *I* don't change. I know *you* haven't. I'm not planning to off-load my child just to suit a whim, as you seem to think I am. She's my daughter and she matters to me more than you, or Rodney, or anything else. I don't care what you think. I will pick out the school very carefully and I hope you and I will visit it together before any final decision is made. The one I have in mind has a good academic record, it's not too big, and I've had a personal recommendation from a couple of people who've sent daughters there. I am sure Millie will settle in and like it.'

'Very well,' he said. 'If that is what you think is best for her. We'll work out something about the fees.'

'Yes, I do think it's best.' After a moment, she added, 'Thank you for cooperating over the fees. You are still coming to supper tonight, with me and Rodney?'

'Yes.' (And doesn't that promise to be a fun evening . . .)

'We can discuss it more, after Millie's gone to bed.'

But there wasn't going to be anything really to discuss, Carter thought. It's all been decided. She's probably right about Millie settling in boarding school. She does have to go to a new school, anyway, in the next academic year. And Millie is growing up. Her needs will be changing during the next few years. You and I, MacTavish, we're going to have to adjust.

On Saturday evening, Tom appeared at Jess's flat with a DVD about saving the Bengal tiger, a bottle of wine, and bag of take-away Chinese food.

'I realise it ought to be Indian food, because of the film, but we ate Indian last time,' he explained.

It all promised to be a pleasant evening until, in the middle of the spring rolls, fried noodles, crispy beef and other delicacies, Jess's mother rang up.

'Are you all on your own darling?'

'No, actually, I've got a friend here. We're just eating . . .'

'Oh? Who?'

'Just a colleague, you might say.'

The conversation did not last long as her mother informed her in conspiratorial tones that she did not want *to interrupt anything*.

'I shall spend the next week,' said Jess to Tom when she rejoined him, 'explaining that she was not interrupting the sort of evening she's imagining us to be having.'

'Funny thing, families,' said Tom, 'did you say Carter's gone visiting his ex-wife?'

'He's got something he wants to talk over with her, about their daughter.'

'You get on well with him, don't you? Didn't you say you got on well with the kid, too?'

'Don't you start,' groaned Jess.

'Just interested. Do you want that last spring roll?'

On Sunday morning, less apologetic and more resentful, the harassed Dave Nugent rang again. 'Sorry to disturb you on a Sunday, ma'am, but there's a lady here insisting that I tell you her husband is missing. She's a Mrs Lucy Claverton. You went to see them recently, she says, and—'

'What does she mean, he's *missing*?' Jess, in dressing gown with the phone in one hand and a mug of coffee in the other, did not want to hear this, not hear of any more problems. She just wanted to rescue what was left of her mangled weekend.

'He went out yesterday afternoon to visit the library and didn't come back, gone all night. She says it's quite out of character.'

Remembering the Clavertons in their neat little home, so eager to chat to her, Jess realised this was probably quite true. Not that people didn't act 'out of character' all the time. They did. But with all the attendant circumstances and the way everything seemed to lead back to the writers' club, the sudden disappearance of one of its members had to be investigated at once.

'Tell her I'll come to her house. If she goes home now, I'll be there as soon as possible.'

Chapter 19

'Dennis wouldn't do it!' sobbed Lucy Claverton. 'He wouldn't just go off and not tell me, not if he meant to be away a long time. And he'd never, never do something like this, just vanish!'

Jess suppressed the urge to reply, 'Well, he has done it.' Instead, she said, 'Do try and keep calm, Mrs Claverton. I realise that is very difficult for you in the circumstances, but I need you to keep a clear head and tell me exactly what happened yesterday, everything, even tiny details.'

'But nothing did!' protested Lucy, waving her hands helplessly in the air, 'not a thing. It was just another Saturday.'

'Did your husband seem worried, or preoccupied? Was he in good health?'

Lucy let her hands drop into her lap and sat up straight, nose raised, a sudden gleam in her reddened eyes. 'He had a cold.'

'I see. How long had he suffered with his cold?'

'No, no, you don't understand, Inspector Campbell. He hadn't had a cold *before*; but yesterday he was definitely going down with one. I'd told him, he ought not to have stayed out nearly all night on Friday.' Lucy uttered an exasperated sound. 'You know what men are like,' she said. 'Really, they have no common sense. Dennis has been obsessed with those owls—'

Startled, Jess interrupted her. 'What do you mean, stayed out all night?'

'Well, not *all* night, of course,' Lucy qualified, 'but until the early hours. I was asleep when he came in. I half woke up, as one does, and I think . . .' Lucy frowned. 'I looked at the clock on my bedside table and it was about three. But I could be wrong because, of course, I didn't have my glasses on.'

'Did you have any conversation with him? Ask him where he'd been?'

Lucy's eyes filled with tears again. 'No, I was too cross. I had been telling him that I don't like him wandering about at night. Apart from anything else, I don't like being left on my own here, not knowing where he is. If only I had asked him, he might have said something that I could tell you, given me some clue as to where he is now . . . but I just buried my head in the pillow.'

'*Why* was he wandering around at night?' Jess tried to sort this amazing statement out. 'How long has he been doing this?'

'Oh, for several weeks. But he doesn't always go far. Sometimes he sits out in the garden with his notebook and a torch. Sometimes he goes further afield. It depends on the location of the owls.'

Ah, yes, the owls. 'Which owls are these, Mrs Claverton?'

'Birds,' said Lucy simply, staring at her. 'You know, tawny owls. They're nocturnal.'

'Yes, I know what owls are – but why was your husband out looking for owls in such cold wet weather? Was this a particular location?'

'There!' exclaimed Lucy with sudden triumph. 'You agree with me it was quite the silliest thing to do at this time of year. He's not a strong man, you know. He's always been a bit chesty. But he wanted to finish his survey. Dennis has always been interested in wildlife but particularly in birds. He has kept track of the garden birds for years. I didn't mind that: it's his interest and everyone needs an interest. He's written some beautiful poems about the birds, you know. But lately, he's got interested in tawny owls; and that's a quite different matter. He has a project. He is trying to make a map of all the hunting areas in the neighbourhood, including the ones they only visit occasionally. When it's finished, he's going to write a long article and submit it to a magazine.' Lucy dabbed her eyes with the handkerchief clenched in her fist. 'I don't know why he couldn't have chosen barn owls, because then he'd be near buildings. But no, it had to be the tawny ones, which live out in woods and cemeteries and deserted places. On Friday night he went out again. He promised it would be the very last time he'd need to do it.'

'And returned, you think, at three in the morning, Saturday morning?'

'Yes, that's it.' Lucy seemed grateful that Jess was following her account. 'Well, I was still cross, you know, so at breakfast I didn't ask him how he'd got on. But I could see he had picked up some sort of cold. He sat huddled over the fire, looking miserable, all Saturday morning, and didn't want any lunch. I persuaded him to have some soup. Then he got up and said he was going to the library, to look up something or other about the owls. Well, our library is run by volunteers now, you know. It's open on a Saturday until four o'clock, when it shuts until Tuesday. So, Dennis said, he had to go out before four that Saturday or he wouldn't be able to look up whatever it was until next Tuesday. I could see that made sense. I still didn't like him going out, not looking and acting the way he did. But he went and – and he didn't come back.'

Lucy broke down and sobbed.

A little later, fortified by tea, she was able to begin again. 'You will wonder why, when he didn't come back on Saturday night, I didn't contact the police at once. But I thought he'd gone off somewhere to track down an owl, or something to do with owls. I was so angry, really angry, because he'd told me that Friday night would be the last night he'd have to go out. I did try and find out where he was. I went to see Isolde.'

'Isolde Evans?' Was Isolde another owl fan? wondered Jess.

'She's on the rota of volunteers to run the library. I thought she might have been there – at the library – on Saturday afternoon. She's a supply teacher and can't always be available on weekdays. I had to go to her house, because obviously the library was closed by then. It was about eight o'clock yesterday evening when I went there. Isolde was working on her novel. I apologised for disturbing her because I know what it's like when someone comes in and breaks the flow of creativity. But she was very good about it. She confirmed that Dennis had called into the library and asked about books on wildlife. But he hadn't stayed very long, she said. She doesn't know if that means he found out what he was looking for – or if he didn't. But he left the library quite suddenly and, well, that's the last anyone appears to have seen of him.' Lucy had concluded her account and now sat, waiting for Jess's reply.

'He didn't speak to Isolde, or anyone else, before he left – or while he was at the library.' Jess was still trying to get her head around the idea that Dennis Claverton wandered around the landscape all night. Dennis, of all men . . . It seemed that there was almost as much coming and going in this corner of the county at night as there was by day. Unknown prowlers around Murchison's house at Lower Weston. Dennis on his owl patrol who knew where . . .

'Isolde says, she doesn't know if Dennis spoke to anyone because she was so busy. Everyone wants a book to read over the weekend, don't they? So she was rushed off her feet. She thinks he called out "Thank you!" or something like that, as he left, but she was helping someone. They have these machines now, you know. It's not like taking a book out in the old days. Now everyone's got a card and swipes it through a machine. The machine reads the book's details and logs it out. It's a sort of computer, I suppose. I can't get on with that sort of technology and nor can a lot of other people, so Isolde has to stand by and help them.'

'Does he have his car?'

'Yes, he's taken the car. Not that it's so very far to the library but, as I told you, he was definitely going down with something and not feeling too good. He wanted to be quick. He did offer to stop by the supermarket if I wanted anything, but I told him not to bother. He said he wouldn't be gone more than an hour.' Lucy's face crumpled. 'But he didn't come back at all.'

'You still didn't contact the police on Saturday night, last night?'

'No, because of the owls . . . I thought he'd rushed off looking for some, despite his promise. I thought he'd be back, as he had been the night before, in the early hours of this morning. But when I woke up, he wasn't there.' In a sudden burst of energy, Lucy shouted, making Jess jump in her seat. '*I hate those owls!*'

'We'll do everything we can to find him, Mrs Claverton, and if you remember anything else . . .'

'There is something else!' said Lucy.

There always is, thought Jess wearily. People never tell you everything. They either forget some detail, or decide that it's not worth recounting, or it's something they don't want you to know. 'Yes, Mrs Claverton?'

Lucy leaned forward and spoke in a conspiratorial whisper. 'Isolde told me that dreadful man, Higson, is going round talking to members of the writers' club. You know, Higson, the father of the girl who was found in the river?' She waited for Jess to nod. 'Isolde has already seen him. Luckily, she was with Jason when Higson turned up. He's terrifying, Isolde says.'

'He threatened them?' Jess asked sharply.

'I gather he didn't speak much to Isolde at all. He was more interested in Jason, because Jason knew his daughter. They were at school together. Jason told Isolde, after Higson had left, that he, I mean Jason, had dated Courtney for a while. But her father warned him off. He didn't actually make any threats, or I don't think so,' added Lucy. 'Isolde didn't really say that. He just looked frightening. Isolde was scared stiff and so glad she was with Jason.' Lucy gazed fearfully at Jess. 'You don't think the Higson man could have anything to do with Dennis's disappearance?'

Clearly this weekend was now completely written off. Jess might just as well give up and surrender what was left of it. She set off for Isolde's flat. She wouldn't have time to talk to Jason Twilling also today. But tomorrow she'd send Bennison to see him again. He was the first person Teddy Higson had gone to and they ought not to overlook Twilling, either.

Isolde was spending the day at home and washing her hair. To

Jess's surprise she opened the door wearing jeans, instead of one of her ethnic long skirts. A towel was wrapped round her head. Without her glasses, she blinked myopically at her visitor, before identifying her and inviting her in. Jess followed her up the un-carpeted stairs. They made less noise this time, because Isolde was not wearing boots but crocheted slippers, with a strap across the top of the arch. As footwear with jeans, they looked very odd.

'You don't mind waiting five minutes while I dry my hair, do you?' she asked earnestly, peering into Jess's face. 'Because otherwise it gets all tangled.'

So Jess sat and waited while Isolde combed her mermaid locks and wielded the hairdryer. The flat was marginally warmer today. Presumably this was because Isolde was home.

'Oh dear,' said Isolde, when Jess had explained the reason for her visit. 'Yes, Lucy came to ask if I'd seen him. But Dennis has still not come home? Whatever could have happened to him? He's a very quiet sort of man.'

Isolde had donned her glasses. She'd also added a patchwork waistcoat to her outfit and a necklace made of assorted buttons strung together. She must make nearly all her clothes herself, Jess realised. She was twisting a strand of hair around her forefinger and frowning.

'Poor Lucy must be going out of her mind with worry. I think I might go over there and sit with her for a bit.'

'That would be kind,' said Jess. 'I understand Dennis Claverton called in at the library on Saturday afternoon?'

'Yes, about a quarter past three. We close up at four on a Saturday because we are all volunteers and have other things to do.'

Isolde's account of Dennis's visit tallied with that Jess had heard from Lucy. 'I wish,' Isolde added, 'I'd paid more attention to him. But because it was nearing closing time, there was the usual last-minute rush and I just didn't . . . He didn't stay very long.'

Jess moved on to her other question. 'I understand Teddy Higson has been in touch?'

Isolde shuddered. 'Yes. He'd actually come to see Jason; but I was at Jason's house when he arrived. We'd all been warned he was seeking out the members of the writers' club, so I'd gone over to discuss it with Jason. I was so scared, you see. What could I do if Higson turned up here while was on my own? Then Higson turned up there! He spoke to both of us, so I hope he won't bother me again. He's an awful-looking man and just stares at you.'

'Did he threaten either you or Mr Twilling?'

Isolde struggled visibly with the instinct for dramatic embroidery, but heroically remained honest. 'No, he just looked, you know, so dangerous. We told him we were very sorry about his daughter; and that we'd tell him if we heard anything.'

'I hope,' said Jess, 'that you'll tell the police first.'

'Of course!' promised Isolde. 'But when someone like Higson is standing over you, in a tiny kitchen, you agree with everything he says, don't you?'

Jess had just left the house when her mobile phone rang. A glance at it told her it was Ian Carter.

'Just to let you know I've got back,' his voice said.

'Oh, right, good visit?' A cold wind was blowing around Jess where she stood in the street outside Isolde's home, discouraging any attempt to loiter in a long conversation.

'Eventful. How are things at your end? I'm sorry I took off like that. I hope nothing's happened while I've been away.'

'Well,' Jess informed him, 'Charlie Fallon, the old fellow who lives in Murchison's wood, has been attacked by someone prowling round Murchison's property and is in hospital, in a coma. That happened during the night, about one thirty, so in the very early hours of Saturday. And Dennis Claverton has gone missing. That happened on Saturday afternoon and there's been no sign of him yet. Oh, and it's possible the murder weapon is a saddler's awl. There's one missing from the antique tool collection on the walls of the Fisherman's Rest. We haven't found anything like that and I think it's wise to assume it's still in the murderer's possession.'

There was a silence then Carter said, 'Blast.'

'I'm annoyed, too,' Jess replied with heroic restraint.

'Where are you now, at home?'

'No, standing on a draughty corner outside Isolde Evans's flat. The last place Dennis was seen was at the local library on Saturday afternoon. Isolde was working there as a volunteer and spoke to him, that's how we know that much. After that, so far, no one has come forward with any more news of him. He didn't give any indication at the library as to what he intended to do next. But his wife thinks it has to do with owls. He's been conducting a survey of the owl population and wandering about the countryside.'

Carter muttered something inaudible, then asked, 'Where is Isolde's flat?'

She told him.

'That's not far from my place,' he said. 'Come over here and

I'll make you some tea or coffee or something. You can tell me all about it.'

Shortly afterwards, sitting in Carter's one comfortable armchair, Jess explained in greater detail everything that had been happening over the weekend.

Carter had grown gloomier as he listened. 'I shouldn't have gone off like that,' he muttered. 'I'm really sorry, Jess.'

'What for? You didn't know someone would attack the old man or that Dennis would decide to go walkabout. I still can't get round the image of Dennis prowling about the countryside, making notes at all hours of the day and night.'

'Night?' asked Carter sharply.

'Yes, he—' Jess broke off. 'He couldn't have been the one who was hanging around Murchison's place at night, could he?'

'He might not be the regular prowler,' Carter said slowly. 'But, on the other hand, there must be owls in that woodland. It's just possible, I suppose, that Dennis could have been there on Friday night and saw someone else hanging around.'

'Or even witnessed the attack,' Jess said soberly.

'If he saw the old man attacked, why didn't he come forward straight away, on Saturday morning?'

'He wasn't feeling well, Lucy says. She believes he was going down with a cold. He sat huddled over the fire. Then he muttered something about having to go to the library before it closed at four, to look up something about the owls. He took his car. Then he disappeared.'

Carter glanced at his watch. 'Have you got a number for her? Right, just check, would you, that there is still no news? Then, if there isn't, and I suspect there won't be, you and I will go over to Rosetta Gardens and have a word with Mr Higson – if he's at home.'

Lucy had confirmed that there was still no news of Dennis. 'But I've got company because dear Isolde is here. She's offered to stay the night because she doesn't have to go to work tomorrow. The school she was working at has broken up for Christmas. But I've told her, I'll be all right on my own overnight.'

Jess set out with Ian Carter for Rosetta Gardens. On the way he asked, 'What was that about an awl?'

'A saddler's awl, about twenty centimetres in length, or a little longer. Gordon Fleming tells me it has a wooden grip at one end. Used to make a hole in leather when stitching heavy harness.'

'And they had this dangerous thing on the wall, on display?' Carter asked incredulously.

'It was mounted in a locked glass-fronted case, together with other small items. The case is fixed securely to the wall. The pointed end had been driven into a cork. Gordon admits the display case lock wasn't a strong one, no real problem for a determined thief. A knife from the dining room could have forced it. The display case was in the little corridor leading from the main bar round to the toilets. That building is all twists and turns. The corridor runs off the bar, makes a left turn, and the facilities are at the far end. The case was on the wall out of direct sight from the bar. Anyone going to or coming from the toilets would pass it. Gordon can't say how long it's been missing. The chef happened to pass by and noticed the display case door was ajar. Then he saw the awl was gone.'

'They must have a daily cleaner? She didn't notice it, obviously.'

'I did ask about a cleaner,' Jess told him. 'Maggie Fallon – that's Amy's mother – comes in the mornings and mops the tiled floors, runs a vacuum over any carpets and generally tidies up the bar. She had not come the morning following the attack on her father-in-law, because she had gone to the hospital with the rest of the family. I don't suppose she even glances at the tools display on the walls.'

'You know, Jess,' Carter said slowly, 'something happened at that celebration meal the writers' club took with Neil Stewart, when the writing course finished. I don't know what, but that visit to the Fisherman's Rest pressed a button and led to Courtney's murder. I wish we could find that awl.'

'Could be in the river,' observed Jess. 'Murderers do try and get rid of the weapon. Although this one could be hidden quite easily, you know, stashed somewhere.'

'It would be safer if the awl were in the river. I, like you, suspect it might still be in the possession of the killer. We still don't know why Courtney was killed. Ah, here we are . . .'

They had reached Rosetta Gardens. It was now around nine in the evening and the area didn't look any better by darkness. Most of the residents were either indoors or had gone about their lawful, or unlawful, business. But luck favoured them, and Teddy Higson was home.

'What do you want?' he greeted them ungraciously, when he opened his door, can of lager in one hand.

'Just a quick word, Teddy,' said Carter.

'What about? You found the scum that killed my girl?'

'Not yet. Can we come in?'

'Make yerselves at home,' said Higson sarcastically, turning his back on them. 'You know your way about, dontcha? Been poking about in here while I was away.'

They'd followed him into the living room where the television was on full blast. They doubted Higson had been watching it because the programme was about baking cakes. He probably just liked the background noise. Carter didn't bother to ask; he just turned the set off.

Jess said, 'The flat was searched, with a warrant, to see if there was any clue to what happened to your daughter.'

Higson gestured towards them with the can. 'Helped yourselves, too, didn't you? Where's my old mother's clothes?'

'They'll be returned to you, Mr Higson. We also found a large number of cigarettes in sealed packets. There is good reason to believe them smuggled.'

'I don't know anything about them.' Higson's features contorted into a threatening scowl. 'You set Customs and Excise on to me, didn't you? A couple of 'em was here asking about them smokes. I told them, I don't know anything about it and you can't prove otherwise. I wasn't here when they was found. All I know is, when I went inside, there were no cigarettes here. I've been enjoying Her Majesty's hospitality. I ain't been making no trips to the Continent, and I don't know anyone who has. I'd like to know who dumped them here, and all. Someone taking advantage of my girl's good nature, I wouldn't be surprised. Them Excise fellers went away in the end, but it'll be marked down against me, I know how it goes. So, what do you two want now?'

Carter drew a deep breath. 'I'll make it quick, Teddy. Have you been harassing the members of the writers' club?'

'No,' said Higson. 'I ain't harassed no one. I went to see a couple of people. That bloke who owns the house where my girl was found – in the river at the bottom of his garden – I had a word with him.' He paused. 'I went to see where they found her and put some flowers, mark of respect. But he came out of his house wanting to know what I was doing, so I introduced myself and we had a bit of a chat. I didn't harass him.'

'You also went to see Jason Twilling,' Jess said.

Higson snorted. 'Twat.'

'But you went to see him?'

'Yes, he used to be friendly with my princess, when they were younger – at school, like. I thought he might have known something about her since then. But he didn't know nothing. He's a berk, that one, always was. Writes books. He had a bird there with him, and she was even soppier. A real nutcase, if you ask me. She was all dressed up like something outa history, long skirts and such – and she'd been cooking her boots in the oven.'

'Cooking *her boots*?'

'That's what I said. She'd got 'em wet, I suppose. It was raining cats and dogs that evening. She'd stuck them in the oven and they'd got singed, made a terrible stink. Anyway, she was another of them writers.'

'Isolde Evans?'

'That's it. Daft name for a daft person.'

'Anyone else had a visit from you?'

'Bloke with the side-whiskers and fancy pullovers, Posset.' Higson squinted at them. 'He knits the bleedin' things himself.'

'What about the Clavertons?'

Higson shook his head.

'Dennis Claverton is missing, Teddy,' Jess said quietly. 'If you have any ideas about that . . .'

Higson stared at her for a moment. 'No, I ain't. Can't your lot find him?'

'We will soon,' said Jess with a confidence she didn't feel. 'We'd appreciate it if you stayed away from Mrs Claverton, who is very distressed at the moment, and also stayed away from Mrs Porter and Mr and Mrs Blackwood.'

Higson drained the last of his can of lager. 'I can tell you something about that writers' club, as they call themselves.'

'Yes?' Carter and Jess spoke in unison.

'They're a bunch of loonies,' said Higson. 'Here, what you turn off my programme for? I was watching that.'

Chapter 20

Mike Lacey was on his way to visit an equine patient on Monday morning. It had stopped raining, thank goodness. They could do with a break. From the 4 x 4 he could see over the hedges and stone walls, across the fields to either side of the lane. Everywhere the ground was sodden and patched with pools of standing water. The whole terrain had become a giant sponge, so water-logged, he reckoned, the soil couldn't absorb any more.

The horse requiring Mike's attention belonged to Ginny Hargreaves; who lived with a resident housekeeper in a large, secluded house. Her husband, rarely seen, was a high-ranking civil servant of some kind. No one seemed to know what kind. He lived all week in a London flat and appeared at weekends – but not always then. Ginny herself was a moderately successful land-scape painter. Mike doubted she was doing much of that in the present inclement weather.

The stables, at the rear and side of the property, were reached by a turning, just wide enough to get a horsebox through. Approaching from this direction, Mike knew you reached the obscured opening before you got to the main entrance to the house, and you needed to keep your eyes open. The track, shielded on either side by trees and undergrowth, was labelled PRIVATE. NO ACCESS. But that didn't stop people occasionally turning in there.

For this reason, Mike slowed and negotiated the entry with care. It was as well he did, because no sooner had he rolled under the overhanging canopy of branches than he saw a figure running full pelt down the track towards him. He braked.

It was Ginny, long ash-blond hair flying, waving her arms and giving every sign of distress. She was dressed as usual in breeches and boots and muddy quilted gilet. But to Mike (who secretly admired her above all women), she looked as she always did – splendid. He let down the side window and leaned out. 'What's wrong?'

He hoped the horse had not collapsed. It was an elderly animal, wheezing a lot of late, and you never knew. Ginny was devoted to the old brute.

She came up alongside his door, panting, heart-stoppingly flushed, and breathless. She gripped the window rim. 'You've got to come . . .' she gasped.

'Major?' he asked. (That was the name of the horse.)

'No, not Major – he's no better but no worse. It's – you've got to come and see, Mike! It's awful, horrible!'

Mike climbed down from his vehicle with sinking spirits. He'd already had one deeply unpleasant experience recently with finding that kid floating in the river. He hoped it was to be nothing as bad as that.

It was to be worse. A car was parked at the side of the track, pulled in well under the trees. Ginny stood back, pointing, and allowed Mike to approach it on his own, which he did with great caution. He could see a dark outline in the driver's seat, slumped forward over the wheel.

'Oh no,' he muttered, 'not again.'

It could be, he told himself, that the driver had felt unwell, turned in here to get off the narrow road, and had a heart attack. These things happened. He stooped to peer in. The man collapsed over the wheel was dead, no doubt about that, but not from any heart attack. He'd been stabbed, in the neck, temple, even, it appeared, straight through the eardrum. The attack had been frenzied. Blood had seeped out from the multiple wounds; from the stab wound in the neck it must have gushed. Perhaps an artery had been severed. It had dried in gory clumps and trickles. This had happened some hours previously – possibly twenty-four or more.

He returned to Ginny and put his hands on her shoulders. She was still shaking. 'Take it easy,' he urged. 'Have you phoned the cops?'

'No . . .' She shook her head. 'Oh, Mike, who is he?'

'No idea. But listen, I'll phone the police and we'll wait here until they arrive. When did you last come down this track?'

'Well, actually, not for a couple of days. I haven't ridden Major out because the weather has been so foul and he's unfit, as you know. I've just led him round the yard or turned him out into the paddock between downpours. But the paddock's all soggy and not really the best place for him.'

'Yes, yes, but the cops will want to know exactly when was the last time you came down here? Before finding this – this car.'

'Oh,' Ginny made an effort to pull herself together and think coherently. 'Yes, it was Saturday lunchtime. There was no car here then. People do pull in, as you know, even though it says it's private. I walked down as far as the lane to see what the surface was like. The trees shield it from the rain and their roots have taken up a lot of the water so, as you see, the surface here is pretty good, considering. There was no one about, no car, no – anything.'

'Fine. You go back to the house and either have a hot drink, or a whisky or something. I'll wait here and when the law gets here, I'll come and fetch you.'

'Oh, Mike,' cried Ginny, throwing her arms round him, 'I am so glad you are here!'

Which almost, not quite but almost, made up for everything.

By time the forensic team had finished at the scene, statements had been taken from Ginny Hargreaves and Mike Lacey, and not only the body removed but also the car itself loaded on to a trailer and taken away for further examination, they were well into late afternoon. The crepuscular gloom that made winter days so short had already descended.

Ian Carter stood with Jess Campbell in the mortuary and gazed down at the pathetic, mutilated face and head.

'It's Dennis Claverton,' Jess said quietly. 'Poor chap. His wife will still have to be brought here to identify him officially. She'll go to pieces when she's given the dreadful news. Why on earth should anyone want to murder someone so inoffensive?'

'Inoffensive – but given to roaming round the countryside by night,' Carter reminded her. 'A dangerous thing to do.' He turned to Tom Palmer. 'Any idea when he died, Tom? I know you haven't carried out any examination. He was last seen in public on Saturday afternoon, a little before four o'clock, at the library in Weston St Ambrose.'

Tom frowned. 'Then I suggest he died on Saturday, probably not more than an hour or so after he was last seen. Rigor has had

276

time to establish itself, but also wear off – it's almost completely gone. Let's suppose, as a working hypothesis, that it spread through the body during Saturday night, lasted all Sunday, and passed off during Sunday night. That would bring us to this morning, early, when the body was discovered. Now, as you can see, the poor guy is on the way to being as limp as a haddock.' Tom raised one of Dennis's hands and it dangled pathetically at the wrist. He tucked it back under the sheet.

'So yes, at an educated guess, early Saturday evening could be time of death. Keep in mind I've not conducted any close examination and there are conditions that can affect progress. If the body has been in open countryside, in an unheated car, for at least forty-eight hours, that could affect rigor.'

'How about weapon?' Jess asked quietly.

'Similar to the last murder victim you brought me, the girl. A needle or skewer-shaped weapon.'

'How about a saddler's awl?'

Tom stared at her. 'I've never seen such a thing. But I've seen nautical tools that might cause damage like this, a marlinspike or a sailmaker's awl. If your saddler's tool is anything like that, yes, definitely a possibility.'

'I'll take a policewoman with me, and go and break the news to Lucy Claverton,' Jess said, as they left the mortuary. 'Someone will have to stay with Lucy tonight. Tracy Bennison might be a good choice.'

'Are you sure? Jason Twilling collapsed when she interviewed him!'

'That was quite different!' Jess told him. 'I'm the one who will have to break the news. Bennison is sympathetic and sensible.

She's also bright. Apart from any state of shock Lucy will be in, there is the possibility that Dennis did say or do something that would give us a clue to what's happened. His wife may have temporarily forgotten it. But she could remember at any time. The killer can't risk that and Lucy alone in that house is too vulnerable. She'll require round-the-clock protection. Bennison has judo as a hobby.'

'I knew he wasn't coming home,' Lucy said. 'After a bit, I just knew. I felt Dennis was not just a missing person – he'd gone, gone somewhere out of this world. I've told myself that I have to accept that, awful though it is.' She sat by the gas fire, hunched, and hands clasped. 'You'll think it peculiar of me, but I feel that Dennis wants to speak to me, but he can't. There's a wall between us.' She looked up. 'But there won't always be. We'll meet again one day, but it won't be in this life.'

Jess had brought Tracy Bennison with her as planned. Having made them all tea in Lucy's kitchen and brought it in, Bennison now sat on the other side of the room watching sympathetically. At Lucy's last words she raised a hand and surreptitiously rubbed it across her eyes.

Jess, also deeply moved, looked around her. It seemed that the little sitting room she remembered well from her previous visit was suffering its own bereavement and shock. There was Dennis's chair by the hearth, with a dent in the seat, but in which he would never sit again. His reference books and magazines on birdlife were neatly stacked on a little table alongside it. On her way into the room she had passed Dennis's jacket hanging on a hook in the hall. On a brief foray into the kitchen to have a word with Bennison during operation tea, she'd seen a mug hanging on the mug-tree, decorated with an owl and with 'Dennis' written on it.

'I realised from the first that something terrible had happened to him,' Lucy went on. 'Dennis would not have gone off like that, not for hours and hours, days . . . I know I said he might have gone owl hunting on Saturday night, but he would still have come home before morning.' She raised her white, tear-streaked face to gaze earnestly at Jess. 'Why would anyone do something so wicked? Dennis never hurt anyone. He couldn't.'

'I don't know, Lucy,' Jess said quietly. After a pause, she went on, 'There is the question of official identification, but that can wait until tomorrow.'

Lucy swayed and both Jess and DC Bennison started forward. But Lucy steadied and Jess signalled to Bennison to sit down again. Jess had had rotten jobs like this before. Very often it was the outwardly strong personalities who buckled under the shock. Apparently fragile little women, like Lucy Claverton, often showed astonishing reserves of strength. Initially, she had collapsed in a heap. A doctor had been called and examined her; but she wouldn't hear of going into hospital for observation. The doctor had left something to help her sleep that night.

'I know how difficult it must be to think clearly at the moment, Lucy,' Jess told her. 'But if you could run through in your mind everything that happened on Saturday, and has happened since Saturday.'

'I think about nothing but that Saturday,' said Lucy simply. 'And nothing has happened since – until now. Isolde came over and sat with me on Saturday evening but I didn't want her to stay the night. She meant to be kind, but kept talking, you know . . . The only things we have in common are books, and writing, so that's what she talked about until I thought I'd go mad. If she'd stayed any longer I'd have shouted at her. I didn't want to do that, so I sent her off home about half past nine in the evening.

'She came back on Sunday and made lunch for us both. We're both vegetarian, so it was easy for her. I didn't want to eat it, but she insisted. This morning she came back again—'

Lucy broke off and Jess took her hand. Lucy drew a deep breath. 'To think poor darling Dennis was lying dead all that time . . . Isolde said I mustn't lose hope. But I knew there was none. I didn't want to upset Isolde, so I pretended to go along with it, stay hopeful, I mean. Isolde said I should carry on as usual because routine would be good for me.'

'There is something in that,' Jess told her.

'Well, I tried, more to please Isolde than help myself. She asked what we usually did on Monday mornings and I said . . .'

This time the silence lasted longer and Jess waited patiently.

'I said, odd though it might seem to some people, Dennis and I usually went to that new little supermarket we've got on Monday morning. You see, if you go early, before they put out all the fresh stuff on the shelves, you can get some very good bargains on fruit and vegetables left unsold over the weekend. There's nothing wrong with them, only they've gone over their date. It's quiet, too, on a Monday morning, not busy like Friday and Saturday. So Isolde said we'd go because that was my routine.

'She had her little car and we went in that. I didn't buy much. I just picked up things at random, paid and stuffed everything in a carrier bag. Denise Garley wasn't on the till, thank goodness. She'd have asked where Dennis was and, you know, if Denise Garley finds out anything, then the whole of Weston St Ambrose knows inside a couple of hours. She is an awful gossip.

'Then we came back here and had some coffee and a sandwich, and I managed to get Isolde to go home. She'd started talking again, offering all sorts of possible explanations. She kept asking if Dennis had given any indication of being under stress, as she put it. She said that people who get very stressed have been known to wander off – suffer from amnesia, you know. Well, I suppose that can happen but I don't think Dennis had been stressed, just going down with a cold. Anyway, I was the one who was stressed! I almost pushed poor Isolde out of the door. I feel so mean talking about rejecting her help like that, but I wanted to be on my own.'

'I understand,' Jess sympathised.

Lucy looked up at her with red-rimmed eyes. 'And then you came,' she said simply. 'I knew, when I saw the cars draw up outside and that you had someone with you, that you had brought bad news, the worst news.'

'Is there anyone, a family member perhaps, you could go and stay with for a little while?' Jess asked.

'No, nobody. My sister lives in Australia. Dennis was never close to his brother and anyway, last year his brother died. He was quite a bit older than Dennis and lived in Spain. He had a Spanish wife and his children were born there. We'd never even met them. We don't have children. It sounds a hard thing to say, but we didn't really miss not having children. I don't mean we wouldn't have loved any children we'd had dearly. But we didn't have them and we managed very well without them. We had each other. Now I don't have Dennis, so I don't have anything. But I tell myself, I was very fortunate to have been so happy all these years.'

Jess hesitated before she said, 'Don't be afraid to let yourself grieve, Lucy.'

'I'm in shock, aren't I? I know I am. I feel cold and sort of numb. I know I'm rambling on to you. I wish I could think more clearly, think of something to help you catch – catch whoever did this. But really,' Lucy went on, 'I haven't known quite what I've been doing these last couple of days. I've hardly slept. I've been in a sort of haze. When I got into Isolde's car this morning, after we'd been to the supermarket, I put my carrier of vegetables and fruit down by my feet. Then I somehow kicked it and they all spilled out, so I had to scrabble about and put everything back in. So clumsy of me.'

'Your mind was on Dennis, Lucy,' Jess told her. 'Routine can be a support, but, well, perhaps going shopping wasn't the best idea.'

'I should get in touch with Isolde,' Lucy was saying now. 'I must tell her what's happened. I don't know how I'll be able to find the words.'

'I can do that,' Jess said. 'I'll be talking to her anyway.'

Lucy blinked. 'Why? Oh, because she saw Dennis on Saturday afternoon. I've already asked her if he said anything at all, when he was at the library, about where he was going next. Isolde was really upset but couldn't tell me a thing. She'd spoken very briefly to him about some wildlife book he wanted; and then he left. She supposed he was going back home, coming here, that is. And he should have been coming straight back here, shouldn't he? Why on earth he should be out there – where he was found . . .'

'We'll find out, Lucy,' Jess soothed her.

'Well, if you speak to dear Isolde please could you find some way of telling her I'm all right here and don't need her with me. It sounds so ungracious, but—'

Jess interrupted. 'DC Bennison will stay here with you, so I'll tell Isolde it's not necessary.'

Lucy looked at her gratefully, then suddenly said, 'Would you tell her, too, that I've got something of hers? So that she won't be looking everywhere for it.'

'I'll tell her that, if you like,' said Jess. 'What is it?'

Lucy looked vaguely round the room and then pointed at a sideboard. 'Some jewellery. It's in the top right-hand drawer, that's where I put it. It was in my plastic carrier bag when I got home and unpacked, lying in there among all the vegetables. When I spilt the contents of the bag in the car it must have been under the seat and when I scrabbled around for odd bits of veg, I scooped it up and pushed it into the bag. But I didn't find it until Isolde had left here, and I unpacked what I'd bought.'

Jess stood up and walked over to the sideboard. 'This drawer?' She pulled it open and suppressed a gasp. Then she asked, 'Have you got a little paper bag anywhere, Lucy?'

DC Bennison followed Jess to the front door. On the step Jess paused, the paper bag gripped in her hand, and said quietly. 'Let no one in, Tracy. It doesn't matter who it is. If the telephone rings, answer it yourself. Tell any inquirer that Mrs Claverton can't come to the phone. Persuade Mrs Claverton to take those pills the doctor left and go to bed.'

'Yes, ma'am.' Bennison, clearly eaten up with curiosity, eyed the paper bag. 'Because of that? Because of what was in that drawer?'

Jess looked down at the bag. 'Because of this. Can't tell you now. I have to show Superintendent Carter. Remember, let no one in!'

Chapter 21

'I slid the bag over it, so that I didn't touch it,' Jess said, 'but it's definitely the pair to the one Courtney was still wearing when she was taken from the river.'

They were gazing down at the gold hoop earring that had been lying in the drawer where Lucy Claverton had put it ready to return to Isolde Evans. As soon as she had left Lucy's home, Jess had phoned Carter and arranged to meet in the incident room. Briefly she had narrated what had happened when she'd informed Lucy of her husband's death – and everything Lucy had told her. Now the earring lay between them on the desk, gleaming in the electric light.

'Lucy doesn't realise the significance of it,' Jess said. 'Bennison is with her and won't leave her tonight. I've impressed on Bennison that no one at all is to be admitted to the house, nor is Lucy to take any phone calls. I hope Lucy has taken the doctor's sleeping pills.'

'Well, we know this earring didn't come off in the river,' Carter said quietly. 'We now have to face the possibility – crazy though it seems – that it came off while Isolde was manhandling Courtney – dying or dead – into her car. Murchison will be able to confirm these are the earrings, or identical to the earrings, he bought for Courtney. Good grief: *Isolde Evans*? Why on earth . . .'

285

'Unrequited passion,' said Jess bleakly. 'Isolde is in love with Graeme Murchison. That's how she would see it. We might call it an unhealthy obsession but if you'd heard her talk about great love affairs, as I have, she really believes that two people can be meant for one another and no one should come between them. Courtney came between Isolde and her soul mate – as she thinks – Murchison.'

'So, are we to believe she's been stalking him?' Carter asked, still gazing down at the earring. 'She's been driving out to his house and parking up in the lane, just sitting there, communing with him in her mind?'

'And while she was doing that, perhaps Dennis saw her? He's been driving round the countryside on his owl survey.' Jess uttered a snort of disgust. 'And ever since she killed him, Isolde's been hanging around poor Lucy, ostensibly to help and console, but really because she's wanted to keep Lucy under her eye. She wanted to know if and when we found Dennis's body. Lucy says Isolde kept talking, although it must have been clear that making conversation was the last thing Lucy wanted to do. For my money, Isolde has been trying to find out if Dennis said anything, gave any clue to his wife that Lucy might have forgotten or thought trivial – but, once Dennis was known to have died, might suddenly spring to Lucy's mind.'

Carter slipped the earring into an evidence bag. 'This will have to go over to forensics first thing in the morning. More urgently, we've got to warn Murchison and find Isolde! We'll try her home address first.'

But neither of these two things proved straightforward. Murchison was not answering the phone. When they arrived at Isolde's address, her car was missing from its usual parking spot in the street. The people living in the ground-floor flat were at home, however.

'I saw her drive off about an hour ago,' said a thin-faced young woman with hair dragged back and secured into a ponytail. She had a metal stud through her lower lip. 'I've no idea where she's gone or when she'll be back, sorry. She does sort of, you know, come and go. She's a funny old stick – well, not really old. I don't suppose she'd be more than thirty, but she's not like anyone else I know. She keeps really peculiar hours. I mean, it's not like she's the sort to go partying. She dresses in odd bits of clothes and looks a real weirdo. Doesn't she, Gary?'

Her partner grinned. He had studs not only in his lips, but his eyebrows, ears and nose. 'I reckon she's got a secret lover somewhere. That's right, in't it, Kim?'

'You ought not to say things like that, Gary! You don't know!' Kim reproved him.

'So where does she go in the middle of the night?' he defended himself. To Carter and Jess, he said, 'She works all over the county, supply teaching. So some days she doesn't work at all. Even when she does, she comes home in the afternoon, and then, much later, about eleven, eleven thirty, she goes out again, takes the car. She often comes back about two in the morning or even later. She can't sleep much.'

'She writes novels,' Kim told them. 'She belongs to a writers' club they've got in Weston St Ambrose. I've never read any of them, her books. I'd really love to, although I'm not much of a reader usually. One evening a week she goes and meets up with these other people who are writers. Can you imagine it? All of them writing books? Perhaps, when she goes out at night, she's doing some research or something – stop laughing, Gary! It's the police asking so it must be serious.'

'Yeah,' said Gary, 'what's old Izzy done?'

'We just want a word with her,' said Jess, to their clear disappointment.

'What do we do now?' she asked Carter when they'd left.

'We keep going until we find her. We alert all cars to look out for a silver smart car, woman driver. She's out there, armed with that awl, and if she's killed two people, well, she's got nothing to lose! If she has returned to the Claverton house since you left, she'll have realised a policewoman is still there. So, she'll know Dennis has been found and his wife told of his death. She won't have hung around. Where else might she go?'

'I'm pretty sure,' Jess said firmly, 'that she's gone to Lower Weston. It's after dark and that's where she's been going regularly at night. It's her pattern. It's what she'll do.'

'Just remember,' Carter growled, 'if we're right, she may have lost any grip on reason. We have to find Murchison.'

As they left Weston St Ambrose the all-too-familiar pattern of raindrops hit the windscreen and soon the wipers had to work hard to clear the rivulets of water running across the windscreen. Only one other vehicle passed them, travelling in the opposite direction.

'Filthy night,' muttered Carter. 'If Isolde set out before us, she's already there. What's she going to do? Sit in her car, with the rain beating on the roof, and do nothing? She'll try and get into the house.'

But there was no response at the Old Manor, and no sign of

Isolde's car. The gates were locked, the house was dark, and the dogs barked without attracting anyone's attention.

'He's not here,' said Carter, shaking the gates in frustration. 'And neither is she, from the look of it.'

'How about the Fisherman's Rest? Murchison could have gone over there to eat.'

'It's Monday and they don't do food, remember?'

'He owns the place. I'm sure they'll find him a sandwich,' Jess argued.

During this time, Graeme Murchison had been at the Fisherman's Rest, but not in search of a sandwich. An hour earlier, Gordon Fleming had phoned him.

'The water's got into the bar! You'd better come and take a look, Graeme. The whole bloody place is flooded out. I'm trying to take stuff upstairs. Harry Fallon is here helping and a couple of the regulars have turned up and pitched in, but we've got no chance of moving any more than we've shifted already.'

Murchison pulled on a waterproof and jumped into his 4 x 4. They had been expecting this and he knew that Gordon had moved a lot of stock upstairs over the last few days. He could load up and bring some more back to his house. But from what Gordon had said the fact was that they would be out of business for the foreseeable future. They had after all been expecting it. The flooded river had been nudging at the back door for several days.

It was dark; the moon was lost behind clouds, and the rain beating down incessantly. He turned into the car park of the pub and jumped out, landing in a puddle. The water was spreading over this area, too. The wind had got up and it was freezing cold. He wondered if the rain would turn to snow before Christmas. The pub was in darkness. The electricity must have failed or been switched off for safety. Someone had hung up a storm lantern by the main entrance, as a substitute, to help anyone trying to find his way around outside. It swung wildly to and fro, like the old wreckers' lantern, luring ships on to the rocks.

As Gordon had told him over the phone, Murchison found there were helping hands already there. When he arrived at the door, Harry Fallon and one of the regulars came staggering out, carrying the coffee machine that usually stood on the bar.

'You got no chance,' gasped Harry by way of greeting. 'You'll have to write it all off. Reckon the insurance'll pay up?'

Murchison made his way cautiously inside. Gordon's pale oval face loomed out of the gloom, splashing towards him through the lake that had formerly been the main restaurant area. 'Where's the rest of the stock?' Murchison demanded.

'Mostly upstairs,' his manager panted. 'I started moving that out days ago, everything bottled, that is. Anything in the cellar is lost. Chef and his assistant are here. They're trying to rescue pots and pans from the kitchen, and any equipment they can. But they've only got a couple of handheld torches. Both of them have already fallen over and got soaked.'

A loud crash from the direction of the kitchen, followed by colourful profanity, suggested either Chef or his assistant had taken another unwished-for bath.

Murchison stumbled and, feeling his way towards the kitchen, cannoned into a body. Someone swore. Torchlight played over him and he recognised the torch's holder as the chef.

'Leave it all!' Murchison ordered. 'We'll have to wait until morning.'

'Can't leave knives and things!' argued the chef. 'Anyway, my set is worth a lot of money.'

'Well, get them out and anything like that, but someone's going to get injured if you carry on trying to move stuff in the dark.' Another figure, identifiable from its repeated cries of distress as the sous-chef, struggled towards them, carrying a rattling cardboard box, apparently full of miscellaneous utensils.

'Give that to me!' Murchison ordered, taking it out of his arms. 'Thanks for all your efforts, but just leave it for now. Come back in the morning. With luck, we'll have got a pump rigged up by then and can clear some of the water out.'

'Not if the river keeps pouring it back in,' opined the chef.

Murchison, with the box in his arms, made his way back through the building and out into the car park. He knew that chefs were attached to specific tools of their profession, and carried their personal set of knives around with them from job to job. He ought not to be surprised at this chef's insistence on rescuing all this stuff. He carried the box to his Range Rover and loaded it up. He'd store it at the Old Manor. There was plenty of room there.

He started back across the rain- and windswept car park towards the building, but before he reached it a voice stopped him in his tracks.

'Graeme!' it called, high-pitched and with a kind of desperate edge to it.

It was a woman's voice. That was the first shock. He'd seen no women at the pub since his arrival. Nor could he see where exactly the voice had come from.

'Graeme!' it called again, more desperately.

His first thought was that this was someone in trouble and he tried to locate the spot. 'Where are you?' he shouted.

'Over here!' The wind caught the words and whirled them away.

It seemed to him, although he still couldn't be sure, the woman in distress – whoever she was – was over there by the gate that, in normal times, gave access to the garden and children's play area. There was a tall hedge between the garden and the car park, and the owner of the voice must be standing right there by it, indistinguishable from it in the gloom.

'Who is it?' he called sharply.

'It's me, Graeme,' the voice replied, again half carried away by the wind so that it seemed to float off into the darkness and rain.

Something shimmered and moved. For a split second the moon edged out from the cloud cover and he could distinguish a figure with long hair tossing in the wind. It raised a long thin white arm and beckoned to him. Murchison felt an atavistic moment of pure panic. He gasped, 'Courtney?'

Of course, he knew it wasn't, couldn't be, Courtney. Courtney was cold in a mortuary drawer. But the voice had hardly sounded human, more like that of some tormented soul.

'*No!*'

The voice had lost its ethereal quality. It was hard and angry now, almost a shout. 'She's *gone!*'

Something moved again in the murk and driving rain, coming towards him, looming ever larger. As it did it became more distinctly human, tall and thin. But he still couldn't identify her.

'Who are you?' he demanded. 'What on earth are you doing there? What do you want?'

'It's Isolde, Graeme,' said the woman. 'Isolde Evans.' The note of entreaty was back in her voice. 'You know me, Graeme.'

For a moment he couldn't put a face and the name together. But it was such an unusual name that he knew he ought to recognise the owner of it. The writers' course at the college! There had been a woman called Isolde on that. She was one of the writers' club. She'd been one of the party who'd eaten at the Fisherman's Rest after the last lecture. He recalled a tall, thin female wrapped in strange garments. She wrote, he was fairly sure, romantic fiction. At that moment a fresh gust of rain and wind caused the storm lantern to rock violently and it threw a ray of light across her. Yes, it was the same woman, not clad like a creature from the *Morte d'Arthur* this time, but in jeans and some sort of jacket. Her hair, which he'd previously only seen worn in a long plait, hung loose and wet locks whirled in the wind around her head like the snakes around the Medusa's.

'What do you want?' he demanded, trying not to sound as appalled as he felt. 'Look, if you've come to help, I appreciate it, but you can't. Just go on home. We're locking the place up and waiting until morning.'

'But I *can* help you, Graeme,' the woman, Isolde, persisted. 'I can help you in so many ways. I'll look after you and I can make you happy. You don't have to be alone. I knew, when I met you on the writing course, that destiny had brought us together. It's meant to be, can't you see?'

Murchison was so taken aback he was momentarily bereft of speech and found even processing what she'd said difficult. The situation was crazy. They were standing here in a deserted car park, in the dark and driving rain, he was trying to cope with an emergency at the flooded pub . . . and this woman was babbling gibberish. She hadn't finished.

'Courtney's gone now.' The speaker was now sounding eminently reasonable, as if explaining something to someone who was slow to get the point. 'She's not in the way any longer, don't you see? She tricked you, Graeme. She stopped you making the right decision. She came between *us*.'

'What the hell are you talking about?' he demanded roughly. 'Look, I'm busy here. Whoever you are, Isolde, or whatever, just go home, can't you?'

'We're meant to be together, Graeme. Can't you see it?' The voice still pleaded but differently. An obstinate note had entered it.

It was then, in a spark of realisation, the awful truth swept over Murchison. It was a truth colder than any winter winds or driving rain. He stood in this deserted car park with a murderer.

'You killed little Courtney!' he gasped. The horror of it almost froze his mind. He wanted to shout at her, 'You murdering bitch! She was only a kid – she was harmless!' But the words stuck in his throat. Then the sheer craziness of the situation suddenly became a threat. Danger crackled in the air, making him painfully aware how vulnerable he was. This mad creature wouldn't listen to reason. She was clearly deluded, totally off her trolley. Any move he made might provoke her to do something, he had no idea what, but something he'd rather she didn't do. She might – in her delusion – come running to him and throw her arms round his neck. Heaven forbid!

'She wouldn't leave you alone, Graeme,' Isolde said, still with a chilling reasonableness. 'Such a silly little tart, but she was putting you in danger. She didn't tell you about her father. He's very dangerous man. I don't blame you, Graeme, for being attracted to her. She made herself so obvious, so available. She was greedy and wanted you to buy her things. She never *cared* about you. She misled you. But she's gone now.' The speaker's tone brightened. 'I got rid of her. Now we can be together.'

In his shock, anger and confusion, he made a near-fatal error. 'You can't really think I'd want *you*! Even if Courtney hadn't been around, I would never have looked at you!' he shouted. 'Good Lord, woman, you're demented!'

She let out a high-pitched, eardrum-assaulting scream and, still howling like a banshee, leaped towards him.

Murchison swung a wild punch at her but she dodged it. He turned and ran towards his vehicle but, before he reached it, she was on him like a wild animal pulling down its prey. Her full weight thudded into his spine and he fell forward into the dirt and puddles. She gripped him with her hands and legs and he couldn't shake her free. And she was still screeching, right into his ear. It made his head ring and totally disorientated him. Then one of her hands loosened from his shoulder and for a second he thought he was succeeding in shaking her off. But she had removed her hand because she needed it for something else.

Her arm swept down, right by his head, and he felt a stinging pain starting at his cheekbone and reaching down to his jaw. He knew he'd been attacked with some weapon, perhaps the same weapon that had killed Courtney.

He tried to roll over and throw her off him in that way. But the arm swept past his face again. By rolling, he'd caused her to miss her target, but he hadn't got rid of her. She still clung like a limpet. If he could stand up . . . But though he got to his knees, it was only to plunge forward again with that dreadful weight still on his back and that maddened scream in his ears. Could no one in the pub hear it? Surely, someone must hear it.

Murchison braced himself for another sweep of her arm and the weapon she held in her hand. But, unexpectedly, the weight on his back was dragged away, jerked backwards. She yelled again, but this time in alarm. Free of her for a blessed moment, he scrabbled away on all fours, before turning and managing at last to get halfway to his feet, wheezing and struggling to control his breath. Moisture ran down his face and trickled into his open mouth. The salty taste stung his tongue and he knew that much of it was blood. She'd slashed his face, the crazy bitch!

Still crouched like Quasimodo, he tried to wipe his injured cheek and peer into the gloom and crazy world in which he found himself. She was still there, screaming and squealing, but she couldn't reach him. Rescue had come in a form as strange as that in which danger had arrived. Murchison now knew he was in a nightmare, imprisoned in some fantastic mediaeval legend, full of giants and witches. An unidentifiable monstrous figure, large and solid, held his attacker in its grip. Both its great arms were wrapped round her body. She screeched and wriggled, kicking out in vain as she tried to free herself.

The newcomer spoke, his voice coarse and low-pitched, as an ogre might be expected to sound.

'No, you don't!' he grated. 'I got you. You killed my princess!

But I promised her I'd get you – and now I *have* got you! You're going to pay for what you did!'

From his position on the ground, the winded Murchison heard the words and realised the identity of his rescuer. He croaked, 'No!' He threw out his arm and struggled to stand upright.

As he did he was dimly aware of new arrivals. A car had turned into the car park. Its doors slammed. Feet came pounding towards them. He called out to whoever was running past him, 'Help me!' Another voice, dimly identifiable as belonging to that police super-intendent, replied, but not addressing him.

'All right, Teddy!' said Carter crisply. 'Leave it to us!'

Chapter 22

Jess sat facing Isolde Evans. It was a dried-out Isolde in different clothes, but different in other ways, too. She looked older and sullen. The solicitor seated beside her didn't look any more cheerful.

'He doesn't love me,' Isolde said to Jess in a small, tight voice that seemed to issue as from a long way away.

'No,' Jess agreed.

'But he might have done,' Isolde went on, 'if that girl hadn't come between us. He never got the chance. It was all that girl's fault.' She reached up and began to twist a long strand of hair round her finger in the way Jess recognised was a habit.

'You can't force someone to love you, Isolde,' Jess said gently. 'Even if there had been no Courtney, things still might not have worked out for you and Graeme Murchison. Some things just aren't the way we would like them to be.'

Isolde's large pale eyes rested on Jess's face. 'You really don't understand, do you?'

Murchison's voice echoed in Jess's head. *You don't understand . . .*

Aloud she said briskly to Isolde, 'Explain to me, then.'

'I know about it, you see,' began Isolde earnestly. She placed her folded hands on the table. In Jess's brain an image formed of Isolde before a class of primary school pupils, about to tell them a story.

'I learned all about that when I was a child,' Isolde was saying. 'My father and mother were both members of a local amateur operatic society. They loved music and theatre. That's why I'm called Isolde. I'm sure they would have had a long and happy marriage, but my grandmother disapproved of my father. I don't know why. She was a very strong-minded woman and she hadn't wanted my mother to marry him. After they married, she still wouldn't accept him. She interfered all the time. I heard my parents arguing about it. I think that, really, my mother was afraid of my grandmother.

'Anyhow, when I was just five, my father left our house. He came to say goodbye to me. He said, "I'm going away for a bit, Izzy." I thought he must have been going somewhere nice, perhaps to the theatre. They used to take me to dress rehearsals of their amateur productions. I loved that, the costumes, everything . . . But when I begged, "Take me!" he just shook his head. He kissed me and left. I never saw him again.

'My mother and I went to live with my grandmother and things got worse. In the end, my mother got the offer of a very good job in London, so she left me with my grandmother and moved there. She never came back. Eventually she moved up to Scotland, where she married again. She sent me a birthday card every year until my sixteenth birthday, then she stopped. I suppose she thought I didn't need birthday cards any longer.'

Not physical neglect or abuse, thought Jess, but unforgivable neglect, all the same, in the form of emotional coldness. 'How about your father? Did you have any contact with him, after he left?'

Isolde shook her head. 'None at all. I understood, right from five years old, that they didn't love me. Perhaps they never had. I was a sort of theatrical prop, you know, for a stage set of their marriage; and when the marriage was over, the curtains came down and the props weren't needed any longer. But I knew they might have loved me eventually, if it hadn't been for my grandmother. It's like I told you. People interfere.'

'Did you continue to live with your grandmother?'

'Oh, yes. She liked to tell people how she had "given me a home". That didn't stop her saying to me, "You can't stay here for ever, Isolde. You must make your own way in life. I think teaching would be a very suitable occupation for a young woman like you." So, I went to teacher training college and here I am.'

Listening to Isolde recounting this sad story with a kind of clinical detachment, Jess understood that Isolde had learned over the years to armour herself against the pain a loveless upbringing had inflicted on a growing child. Jess wished she knew how to reply, but found words failed her. She felt a helpless anger directed at those three selfish people who had let a little girl grow up to womanhood with no idea of any loving relationship except that read of in books or seen acted out on stage or film. A girl whom no one loved; but who had constantly told herself that somewhere, out there, was the man who would love and cherish her, make up for all the absence of warmth and closeness. Tragically, she had thought she'd found him.

In the end, failing to find the words she needed, Jess decided it was best to move the interview on. 'How did you find out, Isolde, about Graeme Murchison and Courtney Higson?'

Isolde had been sitting patiently, seemingly absorbed in her own thoughts. She looked up and blinked. 'I suspected that things were not working out because someone was interfering,' she told Jess. She leaned forward again earnestly. 'I knew there must be someone coming between us, shielding Graeme from what should be so obvious to him. I tried to let Graeme see that I – well, that I was *there*! But it was as if I was invisible.' Her voice trailed away almost to be inaudible. 'Invisible, just as I was when I was five . . .'

Isolde gave herself a shake and sat up straight, to continue clearly, 'That night we all went to the Fisherman's Rest for a meal, after the last lecture Neil gave us on that writing course? Well, that was the night I realised the problem was Courtney. Of course, I didn't know her name then, or not her whole name. I heard someone at the table, I think it was Peter Posset, call her Courtney. Then I saw how she behaved, flirting with all the men there.'

Isolde paused and added in a harsher voice, 'And I saw how all the men liked her. They all watched her, all the time, and she knew it. There was just one who didn't like her and that was Jaz – Jason Twilling. He told me later he'd been at school with her and dated her – but her father had chased him off. Besides Jaz, there was only one man there, apart from the barman and Peter Posset, who didn't watch her; and that was Graeme. He was so careful *not* to watch her: that was what gave me the clue. It wasn't just that he didn't like girls, you know, like Peter. It was different. I caught her giving him glances, sort of laughing and secret – as if she wanted to share some joke with him. But he just sat there silent, eating or listening to the others, pretending he couldn't see how she looked at him. It was such a – *such a farce!*' Isolde suddenly shouted out the last words and everyone in the room started.

'Yet she flirted with all the men, you said.' Jess grasped back control of the interview.

'That made it worse. She didn't even really care for Graeme!' Isolde's voice rose again, this time to a desperate wail that echoed off the walls of the interview room.

'Did you take the awl from the display case in the corridor leading to the toilets that same night?'

The solicitor, now clearly seriously concerned about his client's behaviour, advised her to stay calm and take care in her answer.

But Isolde had already looked up in alarm and blurted, 'How do you know I took it?'

The solicitor looked even more as if he wished he'd chosen some other profession.

'We have it. You held it in your hand when you attacked Graeme Murchison after he refused your advances. Your finger-prints are on it. The landlord of the Fisherman's Rest has identified it. Did you take it that night?'

'The case wasn't properly locked,' said Isolde sullenly. 'I didn't break the lock. It was already broken, loose. I was – I was very angry. The anger was all . . .' She waved her hand. 'It was all bottled up in me, seeing Courtney, seeing – oh, I just wanted to do something! I didn't plan to kill her then. I didn't take the awl with that intention, not consciously, you know. But I saw the case was unlocked and I simply reached in and took the thing, the awl or whatever you call it. There was a little label in the case saying it was a saddler's tool. Anyway, I put it in my bag and – that was that.

'I wanted to be sure. So I began to watch his house. I would sit in my car and know that Graeme was nearby.' Her voice had gained a wistful quality. 'I used to imagine I was sitting indoors with him, before the fire. That we were holding hands and talking and . . . then we'd go upstairs.' She looked at Jess. 'Do you understand now?'

'Not altogether,' Jess admitted.

'Oh,' said Isolde with a shrug. 'If you don't, you don't, I suppose. Well, sure enough, one evening I saw that girl go into the grounds through a little door in the wall at the back of the property – and that proved me right! But even before then, I'd seen them together. Not around Weston St Ambrose; they were too careful for that. But I saw them one day together at a craft fair. He bought her something off a stall, a box of some sort. I saw them another time, at the cinema in Cheltenham. I realised then how dangerous she was. Then it got worse.'

'How?' prompted Jess, as Isolde fell silent for several minutes.

'I work part time at the library in Weston, you know,' Isolde said. 'People come to the library for books, of course, but they come to chat, as well. It's a nuisance but they do. They stand behind the shelves, the stacks, and think no one hears them. But I could hear them from the desk. Two women were chatting – they thought they were whispering but honestly, that sort of whisper carries right across a room. By then, I knew her name was Courtney Higson. And I heard it, the name Higson! So then I really listened. One of them said Teddy Higson was going to come out of prison before long. She said she knew that, because she lived on the Rosetta Gardens estate. They started talking about how she wanted the council to rehouse her but it was so difficult because she didn't have children and oh, they went on for several minutes. Eventually, she said, well, it was bad enough living at

Rosetta Gardens without Teddy Higson turning up again before too long. She'd never had trouble with him, but everyone knew how violent he could be. No one had ever found out what happened to his wife. He was bound to return to the estate because he still had a flat there and his daughter, Courtney, lived in it.'

Isolde looked up at Jess in triumph. 'So I knew it was the same one! That girl was even more dangerous than poor Graeme suspected. She had a very violent father, who was in prison, but would be coming out soon. He'd be coming back to Rosetta Gardens. He'd find out about Graeme for sure! I knew I had to do something.'

'Tell me about the day she died, Isolde,' Jess prompted again, after Isolde had fallen into another introspective silence.

'Oh, that day,' said Isolde. 'It was a Monday. I was working as a supply teacher at a school in Cheltenham. But when I arrived that Monday morning, there was no one there. No children, no staff: only the caretaker. He said the central heating had broken down and everyone had been told not to come in. It was going to be fixed that day and the next day should be school as normal. I said, that was all very well, but no one had told *me*, or the agency. I'd driven all the way from Weston St Ambrose. He said perhaps they'd forgotten about me because I wasn't a regular staff member. But in any case, he said, it had been given out on the local radio the evening before. Well, of course, I hadn't heard it! I understood what had happened. I was invisible again and no one had even remembered me.

'So there I was with a day to myself. I thought I'd wander round the shops, perhaps go to the cinema in the afternoon. But at lunchtime I was walking past a Chinese restaurant, wondering about getting some proper lunch for myself, when I saw, through the window, Graeme and Courtney. They were eating lunch together and laughing and chatting away! I felt like rushing in and telling Graeme there and then what a mistake he was making. But I didn't . . .'

'What did you do, Isolde?'

The solicitor said: 'You don't have to elaborate, Ms Evans. Remember our discussion.'

Isolde looked at him severely as if he'd interrupted one of her lessons. 'I went and sat in a café across the road and had coffee and a sandwich and waited for them to come out. When they did, I followed them. They went to a car park and got into Graeme's Range Rover and left. I was parked back at the school. So I had to go all the way back there and get my car and drive home.

'I thought they would have gone to Graeme's lovely house in Lower Weston, so I drove there first. I thought they must have got there before me. But just after I arrived, Graeme drove up and he was alone. So I worked out he'd driven her to her own place first, and dropped her off.

'I came back home and I made the decision. I had to act. I couldn't wait any longer. I got the awl ready and I drove out to Rosetta Gardens. I didn't park there because the car wouldn't have been safe. There are some awful youths loitering around there. I parked a little way away, by a gate into a field. Then I went back to Rosetta Gardens and hung around. I didn't have to wait long. Courtney came out of one of the blocks of flats. She started off for some lock-up garages behind the block. I followed. There was no one else about by then. It was dark already and all the youths hanging about earlier had gone – off to a pub or something, I suppose. Courtney was obviously going for her car – and that meant, I was sure, she was going to drive out to Lower Weston and the Old Manor. I saw her in some street lighting. She had changed her clothes. She still had on the funny jacket, with bits of fake fur on it. I'm a vegetarian and I don't approve of people wearing fur, even fake fur. She was tottering along on such high heels it's a wonder she didn't fall over. She'd pinned up her hair, and wasn't wearing jeans, as earlier, but some different trousers.' Isolde hesitated. 'She probably thought she looked glamorous but really, she just looked flashy. She went to the door of one of the lock-ups and began hunting in her bag, looking for her key. She didn't hear me. I can move very quietly, you know.' Isolde peered at Jess to make sure she appreciated this skill.

The solicitor opened his mouth, but, clearly realising the futility of offering any advice to this client, closed it again.

'Go on, Isolde,' Jess said.

'It was easy,' Isolde told her simply. 'I had found a nice big stone and I hit her on the back of the head with it. Down she went. She was unconscious but she wasn't dead. So, I took out the awl – and I drove into her faithless, treacherous heart!'

Jess heard Tracy Bennison, sitting quietly in the corner, give a sharp intake of breath. She gave Bennison a warning glance. The solicitor cast his eyes ceilingwards.

'What did you do then, Isolde?'

'I picked up her keys and put them in her bag. Then I dragged her – and the bag – behind the garages and went for my car. There was still no one around. I had no problems at all. I managed to haul her into the passenger seat. She wasn't a very big girl and

I am quite strong. I drove her to the river and pulled her out of the car, across the bank, and rolled her over until she fell in. I threw her bag after her. It was really hard work and I was panting and sweating, even though it was so cold and drizzling rain again. But I felt – it felt wonderful! She was gone. Graeme was free!'

The glee left her face. She frowned. 'I didn't know about the earring. Lucy says it was in her shopping bag because she picked it up from the floor in my car when she spilled her groceries. But I didn't know it was there, if she did! It's not proof it was in my car, just because Lucy says it was, is it?' Isolde stared angrily at Jess.

'Your car has been thoroughly examined by experts, and there is plenty of forensic evidence that Courtney was in that front passenger area. Besides, you've admitted it,' Jess pointed out.

'I know I've told you about it!' snapped Isolde. 'But you still shouldn't have listened to Lucy, because that was just Lucy interfering, as people always do. Anyway, the river was running very fast. I thought the girl would just be swept away – miles away.

'But then the only thing to go really wrong happened . . . She ended up at poor Neil Stewart's garden, stuck under some sort of bridge or something. I was really annoyed about that!' said Isolde. 'It was as if, even dead, she was being a nuisance.'

Chapter 23

While Jess had been interviewing Isolde, Carter was talking to Teddy Higson. But the interview began with Higson asking the questions.

'That loony woman killed my girl!' His small eyes bored into Carter's and his rasping breath seemed to fill the air between them. 'She stabbed my princess!' He jabbed a stubby forefinger at Carter. 'I 'ad one good thing in my life – my princess. She took my little girl from me and she took my daughter's whole life. What are you going to do about it, eh?'

'It's likely she will be charged with the murder of your daughter. She is being interviewed at the moment. Of course, I can't tell you exactly what the result of that will be,' Carter replied carefully.

'You think I don't know how it works? The shrinks will have a look at her, won't they?' demanded Higson with a scowl. 'She'll be reckoned unfit to plead, is that it? They'll call it manslaughter. She's going to be allowed to get away with it! I'm not having it!' His massive body tilted forward and Stubbs, waiting by the door, tensed.

'Her fitness – or not – to plead will have to be decided on by a judge, after proper professional medical opinion has been obtained. It's not something the police decide. We just do the groundwork.'

There was a silence, broken by Higson's heavy breathing, then he leaned back again in his chair. From the door, Stubbs could be heard to exhale in relief.

'You know what?' said Higson thoughtfully. He raised that stubby finger again and shook it to emphasise the point he was about to make. 'I don't often make a mistake like that. I had her down as batty, like the rest of them writers, but I didn't have her down as batty enough.'

'We all made that mistake, Teddy,' Carter told him. 'What led to you being there, in that car park? Were you looking for Murchison? You were warned to stay away from everyone on that writing course.'

'Yeah, well, if I 'ad,' retorted Higson. 'You'd have got another dead body on your hands, wouldn't ya? She'd have done for him, as well!'

'I admit it was very fortunate you were able to save him,' Carter replied patiently, 'but it still doesn't explain what you were doing, hanging about there in the dark.'

Higson leaned back in his chair and folded his hands over his barrel body. His unlovely features twisted into a rare satisfied smile. He looked like some grotesque travesty of a Buddha. 'I wasn't looking *for* him, exactly, not in the way *you* mean. But I was *watching* him. See . . .' Higson's solid form, arms still folded, tilted forward again but this time in emphasis, not threat. 'See, I worked it out. Whatever happened to my girl all started because of something to do with that place where she worked, didn't it?

'From the stuff in the flat I knew someone had been buying her some very expensive clobber, not to say that computer, couple of tellies, and the nice little motor. So who'd got that sort of money? Not that twat Jason. That Fisherman's Rest. That's where she would have met 'im, whoever he was. Had to be. So, who was he?

'I did think perhaps the writer guy – Stewart. I didn't rule him out; but he's got a wife – the sort who comes running out of the house the minute she sees him talking to a stranger. If he was playing away from home, she was the sort of woman who'd suss it out, straight off! She'd give him hell and he'd start behaving himself. So, not him.

'But there was that guy, Murchison, he was much more likely. He was living all on his tod in a big house, plenty of lolly, and only a stone's throw from the pub. The more I thought it over, the more I was sure it had to be him, didn't it, what bought her all that stuff? But I ain't daft. I knew that didn't mean he'd killed my princess. He might 'ave done!'

The massive finger wagged at Carter again. 'He might very well have done! But not necessarily . . . It still could've happened *because* of him. F'r example: it might have been another boyfriend, someone jealous, someone she'd sent packing when she met the new bloke. If that was who the killer was, he wouldn't stop at murdering my princess; he'd come after Murchison, too. So I watched Murchison – waiting. If the killer come for him, too . . .' Higson nodded. 'Then I'd have him.

'That night, I saw Murchison leave his house and go over to the pub. I followed and I waited outside to see if I could catch him and have a word. Not harassing, mind you! No threats! Just a nice, quiet friendly word. Then that woman turned up. He'd already gone into the pub. The woman came running into the car park. She must have chased after him. She stood under that lantern for a minute or two, and I saw it was that Isolde who was friendly with Jason Twilling.

'Cor,' said Higson with deep feeling. 'She did look a sight. She was all soaked with rain, and her long hair was all plastered round her head. She wasn't wearing them long skirts. She was wearing trousers, jeans, or whatever. But it was her, no mistake about it. Talk about a drowned rat!

''Ullo! I said to meself. What's going on here, then? Because I still didn't think the murderer was going to turn out to be a bird, right? I never would have thought it'd turn out to be that one. I got out of the way – and out of the rain – under an open-fronted shed in the corner of the car park. Woodshed, it was, full of logs. She hung about under that lantern for a bit, like she didn't know what to do, then some fellers came out of the pub carrying something heavy. So she scuttled off, and hid herself over by the hedge. The two blokes, they went across the road into one of them cottages, wiv whatever it was they'd nicked.

'It was help-yourself evening, because next Murchison come out, carrying a box, making for this big old Range Rover he's got. He loaded up whatever it was, and he started to walk back to the pub. Then she jumped from under the hedge, and called out to him. The rest you know, or can work out. They had a bit of an argument. He threw a punch at her but it didn't connect. It upset her, though, because she went for him like a madwoman. If it had just been a scrap I'd have left them to it. Never interfere in domestics; that's the rule. But I saw she had something in her hand and was trying to stab him with it. So I reckoned it was time I stepped in. I pulled her away but she kept yelling at him and from what she was shouting, it was pretty clear I'd found what I was looking for.'

312

Higson unfolded his arms. 'That's it,' he said. 'The crazy bitch killed my princess. So now some doctor's going to say she did it because she's off her head. Well, you can be off your head and still know what you're doing!'

There was a long pause. Carter said slowly, 'There's no need for you to contact Murchison again now.'

'Why would I do that?' Higson returned blandly.

'Because of his friendship with your daughter.'

There was a silence. Then Higson said quietly, 'He looked after her nicely, bought her some good gear, great little motor. She would have liked that. It would have made her happy, I reckon. No, it wasn't his fault there was a crazy woman hanging around.'

The following day the interview with Isolde resumed, and this time Ian Carter sat in with Jess. Isolde seemed in better spirits. The sullen look had gone and she appeared altogether brighter. Her legal adviser, on the other hand, looked even more depressed.

'Can we move on to the events of Friday night?' Jess asked. 'When Charlie Fallon was attacked at Lower Weston?'

'Oh, the old man,' said Isolde, 'is he dead, too?' She raised her eyebrows in inquiry. 'I didn't think I'd hit him hard enough. I wasn't trying to kill him.'

'No, he's not dead, but he is still in hospital and unconscious,' Jess told her.

'He lives in the woods, you know,' said Isolde.

'Ms Evans—' began the solicitor.

'Yes, he does!' insisted Isolde, turning to him. 'In a shack.' She turned back to Jess and Ian Carter. 'I had quite a time avoiding him, on several occasions. He wanders about at night, in the woods and all around the outside of the garden walls, across the old paddock, everywhere. He ought not to be allowed to do that.'

'Friday night?' prompted Jess.

'He was wandering about again, I suppose. I had been waiting in my car on the track alongside Graeme's house.'

'Graeme Murchison's property, the Old Manor?' asked Jess for the sake of the recording.

'That's it,' agreed Isolde. 'I'd been sitting in my car.'

'For what purpose?'

'Just to be there,' said Isolde, 'to be near Graeme. Honestly, you have to *try* and understand! Well, I'd got out of my car to stretch my legs. I thought I'd just walk up the track and round the outer wall of the gardens. But then I heard barking and I realised Graeme's dogs were loose and outside. I don't get on with dogs, large or small. I didn't know if anyone was with them, or they'd just got out somehow. So I turned and began to run back to my car. But just before I got there, the old man jumped out at me from the trees. He gave me the fright of my life! So I had the dogs coming up behind me, and the old man in front of me. What was I supposed to do? When I heard the dogs I'd picked up a large stone, to throw at them if they attacked me. I had it in my hand. So I hit the old man with it and he fell over. I jumped in my car and drove off.'

Isolde sighed. 'It was a dreadful evening. None of it was my fault, you know. People shouldn't wander around at night.'

'You were doing that,' Jess pointed out.

'Yes, but I had a reason. I wanted to be near Graeme!' Isolde replied testily. 'But as if it wasn't enough that the old man was out in the woods that night, would you believe it? I drove out of the entrance to the track, on to the main road, and I nearly collided with Dennis Claverton! He was driving along the road from Lower Weston and had almost reached the turning into the track. I swerved and got round him and he braked, and we didn't collide, thank goodness! You'd think Dennis would have been at home in bed, wouldn't you? Really, there were people all over the place that night.'

Isolde shook her head sadly. 'I didn't know Graeme was with the dogs. If I'd known, I'd have risked waiting and braved them. He'd have called them off and we could have talked.'

'But Dennis Claverton had seen you, you believe?' Jess asked her.

Isolde twitched and dragged her attention back to the matter in hand. 'Oh, yes, Dennis. He must have recognised my car. I was pretty sure he'd interfere because that's what people always do. He might start telling people how I'd been near the woods that night. I knew someone would make a fuss about the old man being attacked and news get round. Dennis would hear it. He'd put two and two together – or someone he told about it would.

'Sure enough, Dennis came to the library on Saturday afternoon, just before we closed. He said he needed to talk to me. I knew what about, but I pretended I didn't. He began to ramble on about owls. Dennis has a sort of thing about wildlife, you know. On Friday night, he said, he went to Graeme's woods because he knew a tawny owl hunted there. As I'd guessed, that's when he saw me. "What were you doing there, Isolde?" he asked – as if it were any of his business!

'I told him I could explain, but, obviously, we couldn't talk in the library. I was far too busy. I said I would meet him, but outside

Weston St Ambrose, so that no one saw us talking. I didn't want to go back to Lower Weston. So Dennis suggested a spot he knew, out in the middle of nowhere. There was a turning, he said, a little lane before you got to the main drive into the property. It was marked up "Private", but he'd never encountered anyone there.

'He got to the meeting place before me. I wanted him to be there first and I'd made sure I was a few minutes late. I parked a short way off and walked to the turning. I could see Dennis's car parked so I went up to the window on the driver's side. Dennis saw me and let down the window . . . he leaned his head out towards me and said, "Oh, good, Isolde. You found it."'

'Ms Evans . . .' warned the solicitor.

Isolde ignored him. 'And I killed him,' she said. 'I was sorry I had to do it. I like Lucy and I'm sorry she's so unhappy. But if she let her husband drive round all over the place at night, looking for owls, she shouldn't be surprised he got into trouble.' Isolde stared Jess firmly in the eye. 'People should just not interfere!'

Chapter 24

Stepping out of the building that evening, Jess turned up the collar of her jacket and pulled it tightly about her against the dank evening air. It was not raining now, a welcome break, but there was a damp mist that touched clammy fingers against bare skin. The car park, when she reached it, was nearly deserted, vehicles dotted about it mostly belonging to staff who had come on the night shifts. It was easy to pick out the lonely immobile figure, gazing disconsolately at his car, hands thrust into his coat pockets. 'Something wrong?' she asked. 'Won't start?'

Ian Carter looked up at the sound of her voice. 'Oh, Jess . . . The car's fine. I was just thinking.'

Jess hesitated. She didn't want to intrude on a private problem. But then she thought, what the heck? I can't just walk away and leave him here miserable. Millie's on his mind. I might not be able to help, but I can listen. He's not like Tom, wanting me to give him directions. Ian just needs a friendly ear.

'I meant to ask,' she began awkwardly, 'how you got on when you went back again to see your daughter.' Hastily she added, 'I understand if you don't want to talk about it.'

He didn't reply directly, instead asking, 'Aren't you meeting up with Palmer for your end-of-the-week drink and pizza?'

The type of lighting that official wisdom had installed in the car park bathed the entire area in a sulphurous yellow gloom. Cars could be picked out but appeared all the same colour. People's faces also resembled one another, eerily fluorescent and unearthly. Their expressions were unreadable.

'Tom and I don't always meet up,' she said defensively. 'It's not written in stone. We haven't fixed up anything for this evening. Anyway, Tom has other things on his mind. Do you remember Madison?'

'Wasn't that some girlfriend he had who spent most of her time with things in petri dishes? I thought she went overseas.'

'She went to Australia, but she might be coming back sooner than planned.'

'Ah, and Palmer hopes it's on his account!'

'Well, actually,' Jess confessed. 'I think it's because her Australian romance has fallen through. Now the thought of her return has Tom really worried. He keeps asking me what he should do. I can't tell him.'

'Poor bloke. Can't say I'm unsympathetic but I'm not the one to advise him either!' Carter growled the last words. There was an awkward pause, then he said, 'I don't want to do the same as Palmer and bend your ear with my woes . . .'

'You're not the same as Tom.' Jess phrased her words carefully. 'I know you have a specific problem in Millie. You're worried about her. I like Millie and I'd like to think she's happy. If you want to talk, I can offer you a drink and scrambled eggs on toast at my place. I've got the eggs and bread. The trouble is, I haven't got the wine.'

'You know what my place is like,' he said. 'I don't think I've even got the makings of scrambled eggs on toast.'

So, somehow, after some more dithering, they ended up at a roadside pub neither of them knew, but where a board outside promised 'Good traditional fare'.

Inside it proved warm, comfortable and not too full. A real log fire crackled in the stone hearth. After they had decided on the chicken and ham pie and mash, Carter took a sip of his modest half of locally brewed ale and told Jess about Sophie's plans for Millie.

'But you're against it,' Jess commented.

'At first I was. Then I reasoned that I'd like it even less if they took Millie with them to France full time. Now I accept it's probably the best deal on offer. Millie doesn't seem to mind the idea of boarding school. The only stipulation she had was that MacTavish must go with her. When she was assured the plan included that wretched bear, she said she thought MacTavish would like it. What still bugs me is the way it was all discussed and arranged without me. I was just presented with a fait accompli.

'I'm not surprised, mind you. That was always Sophie's way of doing things. But I trust her judgement on the school,' he added after a fractional pause.

The chicken pies arrived and conversation was interrupted for some minutes.

I wonder if he still loves his ex-wife, Jess mused as she cut into the pastry crust. Perhaps not, but he's loyal. She's Millie's mother and he does his best to speak of her with respect. Perhaps it would help him if he could bring himself to be less polite about her. Perhaps a shrink would say he's built a fence round his feelings. He doesn't love her now; but he did once. He's been hurt.

But what do I know about emotional dilemmas? Look at

Graeme Murchison. He's a successful, intelligent man who deals in old books and collects antique silver. He chooses Courtney Higson, who collects Barbie dolls. Murchison told me I didn't understand what was between them. He was right. I didn't and still don't.

Perhaps that was always an accident waiting to happen. He's a wealthy, unattached, middle-aged man living buried in the country. The only other men Courtney met were the yobs living on the Rosetta Gardens estate. Maybe Murchison was her Ruslan and she his Ludmila.

Ian's voice broke into her train of thought.

'Your food OK? You're scowling at it.'

'Am I?' Jess felt herself blush and hoped it would be put down to the heat from the fire. 'The pie is fine. I was just thinking.'

'About? he asked, eyebrows raised.

About you, of course . . . Mentally Jess slammed on the brake pedal.

'Isolde!' she said firmly. 'If we had spoken to that couple who live downstairs from her, we'd have learned about her habit of keeping odd hours: going out late and coming home after midnight. It might have made us think. We might – just might – have examined her car earlier. Courtney's DNA is all over the interior. We might even have found the earring.'

'We had no reason to talk to the people in the downstairs flat,' Carter argued. 'We had no grounds to suspect Isolde. We both found her a bit odd. But eccentricity isn't a crime; nor does it necessarily lead to one. Teddy Higson summed it up. He told me he'd realised she was batty, but not just how batty. Nor do we still know, until the experts have finished their assessment, how crazy she is.'

'Not so crazy she didn't know what she doing!' Jess retorted. 'She knew what she was doing when she set out to kill Courtney and when she lured poor Dennis Claverton to that meeting.'

'That's up to judge and jury,' Carter said gently, 'not to you and me, Jess. We're just coppers.' Unexpectedly, he grinned at her.

Jess found herself smiling back at him. 'All right, point taken. I won't talk any more shop. Though I do wonder if we'll see any more of Teddy Higson sooner or later. He's lost the one person for whom he might have made an effort to stay out of trouble.'

'What you and I call trouble, he'd call making a living.' Carter drew in a deep breath. 'What you were saying earlier about Palmer . . .'

'Yes?' She looked up from her plate. In response, he looked down at his.

'I've wanted to ask you out for a drink or a meal for ages. If Palmer isn't an obstacle, I'm quite pleased to hear it.'

'He's not an obstacle,' Jess said.

Epilogue

The Stewarts were eating in their kitchen and discussing the future of Glebe House. 'We'll just have to put it on the market and hope for the best. If we ask a reasonable − well, let's face it, if we fix a low price . . .' Beth fiddled with the stem of her wine glass. 'I'm sorry, Neil. I know how much you've liked living here.'

'I was an idiot,' her husband told her. 'Burying us both in the depths of the country like this. You must be very lonely here.' He stretched out his hand to still the continual rotation of her wine glass. 'I'm really sorry, Beth.'

'I agreed to come and I also hoped . . . well, we were neither of us to know there were murderers lurking round every corner.' She pulled a wry smile. 'Or one murderer.'

'Funny thing,' said Neil thoughtfully, 'I do remember Isolde well from the writing course. She used to sit at the front and write down every word said. But her own work never seemed to improve. Every time she read any of it aloud it was always the same thing: lots of heady love scenes but no depth to any of it. I'm really ashamed to say I just dismissed it all − not openly, you understand. I did my best to say something positive about it to her. I never realised it was telling us all how unhappy she must have been. Now, when I read some of the stuff I've written, I begin to wonder what motivates *me*.'

Beth grabbed his hand firmly. 'Neil, listen! You've got a wonderful imagination and you spin a great yarn. Once we get back to London, you will – we both will – forget all about this – this episode. OK, I know we'll neither of us forget the image of the poor kid stretched out dead on the lawn. But once we're back where we belong, we'll cope. I'll get some kind of a job somewhere and life will get back to normal.' And I can't wait, she added mentally.

Jess and Ian did see Higson again before long. As investigating officers in Courtney's murder, they attended her funeral. The turn-out was impressive and the floral tributes eye-popping. There were not so many young people gathered. But Teddy's wide range of acquaintances had mustered to 'show respect'.

'Funny how traditional gangsters and professional thugs can be,' observed Ian Carter, eyeing the assembled expensive overcoats, gold jewellery and dark shades. Teddy, as they presented their condolences, shook their hands and sprang a surprise of his own.

'I got a job,' he confided hoarsely. 'Legit. Private security company wants an adviser. So I'm gonna advise them, what they want to watch out for and that.'

'Oh, dear,' said Ian Carter, as he and Jess quitted the scene. 'We shall have to keep a close eye on that!'

Charlie Fallon astounded his doctors – but not his family – by making a remarkable recovery. After coming round from his coma, he spent a day in bed before informing hospital staff that he'd had a nice rest, but he had to be off home now.

It was put to him that 'off home' could no longer mean the

shack in the woods. At this Charlie became so agitated that it was feared he'd have a relapse. It was eventually agreed that he could spend his days in the shack, provided he returned to his son's cottage at night to sleep.

'We'll see how long that lasts!' said Mrs Fallon to her sister-in-law.

As Charlie Fallon left hospital, Hedley Morris was admitted. He had been badly beaten up. He denied any knowledge of the identity of his attackers or why they'd set about him. A distraught Amy, in a slip of the tongue, said it 'must be because of those sodding cigarettes!' But later she withdrew this remark and refused to discuss it.

Teddy Higson was asked if he knew anything about Hedley's injuries. He replied simply: 'Who's 'Edley Morris? Never heard of him.'

In spring, the receding river eventually surrendered Courtney's jacket with the fake fur panels, leaving it stranded on the mud. An angler hooked up her bag, with her car keys in it, two weeks later. Her mobile phone was never found.

If you enjoyed DEAD IN THE WATER, look out for the other
Campbell and Carter mysteries in the series…

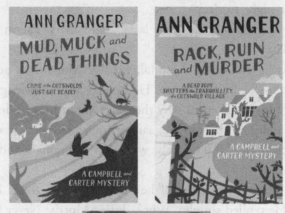

headline
review

For more information visit Ann's website www.anngranger.net or
www.headline.co.uk

Discover Ann Granger's latest thrilling Victorian mystery featuring Inspector Ben Ross and his wife Lizzie...

A hanged man would say anything to save his life. But what if his testimony is true?

When Inspector Ben Ross is called to Newgate Prison by a man condemned to die by the hangman's noose he isn't expecting to give any credence to the man's testimony. But the account of a murder he witnessed over seventeen years ago is so utterly believable that Ben can't help wondering if what he's heard is true.

It's too late to save the man's life, but it's not too late to investigate a murder that has gone undetected for all these years.

And don't miss the previous novels in the series:

A Rare Interest in Corpses
A Mortal Curiosity
A Better Quality of Murder
A Particular Eye for Villainy

www.headline.co.uk
www.anngranger.net